Carrie lifted her foot off the gas and simultaneously tapped the brake. The men behind them were caught by surprise and in a split second they were less than fifteen yards behind the rear of the van. Holliday kicked open the rear doors while he and Eddie tossed everything they could into the path of the oncoming motorcycles.

Both drivers were instantly tangled in net and other debris, and the bikes smashed into each other, bounced, and finally tipped over in a screeching spray of plastic parts and a fury of sparks, tossing the drivers head over heels into a ditch at the side of the road.

Carrie slammed on the brakes as Holliday and Eddie jumped out of the back of the van and ran back along the road. They checked the two drivers. Both were dead.

"These guys aren't cops," said Holliday. "The bikes are BMWs and the riders are carrying Glocks. The bikes, the uniforms—they're phony."

"They were looking for us specifically," Carrie said.

"Who was?" Eddie asked.

"The CIA. They issue Glocks," said Carrie.

"There you go." Holliday nodded grimly.

"Foxes and hounds, and we're the foxes."

continued . . .

Also by Paul Christopher

SECRET
OF THE
TEMPLARS

PAUL CHRISTOPHER

A SIGNET BOOK

SIGNET
Published by the Penguin Group
Penguin Group (USA) LLC, 375 Hudson Street,
New York, New York 10014

USA | Canada | UK | Ireland | Australia | New Zealand | India | South Africa | China
penguin.com
A Penguin Random House Company

First published by Signet, an imprint of New American Library,
a division of Penguin Group (USA) LLC

First Printing, January 2015

 REGISTERED TRADEMARK—MARCA REGISTRADA

ISBN 978-0-451-41570-7

Printed in the United States of America
10 9 8 7 6 5 4 3 2

PART ONE

PORTRAITS OF DEATH

1

Once upon a time, in a land far away, there was a man who taught history at West Point Military Academy and he loved his job and he loved his wife, Amy, even more. He had a favorite uncle, who'd taught him almost everything worthwhile he knew, and a cousin named Peggy, who was funny and full of laughter and, when you got right down to it, was probably his best friend.

But that was once upon a time and that fairy-tale life was over. Amy died a torturous death as cancer ate her alive; his uncle was dead along with the job he loved at West Point. And now, so was Peggy. He was wanted for murder in the country he'd fought for so many times and he had a legion of enemies trying to track him down for the things he knew and the power he had. Power that he didn't want, power that he'd never asked for, power that he wished desperately he had never known existed.

He stood on the high cliffs of the Dorset coast feeling the cold, slanting rain from the English Channel slashing into him, chilling him to the bone. On a clear day, you could make out the coast of France from the muddy pathway, but it hadn't been clear for weeks now.

Lieutenant Colonel John "Doc" Holliday, U.S. Army Rangers (retired), turned away from the cliffs and followed the path back up to the old thatched cottage that he and Eddie Cabrera had rented for the winter, paying six months in advance and in cash. He and Eddie were living completely off the grid now—no credit cards, no cell phones, no wireless devices of any kind. The only communication they had with the outside world was a big Grundig Satellit 900 portable radio with short wave, long wave and police bands.

Holliday turned up the walk and stepped through the little gate and into the overgrown garden in front of the cottage. The old woman who owned the place was willing to have the dead plants and dry grasses cleared away, but Holliday had declined the offer. The tall grass and the windswept undergrowth gave the place a deserted look, which was just what he wanted. The cottage was located on a low hill and there wasn't a neighbor for a mile in any direction. The closest village was Pelham Buckthorpe, a three-mile walk inland, or twenty minutes away on the bicycle that served as their only means of transportation. The nearest constabulary was in Swanage, twenty miles up the coast. "Isolation" was a word he and Eddie were taking quite seriously these days.

Holliday tapped his boots on the fieldstone step and gave a triple tap twice on the worn plank door, announcing his arrival. He pressed down the latch and stepped into the cottage.

Eddie was sitting in one of the old overstuffed armchairs in the living room with an old Purdey Nitro Express elephant gun resting across his legs. The radio stood on the Victorian end table beside him, chattering quietly.

"Anything?" Holliday asked.

"Very quiet, *mi amigo*," replied his Cuban friend. From the kitchen Holliday could smell the rich aroma of some kind of stew. Thankfully the Cuban loved to cook and was good at it; Holliday's repertoire of culinary expertise ran to overcooked fried eggs, charred burgers and barely edible mac and cheese from the box.

Holliday waited until they had sat down for the evening meal to lay out his thoughts. "I was thinking today while I was out for my walk," he said.

"Only poets and sailors' wives should think while walking by the sea." Eddie smiled, mopping up the last of his stew with a chunk of bread.

"Maybe you're right, but I've still been thinking."

"About what, *compadre*?" asked the tall black Cuban, his intelligent brown eyes searching Holliday's expression.

"I've been thinking it's time we parted ways," said Holliday.

Eddie sat back in his chair. "And why would that be?"

"Because it's me they're after, not you. I'm the one they want to kill. I'm the one with the notebook and all the secrets. I have no right to drag you into all this."

"Nobody drags Eddie Vladimir Cabrera Alphonso anywhere he does not want to go. Anything I have done, I have done willingly."

"That's all well and good but I don't think you should share in a burden you never chose."

"No one chooses their burdens, Doc. Fate throws them in our direction and we either avoid them or we do not."

"One of these days they're going to find me

and eventually they're going to kill me. There's no reason you should die too."

"We are friends, Doc, and friends do not abandon each other just because life becomes difficult."

"I still think we should split up."

"And what do I do with myself? There is very little call for river pilots these days."

"You're making this difficult," said Holliday.

"And I intend to keep on making it difficult with every sentence you speak, *amigo*, so why not shut up and help me with the dishes?"

Someone knocked at the door.

Holliday and Eddie both stood up. Eddie picked up the shotgun leaning on the table at his side and both men moved silently toward the door, keeping out of a direct line of fire. Holliday reached the door and stood with his back against the wall. Eddie lowered himself behind one of the upholstered chairs, aiming the elephant rifle over the back and directly toward the door at latch level. Anyone coming through unannounced would be cut into ribbons.

"Who is it?" Holliday called out.

"It's Carrie Pilkington, Colonel Holliday. We spent some time together in Cuba a while back. There's an MI5 kill team fifteen minutes out. We don't have much time."

Eddie cocked the huge-bore rifle. Holliday thumbed down the latch and threw open the door. A pretty woman with dark hair pulled into a ponytail stood there, dressed in climbing gear with a long skein of nylon rope over one shoulder and a gym bag over the other. Her black vest was hung with pitons, clips and locking rings. She was also wearing a 9-millimeter Glock 19 in a sling holster. "Let me in," she said. "I'm dripping wet."

Holliday stood aside and she stepped into the cottage. Holliday closed the door behind her and the young woman dropped the gym bag onto the floor.

"How do you know that MI5 is coming with a kill team?"

"I still have connections," said the young woman.

Holliday remembered. "Black, the Englishman."

"That's right." She nodded. "But we can reminisce later. We've got about ten minutes before they start throwing flash-bangs through the window."

"Where do we go?"

"The cliffs. Put on something waterproof and come with me. Colonel, bring that bag. Forget everything else."

A hundred feet down the path, with the cottage lights blazing behind them, they reached the cliff edge. The rain was coming down in windy sheets from the sea and Holliday could barely hear the waves crashing in on the rocky beach a hundred feet below them. There were already two heavy pitons holding lengths of rope pegged into the chalky soil when Carrie Pilkington opened the bag and pulled out two climbing harnesses.

"Either of you do any rappelling?"

"No," answered Holliday.

Eddie shook his head.

"I hope you're quick studies. Get into the harnesses," she said sharply. From somewhere behind them there was the harsh coughing sound of a rifle-fired grenade launcher.

By the time the two men figured out the truss-like harnesses and fit them around their legs and thighs, Carrie had set the third line. She slipped a self-locking carabiner at their waists through each of the lines and guided them to the edge of the cliff, standing away from the sea.

"Go down backward and ease yourself over the edge and walk down the cliff until you feel comfortable. Then do small jumps outward while letting the line slip through your hands, but keep the loop around your elbow. Ten or fifteen jumps should get you to the bottom."

There was the sound of automatic fire coming from the cottage now. "They're playing our tune, guys. Time to bug out. Don't look down, as the saying goes." She pushed Holliday lightly on the chest and he went over into the rain-filled darkness.

The girl was right. His feet hit the beach with a crunching clatter after less than a minute and a half of unholy terror as he gave himself over to the thin nylon rope and the steel clip on the heavy belt around his waist. Before he had time to slip out of the harness, Eddie and Carrie had both reached the beach.

"Santa Madre de Mierda Cristo!" Eddie exclaimed, breathing hard.

"What now?" Holliday asked.

"There," said the girl, pointing down the beach. A four-man Zodiac with a fifty-horsepower Evinrude had been pulled up onto the stony beach, the engine tilted up on the transom. They ran down the beach and Carrie hopped in first, heading for the bow. Eddie and Holliday pushed the inflatable into the water and jumped into the stern. Eddie lowered the engine and hit the electric start. Carrie took a small GPS unit out of her vest. "That way!" Carrie yelled, her hand pointing just left of center. "Full bore! They'll have us in a minute or two."

Eddie twisted the throttle and they blindly moved out into the choppy water. The flare went up less than thirty seconds later.

"Shit," said Carrie from the bow, looking up from the GPS unit. She watched as the flare burned brightly overhead and began to flutter down on its parachute. They were outlined as though they had been caught in the eye of a searchlight, the light twitching and casting shadows as the flare skirled downward erratically. Finally it fizzled out and darkness shrouded their position.

"Kill the engine!" she ordered sharply. Eddie didn't ask any questions, just followed orders. "Holliday! Get down there and help your friend. We've got to tip the engine overboard—fast!"

Holliday knew exactly why and it raised the hairs on the back of his neck. Eddie had the first of the big cleats loosened and Holliday helped him with the other one. There was a sharp echoing *crack-bang* of a Stinger or its British equivalent as they pushed the outboard into the sea. Another flare went up, this one fired at an angle away from the bow of the boat. A split second later there was a brilliant explosion three hundred yards to port as the infrared heat-seeking surface-to-air missile impacted with the closest source of heat—the flare rather than the Evinrude, which now lay at the bottom of the sea. "You're pretty good at this."

"Don't get excited—we're not out of the woods yet. There's two oars clipped to the gunnels. Set them up and row like hell. They'll figure things out quickly enough."

Eddie and Holliday pulled together, their backs to Carrie and facing the cliffs, which were now no more than shadows through the rain. There was another detonation from the one-man SAM at the summit of the cliffs, but, hearing it, Carrie fired another flare, this one high and to port side again. The infrared tracker in the missile took to the white-hot flare and there was a second explosion with a shock wave that slammed hard enough to hurt their eardrums. A few seconds later Holliday felt the inflatable bump into something.

"We have arrived, folks," said Carrie.

Holliday looked to his right. Rising out of the water was the gray-blue hull of a boat. From what he could see, it was about sixty feet long. "What the hell is this and where did you get it?"

"It's a refurbished World War II motor torpedo boat. A Vosper," Carrie said. She gripped the rope and plastic ladder hanging over the gunnels. "I got it because I know people who like to smuggle cigarettes and other things across the Channel. Now climb aboard and let's get the hell out of here."

2

There are five main bodies that make up the Channel Islands, an archipelago located off the coast of Normandy—the last remaining "bailiwicks" of the Duchy of Normandy. The islands are British protectorates, but are not governed by the United Kingdom or the European Union. Even so, since the citizens of the islands have full UK status, they are also holders of all the privileges of the European Union.

The five islands are Jersey, Guernsey, Herm, Alderney and Sark, with Sark being slightly different from its neighbors since it is ruled by the hereditary Seigneur of Sark. The Channel Islands are an interesting and sometimes confusing place to live. They're also very useful for people hiding money or themselves from various and sundry government agencies since they take both their privacy and their independence very seriously.

Herm is the smallest of the islands. The northern end is craggy and mostly full of cliffs while the southern end is all sandy beaches. Cars are not allowed on the island, nor are bicycles. Quad bikes and tractors are allowed for the locals. Its main source of income is tourism, but there is some farming, animal raising and fishing. There are no customs agents except at the ferry terminal and no local police at all.

Carrie Pilkington guided the Vosper into a small cove on the west side of the island and then led them along the beach to a small fisherman's cottage that had been built on a low rise above the beach. The dawn was just beginning to light the sea behind them and the fog was so thick it was unlikely that anyone saw them arrive.

The cottage was a plain two-story affair with a living/dining area, a kitchen and a bathroom on the ground floor, and a narrow staircase leading up to a pair of small rooms. The roof was slate, the floors were wide planked and the small windows were covered with faded yellow curtains. It had that lonely feeling of a house that hasn't been lived in for a very long time.

Carrie went to the kitchen larder, brought out cutlery, a loaf of sourdough bread, a brick of cheese, a pot of mustard, some butter and the remains of a ham. "Dig in—we won't be here long," she said, sitting down. She began slicing up the bread.

"Where exactly are we going?" Holliday asked, building himself a sandwich. He was starving and realized that he hadn't eaten since the previous afternoon.

"First Guernsey on the ferry and then to France by air."

"Without papers?"

"Leave that to me."

"Last time I checked you were a CIA analyst working out of Langley. What the hell are you doing out in the field?"

"As far as the Company knows I never made it out of Cuba alive, if you remember that little drama."

"Vividly," said Holliday. He and Eddie had gone looking for Eddie's vanished brother and found themselves in the middle of an invasion.

"I was recruited by another group, and I've been working for them for the last two years."

"What group?"

"Officially, it's the Joint International Office of Intelligence Oversight, but it's generally called JOI, when it's called anything at all. In-house, it's just called the Office," she responded.

"Another acronym." Holliday sighed. "What's this one supposed to do?"

"Just what it says. The big intelligence agencies around the world have become their own governments—they do what they want to, and get what they want. They're out of control. We're supposed to rein them in, or at the very least gather intelligence about what they're doing."

"So just who is the Office made up of and why is it interested in me?"

"The Office is a joint committee of high-ranking government and military officials from the UK, the United States, Germany, France and Russia."

"Not China?"

"Not to be trusted."

"Why me and why now?"

"The Vatican has recently allied with P2, Propaganda Due, the old fascist paramilitary group that worked with the Pope after the war and into the late fifties. It was a P2 assassin that killed your cousin and her husband at Qumran—on the Vatican's orders."

"Why?"

"Because they're afraid of what you're looking for and they want the notebook given to you by Brother Rodrigues. They want the money and they want its power."

"Why should we believe you?"

"Because you have no other choice."

*   *   *

René Dubois, assistant director of operations for the DGSE—Direction Générale de la Sécurité Extérieure (General Directorate for External Security)—was sleeping peacefully in his family's apartment in the Saint-Mandé district of Paris when the telephone on his bedside table screeched at him. He opened his eyes and looked at the illuminated numbers on his alarm clock. It was four thirty in the morning.

Dubois sighed. Beside him his wife, Marguerite, didn't even lose the rhythm of her snoring. She was used to such calls. Dubois picked up the telephone.

"Yes?"

"It's Leclerc, sir. We've just had a facial recognition alert from Saint-Malo. It's the American and the Cuban."

"When did they enter France?"

"Nine hours ago," said Leclerc, Dubois's assistant.

"*Fils de pute!*" Dubois groaned. "We have the technology to pick their photographs out of thin air but we can't get a message to Paris for ten hours? This is madness!"

"Don't swear, René. Remember the children,"

muttered Marguerite from beneath the duvet beside him.

"To hell with the children. They have a lifetime of sleep ahead of them. Leclerc, get me a car. I want it at my door in half an hour."

Showered and shaved, Dubois was standing on the curb in front of his building when the big black Peugeot 607 pulled up with Leclerc behind the wheel. Dubois climbed in the back and found a large cup of steaming black coffee in the holder and a thin dossier in a red cover on the seat beside him. He lit a cigarette and leaned back in the seat, closing his eyes and wondering about the idiotic intricacies of a bureaucracy created by the nation that had invented the very word. After a few moments of self-indulgence he opened his eyes, picked up the dossier and began to read.

The headquarters of the DGSE is at 142 Boulevard Mortier in the twentieth arrondissement, just beyond the Père Lachaise Cemetery. It is a château-style fortress on three sides with a high wall and guard stations on the boulevard side. Beyond the entrance, a gravel drive leads around the treed courtyard to the main doors of the building. At this time of the morning, the entire building was bathed in the light of a score of mercury-vapor lamps throwing the courtyard trees into stark silhouette. Leclerc left the car for the attendants to care for and he and Dubois walked up the steps to the main lobby. There was a security post and two ornate staircases. They passed through security and took the right stairway to the third-floor conference room. Dubois, like any other bureaucrat in France, reported to a committee. In his case the committee consisted of four men: Deputy Foreign Minister François Picard, Deputy Minister of Justice Émile Redon, Deputy Minister of Internal Affairs Jean Granville and Deputy Minister of Transportation Henri Jarre. None of the exalted politicians was happy about being dragged from his bed at such an early hour, and their faces showed it.

Dubois entered the room, paused at the door to offer a short, polite bow and then took his regular seat at the foot of the table. Picard, the man from the foreign ministry, was the first to speak. He was a tall, shallow-cheeked man, and of all the deputies around the table he was the only one dressed in a three-piece suit and a perfectly knotted tie.

"I hope you have a good reason for taking us from our homes at this hour, Dubois."

"I believe I do." Dubois flipped open the folder in front of him. "Colonel John Holliday and his Cuban friend have been spotted coming through customs at Saint-Malo."

"*Merde*," said Jarre, the bald-headed deputy from Transportation. "When was this?"

"Seven thirty o'clock yesterday evening."

"That is intolerable!" Redon exclaimed. He was a big man with unshaven jowls and a very large nose. The red explosions of color on his cheeks marked a man who drank too much.

"These men did not come into France on their own passports, Deputy Redon. They were identified through facial-recognition software. By the time the red flag went up they had been gone for some time." He didn't add that the bureaucracy of the Justice Department was so unwieldy that it was a miracle he'd been notified at all.

"Do we know where they are now?" Picard asked.

"No, Deputy Picard, but we almost certainly know why they have come to France."

"The notebook," said Picard flatly.

"We searched the castle Holliday purchased in Talant and found nothing. There was only one small apartment there that had ever been used. The notebook is not there," Dubois said.

"Then it must be somewhere else," said the heavy-set Redon, his tone snide as he looked down the table at Dubois.

"Yes, this was a conclusion I had reached as well," said Dubois.

"And what do you intend to do about it?" Picard asked.

"Find them and then follow them."

"We are talking about a trillion-dollar asset that arguably belongs to France," said Granville, from Internal Affairs.

"There are several Bourbon kings and Napoléon Bonaparte who might argue that, Deputy Granville, but by the law of uti possidetis it is fair game."

"But you have to possess it first." Dubois smiled.

"So go and find it," said Picard. "If everyone is agreed, we shall all meet here at six o'clock each evening for further briefings."

It was an obvious signal to break up the meeting and everybody stood. But before he could slip out of the room, Dubois was cornered by Picard.

"This must have your full attention, Dubois. Nothing else is to be entertained while this notebook or whatever it is remains out of our possession. If you need anything, ask my assistant, Jobert. Anything you need. You understand this?"

"Of course, Deputy," answered Dubois.

Picard nodded.

Dubois had been dismissed. He went down to

his small, drafty office one floor below. Leclerc was waiting for him.

"Well?"

"Full speed ahead. We'll need more computers, a coffee machine and one of those folding beds from the guards' barracks in the basement. This will be a twenty-four-hour-a-day job for at least several weeks. You have no wife, so that will not be a problem. Mine will probably enjoy being without me."

Leclerc smiled.

"Why are you standing there? Get going. But find the coffeemaker first."

The target was a three-story villa on the shores of Lake Como in northern Italy owned by the designer Max Feramiglia. The villa was stuccoed in yellow with a slate roof and brown shutters. There was a large pool in the rear; the lawn leading down to the water was perfectly manicured by a local gardener. The entire place was surrounded by pine trees sculpted into perfect tall cone shapes.

Paulo and Tonio Broganti had been thieves since they were small children in Rome. Over the years they had become more specialized and were now robbers on commission only, stealing specific items from particular people. Mostly it was art, as was the case this afternoon.

In the absence of maestro Feramiglia, the estate by the lake was taken care of by Mr. and Mrs. Tucci. Emilio Tucci took care of the pool and grounds while Helena Tucci was the cook and housekeeper. There was a complex alarm system to cover insurance qualifications, but it was always turned off during daylight hours. This, of course, was the reason the Broganti brothers preferred daytime robberies to those at night.

They drove up to the estate in a van with a magnetic sign saying they were plumbers and went to the side of the house where they knew Mr. and Mrs. Tucci usually enjoyed a light afternoon meal sitting at a small patio table. Both brothers carried bright red toolboxes, which they set down on the patio and opened.

"We're here about the pipes," said Tonio.

"I didn't call a plumber," said Mr. Tucci.

"No, you didn't," said Tonio.

He and his brother reached down into their toolboxes and each withdrew a Pneu-Dart tranquilizer pistol and shot a single dart into the Tuccis' chests. They were unconscious in seconds and would remain that way for several hours.

The two thieves went through the side entrance and made their way to the main salon.

There were a number of paintings that hung there, but the brothers went to one in particular, a Giotto *Madonna and Child*.

The painting, like many of Giotto's mature works, was done on board with tempera. It was held into the frame by eight iron staples, which Tonio quickly clipped using a pair of short-handled bolt cutters. They popped the painting from the frame, then carried it out to the van, where they put it into a foam-lined case specifically built for it. They were at the villa for exactly twelve minutes.

The brothers drove away from the lake and traveled due south to the little town of Lucino. There they switched the sign of the van so that it now advertised a courier service based in Rome and put the painting into a hidden slot in the rear of their own Peugeot estate wagon.

At Lucino they split up, Tonio heading back to Rome and his brother heading to Tuscany for a meeting with the winemaker Meucci.

The Meucci Vineyards were located just north of Siena in the sunlit Tuscan hills. The vineyard had been in the Meucci family for more than two hundred years, producing a Chianti Ruffino called Chianti Meucci.

Meucci himself was every inch the Tuscan: round faced, gray, curly balding hair with a bushy mustache, broad shoulders, strong square-fingered hands and the build of a wrestler. He was sitting in the vineyard office going over bottling receipts when the telephone rang.

"Meucci."

"Is it there?" The voice was familiar to the vintner. Clearly Parisian.

"Yes." Meucci glanced up from his desk. The painting in its special container was resting on top of a row of filing cabinets.

"A man is coming from Geneva. His license plate is GE90619. Give him the painting."

"The financial matters?"

"Already taken care of."

"As you wish."

3

Cardinal Pierre Hébert, Archbishop of Paris, sat in the vestry office of Nôtre-Dame Cathedral after saying a requiem Mass for a dead premier who couldn't even remember his own name in the end. With him was a priest from Saint-Sulpice.

"Tell me exactly what was said," ordered the cardinal.

"Holliday and the Cuban are in France, Your Eminence."

For a moment the cardinal looked surprised. But surprise quickly changed to anger, his lean, austere features hardening.

"Where did they enter and how?"

"Saint-Malo. The ferry."

"When?"

"Two days ago."

"Have they been found?"

"Not yet, Your Eminence. But a task force has been organized."

"Who have they got heading it?"

"René Dubois, assistant director of operations for the DGSE."

"Find out everything you can. I want reports daily."

"Yes, Your Eminence."

The man bowed out of the vestry, closing the door behind him. Cardinal Hébert dressed in simple black priest's daywear, then stepped out of the side door of the vestry. He walked down the short hall until he reached a second door, this one leading into the alley beside the famous cathedral. He stepped into the black Citroën, which was already waiting for him, and settled back into the soft leather seat.

"Paris–Le Bourget," said Hébert.

The car moved off. The traffic was heavy and it took them the better part of an hour to reach the airport. He wasn't concerned; his flight wasn't going to leave without him.

When they arrived at the airport, they drove through the private jet entrance, drove across the tarmac and stopped at the lowered stairway of a dark blue Gulfstream G650 with the gold crown insignia of Hébert et Cie. on the tail.

Cardinal Hébert exited the limousine, climbed

the steps up into the plane and settled into his seat. As the engines spooled up, a male steward in a blue uniform fitted his place with a table, laid out cutlery and went to fetch the cardinal's meal, while a second steward opened a bottle of 2010 Domaine de la Côte de l'Ange Châteauneuf-du-Pape. He offered the cardinal a small sip and at Hébert's nod he filled the glass. A moment later the first steward appeared carrying a plate holding a meal of chateaubriand, haricots verts and gratin dauphinois potatoes, Hébert's favorite. He waited for the jet to take off and settled down to eat. He would be in Rome before he finished dessert.

The cardinal was the younger of the two sons of Jean Hébert. Even before World War II, Hébert was a name to conjure within France. The elder Hébert owned Cément Hébert, the largest concrete plant in the country, in addition to several oil refineries and a fleet of transport ships among many other enterprises. The war itself only served to increase the company's wealth. Hitler's supposedly unbreakable Atlantic Wall was built with Hébert concrete and Hitler's panzers were fueled with Hébert's gasoline. Most war profiteers would have been hung after the war for such gross collaboration, but the truth was Hébert was too important and knew too many people in high places to make any charges stick.

As with many younger brothers of wealthy families, the only way to gain power and prestige in the world was through the Church. With his family's money behind him, Hébert had risen quickly, working hard to cultivate relationships with the right people in the right places and proving himself to be an asset to both the Church and to France. He spent six years in the Vatican working as an assistant to important figures while simultaneously refining his own goals and objectives. When he was named cardinal of Paris, most people thought he'd reached the pinnacle of his career. They were wrong. Hébert was just beginning.

Cardinal Hébert was just finishing his coffee when the jet landed at Ciampino Airport. He stepped down and was ushered into a waiting Lancia Thesis limousine bearing Vatican City plates and began the half-hour journey into the center of Rome. Exactly forty-five minutes later he was being ushered into the Vatican secretary of state's office in the Apostolic Palace.

"Cardinal Hébert," said Ruffino, standing up and coming around his enormous seventeenth-century Spanish desk, hand extended.

"Arturo." Hébert smiled, taking Ruffino's hand. "It has been too long." The Frenchman pointed an index finger upward. "How goes it with our new leader?"

"Our Argentinian Papa wanders around with his big brown eyes wide, wondering how he got here. He speaks good English but poor Italian, despite his name, which means he has no friends in his own court. In the end I think we'll find that he's as much a conservative as his predecessor."

"It sounds like you're not having an easy time of it," said Hébert.

"Except for your news about Holliday."

"Like the cockroach he is, he keeps on popping up everywhere, and no matter how you try to stamp him out, he returns just to spite you."

"Any idea why he's chosen to reappear in France?"

"Presumably because France is where he settled after meeting with Rodrigues the monk. There are some people in the government who think his massive hoard is still hidden there. They've even created a task force."

"You have access to it?"

"Intimate access."

"Excellent. The Church is tearing itself apart, Hébert. These men must be stopped before it is completely destroyed. Sexual depravities with children and gross financial blunders are bad enough, but Holliday is taking aim at the very heart of things—our credibility that trusting the faith that can be honored and believed in. If the faith is rich, then the Church is rich."

The French cardinal shook his head. "It's so difficult to believe—that one man and his friend could do such damage to an institution that has lasted for two millennia."

"It only requires a hole the size of a child's finger to destroy an entire dam, Hébert. And we must remember that it was only one man who began the whole institution that we are a part of."

Soon they were out of Rennes and heading for Le Mans and then Paris. The rental car hadn't made it any farther than the ferry parking lot in Saint-Malo, where they'd exchanged it for an old Renault 4 provided by Carrie's "people." It had the name "Pleine Mer" on the side panels and a poor painting of a leaping trout logo.

"We've got cops on our tail—two motorcycles coming up fast," said Carrie.

"Get off the main road," said Holliday. The A81 was a broad, modern highway, but this early in the day there was very little traffic. "There," said Holliday, pointing to an exit. Holliday looked over his shoulder. "Anything we can use back there, *mi compadre*?"

"Nets, fish traps, floats for the nets, *basura en su mayoría*—mostly junk," replied Eddie.

"That could work." Holliday crawled between the front seats and scrambled into the cramped back of the van. The truck had long oval windows on the doors. Holliday looked back down the side road. The motorcycle cops were closing in, less than fifty yards now, lights flashing and sirens howling.

"Slow down just a bit," called Holliday.

Carrie lifted her foot off the gas and simultaneously tapped the brake. The men behind them were caught by surprise and in a split second they were less than fifteen yards behind the rear of the van. Then Holliday kicked open the rear doors while he and Eddie tossed everything they could into the path of the oncoming motorcycles.

Both drivers were instantly tangled in net and other debris. The bikes, which were traveling at speed, smashed into each other, bounced and finally tipped over in a screeching spray of plastic parts and a dazzling fury of sparks, tossing the leather-dressed and helmeted drivers head over heels into a ditch at the side of the road.

Carrie slammed on the brakes as Holliday and Eddie jumped out of the back of the van and ran back along the road. The bikes were ticking and rattling in their death throes, the smell of gasoline heavy in the air. They checked the two drivers. Both were dead, their necks broken.

Carrie joined Holliday and Eddie.

"These guys aren't cops," said Holliday. "The bikes are BMWs and the riders are carrying Glocks. Police Nationale drive big Yamahas and carry SIG Pros. The bikes, the uniforms—they're phony."

"They were looking for us specifically," Carrie said.

"Who was?" Eddie asked.

"The CIA. They issue Glocks," said Carrie.

"There you go." Holliday nodded grimly.

"Foxes and hounds, and we're the foxes."

The CIA's Department D was located on two floors of the old Tour Albert in the thirteenth arrondissement of Paris, one of the first high-rises in the city. Department D carried out some of the most covert work in Western and Eastern Europe as well as regular surveillance of anyone who was deemed a threat to U.S. national security.

The director of Department D was a fifty-four-year-old named Elliot Foster, a career CIA man who had been recruited right out of Yale. Foster stood on the catwalk outside his second-level office and stared down into the bull pen, a

crossword puzzle of cubicles, glassed-in conference areas and computer arrays all surrounded
by large-screen displays and sealed off from outside electronic or visual surveillance. It was Foster's domain.

For twenty of his thirty years with the Company, Foster had been a true believer, climbing
the ladder rung by rung as he headed for the top.
Everything could be sacrificed to the job, including two wives and three children. But in his
twenty-first year, politics had snuck up on Foster,
and once again he had become a sacrificial goat
and was sent to Paris to prevent him from inter-
fering with the career of a lesser man with better
connections.

After two years moldering in Paris, he was quietly introduced to the Ghost Squad, a CIA within
the CIA using the Company's assets, finances and
people to increase its own power. It was a hyper-
intelligence group loyal to no one but its own
members. And best of all, its leader was a fellow
Bonesman.

Kate Rogers, one of the unit liaisons, climbed
up to the catwalk with a folder in her hand. She
was in her thirties, seven or eight years on the job,
and was being groomed as a field surveillance operative. Foster had made a play for her more than
once and had been rebuffed each time. It didn't

seem to affect their working relationship, for which
Foster gave her high marks. Give her a few more
years, he thought, and he might consider taking
a look at her for the Ghost Squad—if the others
approved.

"What's up?" Foster asked as she approached
him.

"We were stealing eyes from that French Harfang drone they had up and we sent out a couple
of bikes to follow a killer unit."

"This afternoon." Foster nodded.

"We haven't heard from the bikes for almost
three hours. They just missed another check-in."

"The Harfang?"

"Frogs put it to bed. They were looking for
the rental; we had the info on the fish truck."

"We have any assets in the area?"

"Closest is Lyon."

"Get him down to Rennes and sniff around. I
want some news. Fast."

Holliday sat on the outside terrace of La Squadra
Pizzeria and Café on Rue Jean-Boucher in the
town of Hédé-Bazouges, eating the French version of pizza and planning the next move with
Eddie and Carrie. The sun was going down now

and heavy shadows were beginning to swallow the old stone buildings around them. The fish truck was hidden a few blocks away on a narrow side street, safely out of sight. Hédé-Bazouges was ten miles up the road from where they'd taken out the fake motorcycle cops, but everyone knew it wasn't far enough. Not by a long shot.

"The motorcycles will have pingers on them. They'll have to know where they are by now," said Holliday. He turned to Carrie. "How close is the nearest CIA station?"

"They've got a small satellite station in Lyon. Half a dozen people at most."

"It's been an hour. We don't have much time left. We have to find some way out of here. The fish truck is marked."

"I have an idea," said Carrie. She called the waiter over in a perfect Parisian accent.

"Oui, madame?"

"Pourriez-vous m'indiquer une maison funéraire?"

"Madame?"

"Mon oncle est très malade," responded Carrie, shaking her head sadly and putting a tearful expression on her face.

"Mes condoléances, madame. Un moment," said the waiter. He disappeared into the restaurant and came back a moment later with a name and

address written on a scrap of paper: *Mercier et Fils, 46 Rue de la Barrière*. The waiter then proceeded to give Carrie detailed directions.

Rue de la Barrière turned out to be a narrow side street on the western edge of town, its narrow sidewalks laid out with cut flagstone and its buildings two stories high, stone as well. Mercier et Fils had two curved barn doors with a long building beside it, and chapel-like windows set into the old walls. The barn doors had an old hasp and an immense lock.

"I called the number the owner of the restaurant gave me," said Carrie. "It sounds like he's having his calls forwarded to his home. The person who answered sounded like a little girl."

"Eddie," said Holliday, nodding at the lock.

The Cuban slipped a pry bar from the fish van into the hasp of the lock and pulled. It tore off at the hinges and they eased through the doors.

Holliday pulled the string of a naked bulb that was hanging from the roof of the garage. Stuffed inside the dark, cavelike garage was a 1955 Citroën hearse—which really looked like it was no more than an ambulance painted black and the words "Mercier et Fils" in gold Gothic-style script on the side panels. Holliday eased his way toward the left side of the boxy, high-roofed vehicle, opened the door and slipped behind the wheel. The keys were still in the ignition.

"Open the garage doors," he whispered. Once it was done, he switched on the ignition, scratched the unfamiliar shift into reverse and backed out onto the narrow street. Eddie and Carrie closed the doors and then squeezed into the forward passenger compartment.

"Now what?" Carrie said as they puttered out of town at an appropriately somber rate.

"Now we go and visit my old friend Professor Spencer Boatman."

4

Professor Spencer Maxwell Boatman sat at the tiny table set outside the Cour de la Huchette drinking café au lait, occasionally dunking his pain au chocolat into the milky coffee. In most cities, the Rue de la Huchette would have been called an alley, but this was Paris and nothing here was done as other cities. Directly across from where he sat was an even narrower thoroughfare leading down to the Seine called Rue du Chat-Qui-Pêche—Street of the Fishing Cat—which was named hundreds of years ago for the cats who went there to fish for carp when the river regularly flooded in the spring.

Boatman was in his mid-forties but he still had the air of a tall, slim figure from a Renaissance painting by Raphael. His face was long, the features as smooth and sculptured as a statue by Cellini, his hair black but tinged with streaks of silver, his large eyes suffering from heterochromia—one eye a bright blue, the other startling green.

Today he was wearing a pale linen suit, a small blue-checkered handmade Egyptian cotton shirt and Russian calf loafers. He was the kind of middle-aged man who young girls fell in love with as easily as taking in a deep breath. The kind of man people his own age knew to keep away from their daughters. On top of that, he had an IQ of 224, an eidetic memory, doctorates in everything from chemistry and physics to archaeology and psychology as well as a background that included more wealth than several medium-sized countries. To make matters worse, Spencer Boatman had never changed his personality from the friendly unassuming kid he'd been when Holliday had met him at school during his first year at Georgetown when Boatman was graduating with a master's degree in chemistry at sixteen. The scholar was reading C. S. Lewis's *The Abolition of Man* when Holliday sat down across from him.

"Doc. Strange place to meet."

"I keep the apartment above the bar as a safe house when I'm here in Paris. My two friends are getting some well-earned sleep." Holliday paused. "You weren't followed, were you?"

"I should think not. I've had the bloody CIA,

MI6 and the idiots at GCHQ Cheltenham following me around and wooing me for years. I've even had the froggies and the Russian FSB sniffing around me just to make sure I'm not working for someone else. I know how to give them the slip."

"I need to ask you a question."

"So you said when you called me in the middle of the night."

"Have you ever heard the phrase 'The King of the Jews is dead. The Messiah is risen in the East'?"

It was the Aramaic phrase carved into the wall of the cave at Qumran, where Peggy and Rafi had been murdered.

Holliday could see Boatman's mind at work, the sounds of Quai Saint-Michel fading away in his ears until there was nothing except that memory working in the deepest part of his brain. Suddenly Boatman's eyes lit up. Holliday could almost see a lightbulb coming on above his handsome head.

"The traitor at the feast is given the robe, the feast is eaten and the greatest is least," said Boatman. "It's a quotation from Scroll 59 of the Dead Sea Scrolls, the one that was stolen in 1949 by a professor from the École Biblique et Archéologique Française in Jerusalem. It suggests that Judas wore the kittel, the robe that marked him as Christ during the Last Supper, and that it was Christ who took Judas's place. Since there was no way of identifying people during that period, it's more than likely that the story is true: Judas took the place of Christ, thus allowing the prophecy of the Resurrection to occur and for Christ to continue his teachings and his travels to the East. As I said, the scroll containing the facts of this story was taken by an archaeologist from the École Biblique et Archéologique Française in Jerusalem."

Holliday nodded. The Judas-Christ switch was a theory he'd heard more than once before. "Does anyone know where Scroll 59 is now?"

"There are lots of stories, but there's one man who might tell you for sure. He's here in Paris. His name is Peter Lazarus. He knows a great deal about stolen and looted art and artifacts. In fact, that's his job."

Elliot Foster stared down into the bull pen and scowled. He'd sent out one of his best teams of field men on the tip they'd received from their mole in the French Police Judiciaire and the two men had missed several of their scheduled call-ins.

Foster heard a clattering of heels behind him

and turned. It was Maggie Teal, the hard-faced sixtysomething head of station for Paris. She was wearing expensive heels, a Prada suit and a remote headphone. Like Foster, Teal had risen to power the hard way with years of hard work, dedication and an ability to sidestep any political shitstorms that came in her direction. Her hair was a steely gray, and there was never even a wisp of a rumor of her involvement with a man. She was as sexless as a hammer but, oddly, had a husky, almost erotic voice, like an echo of Ingrid Bergman in *Casablanca*. The only problem was she was still one of the good guys and Foster knew that there was no armor more impervious than that worn by the true believer.

"What is it?" Foster asked.

"We've got a hit. I put out a surveillance tag on all our video links and put in all of Holliday's known acquaintances in Paris. His name is Spencer Boatman."

"Where?"

"Rive Gauche." Teal paused and spoke into her headphone. "Put it on the grid. I want video and audio and boots on the ground ASAP. Boundary is Quai de Gesvres on the north, Saint-Germain on the south, Pont Neuf on the west and Pont d'Arcole to the east. Cover all the Métro entrances and report every five minutes into Central." Teal turned her attention back to Foster. "Ten minutes and we'll have him in the bag." The woman frowned. "Although I'm still not sure why we want him so bad."

"Above your pay grade, Maggie. Just get him."

"Consider it done."

The disposable in Holliday's pocket buzzed. It was Carrie, her voice urgent. "Get out of there—they had a tag on your friend. You've got about six minutes before the net starts to close."

"What about you and Eddie?"

"Already moving. Get to the Saint-Michel Métro entrance and then get a train at Châtelet to Nation. Walk to the open-air farmers' market at Saint-Mandé. We'll meet there. Go. Right now."

Holliday stuffed the phone back in his pocket. "We've been rumbled. You go any way except the direction you see me going in."

Boatman looked stunned and began to speak but Holliday wasn't listening. He picked up an empty wineglass, wrapped it in a linen napkin, then stuffed it into the pocket of his jacket. He crossed Rue de la Huchette and slipped into the narrow alley across from the bistro. Lost in the shadows, he could see all the way down to the Seine.

Over its thousand-year history, the eight-foot-

wide space had gone from being a drainage ditch
for human waste to an alley and eventually achieved
its final nomenclature as a bona fide *rue*. It had
been a home to slit purses and petty thieves, a
shortcut for Picasso from his studio on the quai
and a way for resistance fighters to disappear during
World War II.

Suddenly Holliday's view of the Seine was
blocked. There was someone else in the alley
coming toward him from the north. A coincidence? Highly unlikely. He took out his linen
package and smashed the goblet against the old
stone wall beside him. There was a muffled shat-
tering sound as the goblet broke, but Holliday
felt the stem firm in his grip. He dropped the
linen, and any pretense of being a passerby vanished. An ordinary person walking up the alley,
seeing a man approaching him with a broken
glass in his hand, would have fled, but this man
continued toward him. So much for coincidence.

When he was twenty feet away, the approaching man reached threateningly into the inside
pocket of his jacket. A normal reaction would
have been to pause, but instead Holliday sprinted
forward, the broken stem of the glass raised to
the level of the man's crotch. The man's eyes
flickered and suddenly Holliday lunged forward,
stabbing at the man's exposed throat. The splin-

tered stem dug into the stretched skin and then swept over the right carotid, gouging through the thick, rubbery artery.

Holliday pushed harder, setting the stem in the man's windpipe. With his free hand Holliday gathered up the cloth of the man's jacket and turned him against the left side of the alley, flattening him against the wall, keeping him standing with the force of his hip as the man bled out against the ancient stone. He let go of the broken glass, pushed his hand under the man's jacket and pulled a pistol out of the hidden shoulder holster.

He stepped back and looked down at the weapon before stuffing it into his pocket. It was a SIG Pro, standard issue for the French secret police. He found the man's wallet in the left inside pocket of his suit jacket, and an ID folder in one of the sleeves identified the man as Paul Richard, a detective in the DST—Direction de la Surveillance du Territoire. So now the French were after him as well as the Company. He felt as if there was a target painted on his back. He hurried down the alley to the end. He was running out of time.

With the inclusion of the French cops, everything had been thrown for a loop. It was a whole new ball game.

He stopped and turned back the way he'd

come. Whatever net had been thrown over the area had effectively been doubled now. He went back thirty feet into the shadowy alley. There was a small lane servicing the buildings that faced the Quai Saint-Michel. He squeezed down the narrow crevasse. It smelled like the garbage that was spilling out of the bins at the rear entrances of the buildings. A rat scurried. Holliday reached a bin marked "Hôtel du Quai." The same name was stenciled on a gray steel door that was propped open with a brick. Holliday pulled it open and stepped into a short hall that led him to a kitchen area filled with steam, turmoil and the odors of half a dozen dishes being cooked. Men in paper hats and aprons were moving from station to station fetching, chopping, tasting and flambéing, while a fat man with sweat streaming down his face wearing a tall chef's hat bellowed orders. A skinny man looked up, a bloody cleaver raised in his hand above a butcher block with a slaughtered suckling pig spread-eagle across it. He scowled. Holliday flashed the ID folder and the man dropped his eyes and his scowl.

Holliday pushed out through the swinging doors into a dowdy restaurant that was barely larger than an average living room. The walls were yellowing and decorated with cheap prints of Parisian scenes. The floor was covered in carpeting that had probably been a rich red but had aged to an ugly dark brown after decades of use. There were three diners all eating soup and none of them looked very happy about it.

Holliday threaded his way between the tables and left the room walking between two faux marble pillars and into the lobby. The lobby was small, dark, decorated in much the same manner as the restaurant. A dark-complexioned man was reading a magazine and sitting behind the counter. The man was reading *Der Spiegel* and smoking a foul-smelling cigarette. Holliday recognized the stink of the cigarette—it was an F6 brand. The man behind the desk was German.

"Ein Zimmer. Keine Fragen gestellt," Holliday said and flashed the ID folder again. The man behind the counter put down the magazine and slapped down a key with a tag on it. Holliday fished three fifty-euro bills out of the dead policeman's wallet, put them down and picked up the key.

"Danke," he said.

"Bitte," replied the man behind the counter, and he picked up his magazine again. Holliday went up two flights and found his room, which faced out over the Quai Saint-Michel. It was small and narrow. The gray wall-to-wall carpet-

ing was thin and burnt here and there by errant cigarette butts. The bed was a single and the art on the wall was surprising: a famous Ronald Searle cartoon showing café life in Montmartre. Searle, the creator of the infamous Girls of Saint Trinians, had lived in Paris for many years to escape onerous British taxation and wound up falling in love with the city. And despite his fame and wealth he lived out his life above a café on the Left Bank.

Holliday went to the window and glanced down. The Quai Saint-Michel was a one-way street that headed west. The broad avenue as well as the parking lane directly below him were choked with traffic. He turned away and went to the house phone on a small beside table. He sat down on the bed and picked up the phone.

"Desk."

"Do you have porters here?"

"Sure."

"Send one up to 346."

"Sure."

Five minutes later there was a knock at the door. The bellhop was in his forties, balding and wearing a cardigan. His fingers and mustache were nicotine stained and he smelled faintly of wine.

"You speak English?"

"Yes, a little."

Holliday peeled off three hundred-euro bills from his own wallet. "You know where to buy cell phones around here?"

"Oui."

"Get me two, bring them back here. Be back in less than half an hour and there'll be an extra hundred in it for you. Understand?"

"Oui, m'sieur."

"Get going."

The man hustled out the door and Holliday settled down to wait. Twenty minutes later the bellhop handed Holliday the two cell phones still in their boxes, collected his bonus and left. Holliday called down to the desk again.

"Find me the number for Peter Lazarus and connect me." Holliday spelled out the name and hung up the phone. The Company might have the cell towers covered, but not the landlines. A moment later the house phone rang. Holliday picked it up. "Dr. Lazarus?"

"Yes."

"I'm a friend of Spencer Boatman. My name is John Holliday."

"He mentioned you. What can I do for you?"

"I have to see you. Now. Spencer is in harm's way and I put him there."

"Eighty-eight Avenue Foch," Lazarus said, a

note of dark humor in his deep voice. "You can recognize it easily enough. There's a plaque on the entrance commemorating it as the Gestapo headquarters during the war." Lazarus gave Holliday detailed information on how to find him.

"I'll need about an hour," said Holliday.

"I'll be here."

It took Holliday twenty minutes to find a room where housekeeping was still working. He slipped into the room as though he owned it, sat down in the armchair and made several mock calls on one of his new "burner" phones. The housekeeper finished, Holliday gave her a ten-euro tip and that was that. As soon as the housekeeper was out the door, Holliday was on his feet and going through the real occupant's clothing.

He found a cheap suit that fit him well enough, a white shirt and a pale yellow tie. His best find was a large wraparound pair of aviator sunglasses. He also found a formless old fedora on the shelf of the cupboard and realized the man was probably in the dining room. He quickened his pace. He went into the bathroom, removed his eye patch, put on the sunglasses and looked at himself in the bathroom mirror. The glasses didn't quite cover the scar tissue from the hit he'd taken at the

Moscow Airport a few years back, but they were good enough. He dropped the fedora onto his head, which shaded his face even more. Satisfied, he left the room.

As Holliday went down the stairs, he prayed he wouldn't meet the stranger whose clothes he had just stolen, then crossed the small lobby and stepped out onto the street. The weather was cool and cloudy. Directly in front of him was a chunky, battered Mercedes taxi with an equally chunky and battered driver behind the wheel, who was reading a copy of *Le Figaro*. Holliday looked to his left and right, saw nothing suspicious and climbed into the rear seat. The interior of the taxi smelled of sausage and cheese. He gave the driver an address on Rue Pergolèse and ten minutes later they were there. He paid the driver, watched him go and then went back around the corner to Avenue Foch. It wasn't much of a cover, but it would probably buy him a little time.

Just as Lazarus had described, there was a narrow porte cochere leading to the interior courtyard. He walked down to the end of it, and instead of garbage bins and bicycles, there was a substantial two-story stone house, its roof covered with sooty clay tiles. The house must have predated the blocks of apartments all around it by at least a hundred years.

There was a man in his late fifties standing on the steps, presumably waiting for Holliday. He was tall and more heavy-set than Holliday, with a square-jawed, clean-shaven face, hazel eyes and long, curly jet-black hair. He was, in fact, a re-markably good-looking man. He was wearing a black turtleneck, black jeans, expensive black loaf-ers and a shoulder holster with what appeared to be a Smith & Wesson .45 ACP automatic pistol.

"Karl Bömelburg's old place," Holliday said, approaching the man on the steps.

"You know your history, Colonel."

"I taught it once upon a time. You're Lazarus, I presume."

"You presume correctly."

"Dressed for friendly chats, I see," said Holli-day, nodding at the shoulder holster and the weapon it contained.

"I'm a cop. How else should I dress?"

"Maybe you're not the person I should be speaking to."

"I'm the right person. Come on in for a min-ute and I'll explain."

Holliday went up the three steps and into the house. The main hall was wide and the white plaster walls were covered with million-dollar paintings.

Lazarus led Holliday to a large room at the rear

of the house, which was set up as a gentleman's study: leather chairs, dark carpets, the smell of pipe tobacco and a large oak desk. There were more paintings on the walls—Sisley, Gauguin, Van Gogh, Braque.

"Quite the collection," said Holliday, seating himself in one of the leather chairs while Lazarus sat down behind the desk.

"And each and every one of them is a phony. Part of an insurance scam from the eighties and nineties. Steal a painting from a museum, a gallery or a private home and ransom back the forgery in its place. Took us almost ten years to crack that one and then only because one of the forgers died."

"Us?"

"I work for a backwater unit of Interpol called the Combined Art and Artifact Recovery Division. CAARD for short." Lazarus laughed, his voice a cool baritone. "Short by name and short by nature. I'm the chief and only investigator and my only backup is a nice young lady named Molly Malone who's half a computer genius and half an Asperger's syndrome idiot savant who collects Barbie dolls that she uses in meticulously detailed dioramas of famous murder scenes."

"Molly Malone . . . you've got to be kidding."

"Her parents thought it was amusing."

There was a long pause. Finally Holliday spoke. "All right, you're some kind of art cop. What does that have to do with me?"

"We'll talk about that later. First we have to pick up your friends and get you out of Paris."

"How about a clue?"

"I want you to help me rob the Vatican."

5

The old farmhouse rented by Lazarus was a few miles from the village of Brévonnes on Auzon Lake, a hundred miles east of Paris in the commune of Aube. The house was large, stone and thatch-roofed, heated with fireplaces in the upstairs rooms and a huge hearth on the main floor. The floors were broad slabs of honey-colored pine and the walls were rough plaster.

The group was gathered around the kitchen's old monk's table drinking wine while Lazarus made them omelettes aux herbes on the massive wood stove in the center of the room.

"We've had enemies in the past, but it seems as though everyone is suddenly on our case," Holliday said, frustration in his voice.

"Most likely because everyone is into everyone else's business these days," said Lazarus, sliding an omelet onto the plate in front of Eddie. "The world operates on corruption of all kinds now and there's no way to tell them apart anymore. Fine art is used for currency transfers in terrorism and organized crime. Intelligence agencies use drugs to finance their black operations and to line their own pockets. It's every man and woman for themselves now. Honor, truth, loyalty . . . words like that have no meaning anymore."

"Pretty cynical," said Carrie Pilkington.

"Pretty naive if you believe anything else. Especially for someone who works for an oversight group and thinks their own intelligence community is corrupt as a priest in a whorehouse." Lazarus shrugged.

Eddie looked up from his omelet. "I grew up under that kind of corruption, Señorita Carrie. Mr. Lazarus is right. It is pervasive. It leaks into every part of your life, from Castro, through the generals and the police who take, right down to the woman on every block who reports your every move to the secret police unless you bribe her with money or food. To live that way eventually corrupts your heart and soul. It eats you alive."

"But what the hell does that have to do with me?" Holliday asked wearily.

"The notebook Brother Rodrigues entrusted

to you," said Carrie, "is not only a massive financial resource—it's also its own self-contained intelligence system—one that crosses borders, religions and factions like a knife through butter. The CIA has been after it for years. They knew about it even before Rodrigues handed it over, and the Russians were sniffing around it as well. Half the reason the Company put me together with you on your escapade in Cuba was to find out more about it."

"And the Vatican wants you dead for two reasons," said Lazarus, finally sitting down with his own meal.

"So on that note let's get down to brass tacks," said Holliday. "Just what is it you want us to help you steal from the Vatican and why should we help you steal it?"

Lazarus paused for a few moments, gathering his thoughts before he finally spoke. "For many years one of the few Gutenberg Bibles left in existence was located in the library in Saint-Omer, France. During the war it was stolen by Göering's people for the fat man's collection. It disappeared until it resurfaced in 1945. Remember that film with Burt Lancaster called *The Train*? Well, there really were trains like that, full of plundered art. One in particular was sent out of France under the command of an SS colonel

named Rheinhard Huff. It was headed for the
salt mines at Altaussee in Austria. But it never
got there. Three months later Huff appeared at
the Vatican. This was back in the days when the
Kameraden network ODESSA had its famous
ratlines for smuggling Nazis through the Vatican
and out of Europe. Huff paid his way with the
Gutenberg Bible and somewhere along the way
a forgery was returned to Saint-Omer. Huff and
the Bible disappeared, never to be heard from
again."

"Presumably that's not the end of the story,"
said Carrie.

"No. But to find that out we have to go to a
small village in Tuscany and interview Huff's
onetime gay lover, an altar boy at the Sistine
Chapel in 1945 named Antonio Nardi."

"And just how are we to get out of France and
into Tuscany?"

"On an Interpol jet, of course." Lazarus smiled.

Doug Kitchen, chief of covert operations at the
CIA's National Resources Division, sat behind his
big desk in his big office on the fifth floor of the
Company's headquarters in Langley, Virginia, reading the report that had been given to him by his
assistant, Rusty Smart. Kitchen looked almost

exactly like the Prince of Wales, right down to the big ears, big nose and thinning gray hair. Rusty Smart didn't look like anyone, which was in his favor. It didn't do to shine too brightly around men like Kitchen.

After twenty-five years with the Company, Rusty Smart knew that people who shone brightly were often targets. For instance, when the president was elected for a surprise second term in office, a lot of the bright and shining boys and girls had vanished overnight. Rusty himself had seen the handwriting on the wall when the president had given the kudos for capturing and killing Osama bin Laden without a single mention of the CIA.

Kitchen closed the file. "No copies?"

"No, sir," answered Smart.

"Thank you for your good work as always, Rusty." It was a dismissal.

"Thank you, sir." He stood and left the room. Christ, how he hated the name Rusty. It had followed him from grade school, when his hair had been the color of a traffic light and his face was covered with freckles. Though it was half gone and a nondescript brown now, the name still stuck.

Kitchen waited until his assistant slithered off to his little hole before he picked up the report and went down the hall to George Abramovich's office. George had replaced Harrison White as director of the Central Intelligence Agency eighteen months earlier. George was a player, which meant that whichever way the wind blew, he blew in the same direction.

Abramovich's office was crammed with nautical paraphernalia—model boats in glass boxes, a brass ship's bell, bits of scrimshaw and even a bicorn hat that supposedly belonged to John Paul Jones. The walls were covered with pictures of Abramovich's climb through the ranks all the way to secretary of the navy. Abramovich himself looked like a boxer gone to flab, his cheeks sagging and his skull retaining just a few wisps of hair. He looked uncomfortable in a suit, and was obviously missing his uniform, which was resplendent with gold and a lifetime's achievement on the broad patch of ribbons on his chest. He looked up from something he was reading as Kitchen entered the room, and handed him the folder.

"Give me the short form."

"Paris lost them."

"Any contacts?"

"A man named Spencer Boatman."

"Who is he?"

"Big-time academic. Oxford don, lot of pull in high places. He does work for MI6 every now

and again. Codes mostly. IQ is in the strato-
sphere."

"How does Holliday know him?"

"They met briefly at Georgetown University
years ago. Boatman was a kid, some kind of su-
perstar. Holliday was twice his age or more,
working the GI Bill."

"Do we know what they talked about?"

"No, sir. I'm afraid not."

"Find out. I don't give a shit how you do it,
just find out. This whole thing is getting out of
hand."

Rusty Smart left the office at six o'clock, his usual
time, but instead of going home to his apartment
in Georgetown, he headed out of McLean and
into Fairfax County. He made sure his car's GPS
unit was shut off before he made his way to Earl
Street and parked at the end of the residential
backwater. Most of the large ranch-style houses
were lit, their curtains pulled against the en-
croaching dusk. He took the Nikon from the seat
beside him, climbed out of the car and headed
down the trail into the park that led off the dead
end. The small bridge was about two hundred
yards in.

Rusty took a few pictures, making sure that he

was alone, then slipped down the embankment, opened up the camera and took out the chip. He reached into his pocket, took out a foil gum wrapper, quickly folded it around the chip, then tucked the little packet deep under the struts of the bridge above. As he climbed back up to the trail he took a green thumbtack out of his other jacket pocket, pressing it into the inside face of the bridge's support post. He then took a few more shots, headed back down the trail to Earl Street and climbed into the car. He drove off and headed for home.

"Go get it," said the older of the two men hiding in the underbrush fifty yards from the bridge. He carried a 35-millimeter camera with a 350-millimeter zoom lens and had photo-graphed all of Rusty Smart's activities at the bridge. His name was Morton Banks and he was an ex-marine MP turned private detective who now worked for only one client.

His companion went and fetched the chip, which Banks then downloaded onto his phone. He returned the chip to his companion, who re-placed it under the bridge. Banks read the first page of the material he'd downloaded. He smiled. The boss was going to be very pleased.

*   *   *

Eddie and Carrie found themselves a safe house in Rome while Holliday and Lazarus met with Antonio Nardi in a café beneath his rooms on the Strada Statale in the Tuscan town of Albinia. A salt breeze blew in from the Tyrrhenian Sea, which was only a few kilometers to the west. Eddie and Carrie had stayed behind in Rome to buy equipment and to do whatever reconnaissance they could.

Nardi was in his late eighties, his face seamed and brown. What little gray hair he had grew over a spotted scalp. He was wearing a zippered hoodie even though it was hot at the table of the streetside café. When he spoke his voice trembled a little, but his English was surprisingly good.

"So tell us about your friendship with Rheinhard Huff," said Lazarus.

"Ah, yes," said the old man, a half smile twitching onto his face briefly. "My good friend Rheinhard Huff." He lit a De Nobili cigarette and sighed. "I sang in the Sistine choir. I was pretty and I was fourteen. I was also an orphan, so I had no one to turn to even if anyone would have believed me. It wasn't the first time I had been used that way. I was almost used to it."

"Huff was gay?" Carrie said.

"Huff was a sodomist. 'Gay' is much too pleasant a word to use for such a creature."

"When was the first time you met him?" Lazarus asked.

"May 11, 1944."

"A month before Rome was occupied. Just in time," Holliday said.

"They brought the train in late that night," said Nardi. "No one was supposed to see except the SS squad and a few of the Holy Father's people. That night I drove Huff and the Holy Father to the train station to watch the unloading."

"The train?" Lazarus asked, stunned.

"Yes. A goods train. Nine wagons, each with its own guard on the roof."

"How did it get into the Vatican?" Holliday asked.

"The way any other train did." Nardi shrugged. "Over the viaduct and then through the big iron doors where the tracks entered at Viale Vaticano."

"And then?"

"Some lorries came and took dozens of crates away to the Vatican Administration Building. I never saw them after that."

"Dear God," said Lazarus. "It wasn't just the Bible—it was everything!"

6

May 11, 1944

Eugenio Maria Giuseppe Giovanni Pacelli, Pope Pius XII, sat in the rear seat of the 1939 Fiat Berlina and watched as the goods train was unloaded. Rheinhard Huff was seated beside him and Nardi, his "special" young priest, sat behind the wheel. The thin-faced Pope noted that there were two kinds of wagons making up the train, dark green French SNCF wagons and the curved-roof German freight cars carrying the spread-winged Deutsche Adler eagle above its routing numbers. The men unloading were all SS.

"What exactly are we looking at here?" Pius asked.

"The best of the best from four years of plunder and the Swiss 'auctions' before that. And I also have a special gift for you, Your Holiness."

"You found one?" asked Pacelli.

"I did indeed. It was lying unnoticed and unappreciated in a French village library where nobody saw it or cared." Huff smiled.

"Wonderful," said Pacelli.

"I have brought you anything of value to be had from any museum or gallery, Jewish or otherwise," said Huff. The soldier and the Pope spoke in German, which Pius had become fluent in as papal nuncio in Berlin, and they assumed Nardi didn't understand a word of it.

"Of which we retain fifty percent of everything sold. A fixed amount will be made available to you and your Kameraden network, ODESSA, whenever you require it," Pacelli said.

"Precisely," said Huff, watching as another crate rolled down the ramp of one of the wagons. "There is also an amount of gold specie in the shipment—an amount we didn't manage to get into Switzerland before Allied intelligence set up shop there."

"Things are that bad for the Reich?" Pius asked.

"There is no Reich, Holy Father. There is only panic. The Führer thinks he can win the war by moving imaginary tanks and men across his maps, and those in high command are rats looking for holes to hide in."

"So the Vatican is a rathole to you, Colonel Huff?"

"This has been planned since the Führer opened the Western Front. The war was lost on that day and most of the SS command were aware of it. The authority comes from Reichsführer Himmler himself."

"And if our gentle Heinrich was told the Vatican did not wish to take part in his plan?"

Huff shrugged. "Do whatever you wish, but the Obersturmbannführer Roedel and his SS Tenth Army will be leaving Rome in two weeks. They can either do it by driving the panzers through Saint Paul's and the Sistine Chapel on their way north, or down the Appian Way. The choice is entirely yours."

"You threaten the Holy See?"

"For ODESSA and its Kameraden—certainly."

"He actually threatened the Pope?" Lazarus asked. "You heard him?"

"It was common knowledge and he left enough armed men to make good on the threat. There were soldiers dressed as priests everywhere. Huff would have shot the Holy Father in the blink of an eye." Nardi smiled and puffed on his cigarette. "Although I think it was a ruse, a way for the

73

Pope to give himself an excuse if the story ever was made public—which it eventually was, of course."

"Blackmail," said Lazarus.

"It was mutual, I can assure you." Nardi smiled. "In the end both of them benefited. After Ber Ruffinono Nogara, director of the Special Administration of the Holy See, closed the doors of the administration building cellars all the gold and paintings and sculptures and priceless manuscripts no longer existed."

"I'm surprised with all that information you weren't killed years ago."

"It's because I never made a fuss about things. What I didn't see that night I picked up from conversations Huff had with various people. Huff never knew it, but I spoke quite a bit of German and understood pretty much everything he and the Pope talked about that night. If you did not have any power, the Vatican and the Nazis chose to believe you were simply invisible. I made sure I was one of those people. I had my uses, but I had no power. Huff would say things with me in the room simply because he assumed I had no idea of what was being said." The old man paused and crushed another cigarette into the stained old Cinzano metal ashtray on his bedside table. "And I've probably said too much now. And it's also my bedtime, so if you gentle-men would be kind enough to leave the money you promised me on the table behind you, I can take to my bed."

They did as Nardi asked and left the little rooms over the café. They drove out of Tuscany and back to Rome the following morning.

The apartment Eddie and Carrie had rented was close to the Vatican and located on the top floor of a large block of flats on Via Rusticucci. It had four small bedrooms, a bathroom, a sitting room, a dining room and a kitchen. Holliday took the key down from its hiding place above the door. The moment he stepped into the hallway he knew something was wrong. There was a familiar stench in the air. The metallic throat-catching odor of blood and the dark smell of human feces.

"Oh, shit," Holliday whispered, glancing toward Lazarus. He'd smelled that smell from the jungles of Vietnam to the hot desert sand of Iraq and the harsh mountains of Afghanistan. Somebody had died here and not too long ago.

They found Eddie in the kitchen. He was slumped with his back against one of the cup-board doors beneath the sink. His shirt was bloody from the right side of his chest to his waistband. The wound bubbled slightly as Eddie breathed in and out. He was alive, but not by much. Holliday knelt down beside his dying friend.

"Who did this to you?"

"*Una perra*. She was a traitor. She was playing both sides, *mi compañero*. Phone."

Eddie smiled weakly, blood leaking out of the corner of his mouth. His breath was coming in harsh little gasps. "I think I gave the *puta* as good as she gave me." He lifted the blood-covered butcher knife feebly and then dropped it. *"Hasta luego, mi colonel."* The bubbles stopped frothing from the wound in his chest. Holliday crouched beside his friend for a moment, and then closed Eddie's eyes.

"Too many times, too many times," he whispered, hard, cold tears forming at the death of his friend, a man he'd loved like a brother. The whole thing had been a setup right from the beginning. Carrie's objective had always been the notebook. She'd led them along like the Pied Piper. He felt like an utter fool.

They found Carrie in the bathroom. There was a Glock 19 on the tile floor beside her. With one motion Eddie had sliced her from waist to heart. Her organs and intestines spilled out on her lap as if on the floor of a slaughterhouse. Holliday rummaged around her corpse, uncaring of the blood that was getting all over his hands and arms. He eventually found her cell phone and scrolled down to the last call she'd made.

"Seven-oh-three. McLean, Virginia. The Company."

"Why not the Paris division?" Lazarus asked.

"Because she was working for a black cell inside the CIA. There've been rumors about it for years. The little bitch here even mentioned it to me on her way to Paris."

"So what do we do now?" Lazarus asked.

"We are on the top floor of a building without elevators. We'll have to clean them up as best we can."

They dragged Eddie into the bathroom and loaded him into the bathtub, followed by the body of the woman. Going back to the kitchen, Holliday rummaged around in the cupboard under the sink. He found a bottle of ammonia and a box of lye soap. He looked through the drawers and discovered two boxes of cling wrap and took it all back to the bathroom.

"See if you can find me a dry-cleaning bag and a roll of any kind of tape, preferably duct tape."

Lazarus left the bathroom and Holliday started on the bodies. He filled the tub until the remains of the Pilkington woman and Eddie were covered, and then stopped the water. He poured in the half gallon of ammonia and sprinkled the box of lye over the interior of the old claw-foot tub. He took the cling wrap and covered the tub from side to side and end to end. Lazarus returned with two dry-cleaning bags and a roll of duct tape.

"Help me with this," Holliday said.

They spread the bags out over the top of the bathtub as tightly as they could, taping as they went.

"If we're lucky, the lye and the ammonia will keep the stink down for a day or two and the dry-cleaning bags and Saran wrap should keep it down for a day or two more."

"Then what?" Lazarus asked.

"We find another hidey-hole. And then we see what's in the basement of the Vatican Administration Building."

7

Rusty Smart sat in the living room of a safe house on Fort Myer Drive just across the Potomac from D.C. The room was cluttered with plasma-screen computers and printers, and there was a complex communications setup that included satellite phones and stolen image-tracking links with five Keyhole units. There were three other men in the room with him: Tom Harris, James Black and Paul Streeter—all members of a ghost unit running out of Langley headquarters.

"They're in Rome. Carrie shot the Cuban but he managed to kill her anyway. Holliday and his new friend found them and tried to keep the stink away," Rusty Smart said.

"What about Nardi?" Streeter asked.

"We managed to find him but we were too late. Holliday and his new friend had gotten to him first."

"So now what do we do?" Harris asked.

"Without the old place, they're going to have to find a new bolt-hole," Smart said. "First we find the bolt-hole and then we follow them. If they were talking to Nardi, they know about Huff and his train. But if we don't get Holliday's notebook, this whole thing is going to fall apart."

"I don't get it," said Harris. "This isn't our kind of thing. You make Holliday sound like some kind of boogeyman. Why is he important anyway? I've gone over the file, and there is nothing strategic about him, or world-shaking. So what goes?"

"This group, or one like it, has existed inside the U.S. intelligence community since Donovan's Office of Strategic Services back in World War II. Holliday's connection is through his uncle, who was a liaison officer between the OSS and British military intelligence. He found a Templar sword at Berchtesgaden, which turned out to be part of a code that led to the collected wealth of the entire Templar system. Holliday's initial investigations into the sword led him to one of the last true Templar monks, who, on his deathbed, gave Holliday the notebook containing every code and account number for Templar funds throughout the world. There are a lot of other people who have been chasing the notebook, including the Vatican. Our group's thinking is that there is some connection between Huff and the Vatican and between the Vatican and Holliday. The notebook is the key to all of it for some reason. And we have to find out what that reason is before the shit hits the fan."

Holliday and Lazarus found rooms in a cheap flophouse hotel on Via dei Serpenti. They found a local secondhand store, outfitted themselves and headed off to the Via di Monte d'Oro, a side street off Mercato delle Stampe. Holliday followed Lazarus down the narrow street to a four-story granite building with a plain black-and-gold sign above the door that read "Saxon Peck Rare Books, Maps, Charts and Collectibles."

Lazarus opened the door with the old-fashioned spoon-handle mechanism and they went inside. The interior smelled of exactly what the sign had said. Rich scents of old leather, brass and books in addition to the wonderful smell coming from the espresso machine at the rear of the shop.

The long shop was divided into two parts, with books dominating the floor-to-ceiling oak cases and rarer objects behind glass and display tables that ran in three aisles. At the rear of the store was a small area of peace and quiet, with three leather chairs arranged around an ornate four-legged circular table, almost certainly seventeenth century and definitely British. To the left, a black cast-iron spiral staircase ran up to the floor above.

On one of the railed wooden ladders sliding down each of the bookcases a short, heavy-set man with snow white hair was rearranging books on the upper shelves. Eventually he ran out of books to rearrange and came down the ladder. He turned and saw Lazarus. His ruddy-bearded face suddenly beamed.

"Peter, my boy! I haven't seen you in years. Still looking for old paintings and such?"

"Quite a number of them, actually, Lord Peck."

Peck's gaze fell on Holliday. "And you must be Colonel Holliday, the man I've been hearing about for so long."

"Today is the first day I've ever heard your name," said Holliday.

"I knew of you through your uncle Henry. He and I were classmates at Oxford and colleagues during the war. I was also a friend of Rodrigues."

Holliday was stunned. "You knew Rodrigues? How did that come to pass?"

"It's too complicated of a story to go into now. Let's just say we were brothers together and that I know he gave you the notebook."

The old man looked at his watch. "Just about time to close up," he said. He bolted up the door, then turned out the lights in the windows. He turned around and smiled. "The two of you look terribly tired. Now, come. I'll make us a cup of my special espresso and we can talk all about it."

Lazarus had filled Holliday in about Peck on the way to his store. Peck was the second son of the Duke of Rutland, a so-called insurance heir. If his elder brother, Thomas, had died before him, Peck would have inherited everything. As it was, Thomas had lived and inherited everything instead. He had sunk millions into Rutland Abbey for the sake of appearances, and in the end was forced to sell everything. Rutland Abbey was now owned by the National Trust, which ran five-shilling tours on weekends.

Peck, on the other hand, had met a rich Italian countess at one of his brother's lavish summer weekends in the country. They'd fallen in love, decided to marry, and with nothing left to keep him in England, Peck moved to Rome, where he had been ever since. His dearest wife had been the light of his life for the better part of forty years. When she died, he inherited her entire fortune and opened his store. During those four decades of life with her, he had become the world's leading expert on ecclesiastical documents, especially those regarding the Vatican. He also had what was perhaps the largest collection of Renaissance and eighteenth-century technical books.

Holliday and Lazarus settled into the old leather chairs while the old man brewed them three cups of dark espresso spiked with an exotic plum brandy.

"I know you wouldn't come to visit an old man simply out of friendship. So you must have a question."

"We both have questions," said Lazarus.

"You go first," Peck said.

"What can you tell me about this?" Lazarus said, reaching into his jacket pocket and handing a small image Nardi had given them on their trip to Tuscany.

Saxon Peck stared at the postcard-sized photograph and smiled. "I can tell you just about everything there is to know about it," said Peck. "The title is *Three Men Talking in Front of a House*, by David Teniers the Younger. The painting is Flemish. It was originally owned by H. L. Larsen, and in 1943 it was auctioned by Van Marle and Bignell to E. Gopel, Den Haag, who were dealers. That same year it mysteriously was gifted to Herr A. Hitler and turned up in the Führermuseum in Linz. Later, it was taken out of Germany by an SS colonel named Rheinhard Huff. It eventually wound up in the Vatican and was last seen on the wall of the cardinal secretary of state's office. The man's name is Ruffino, I believe."

"What do you mean, 'last seen'?" Holliday asked.

"On a visit by the present bishop of Linz to Ruffino's office, the prelate commented that he'd last seen the painting in the Führermuseum during the war. Knowing the powers of such rumors, Ruffino immediately had the painting taken down, and within two or three weeks had replaced it with a second-rate copy. The bishop of Linz took the responsibility of not being able to know the difference between the real thing and a cheap copy."

"Nardi made it sound as though the train had been a big secret," said Lazarus.

"For the most part, it was," said the white-haired old man. "It wasn't until the fall of Rome that our intelligence people got wind of the story. Even then we didn't know the details." Lord Peck paused. "All we do know is that a number of paintings and other artworks were used by members of ODESSA to finance their escape through the Vatican ratlines."

"So nobody really knows how much of the art is still there?" Lazarus asked.

"No," Peck answered, shaking his head. He fished around his waistcoat pocket and brought out a darkened, gnarled briar pipe and a kitchen match. He lit the match and held it over the bowl of the pipe, sucking until it began producing clouds of aromatic smoke. He turned to Holliday. "Now, you said you had a question?"

"What can you tell me about a Templar Knight named Sir Martin Fitzwilliam?" Holliday asked.

"Sir Martin Fitzwilliam. Fitzwilliam was a monk of the Abbey of Saint Andrew. All we know of him is that he vanished sometime shortly after the taking of Jerusalem in 1199. He is notable for refusing to take part in the massacre that followed the siege and was last seen heading into the desert alone. According to Roland de Vaux, Fitzwilliam's family sigil—a single lion rampant below a Templar Cross—was found scratched onto a staircase in the ruins of the scriptorium at Khirbet Qumran."

"Who is Roland de Vaux?" Lazarus asked.

"You mean, who *was* he," said Holliday. "From the early twenties onward he was head of the Je-

SECRET OF THE TEMPLARS

rusalem Archaeology Institute. He was also the first man to dig for the Dead Sea Scrolls."

"He had a theory, I believe," said Peck.

"Yes," said Holliday. "De Vaux surmised that, instead of heading east, Fitzwilliam returned to France and gave a scroll to Bernard of Clairvaux, who was a student of languages and knew the scroll for what it was. He gifted the scroll to the Vatican and Pope Innocent III, and it hasn't been seen since."

"What was in the scroll?" Lazarus asked.

"Supposedly it was the Gospel according to Christ himself and described his travels in the East. Apparently the 'East' included India, Tibet and China."

"Such a document would be heresy. It would belie the whole story of the Resurrection. It would destroy the very foundation of Christianity," Peck said, tamping his pipe with a nicotine-stained thumb.

"I don't see what this Fitzwilliam fellow and a train load of looted Nazi art have to do with each other," said Lazarus.

"I'll tell you," said Peck. "The actual Vatican Bank wasn't organized until 1942 by Pope Pius XII. Prior to that, all Vatican real wealth—bullion, art, gemstones and monetary offerings of all kinds—were held by the Administration of the

Patrimony of the Apostolic See, which managed the funds remaining at the disposal of the Pope. In other words, the private funds used to run the Vatican itself. All of this was kept in the Vatican Administration Building, which is where the trucks from Huff's train were unloaded."

"Nardi said the trucks off-loaded through the side entrance of the administration building's southern wing. Why would they have unloaded there?" Holliday asked.

"Come with me and I'll show you," said Peck.

The old man led them up the circular staircase to the second floor, where instead of bookshelves lining the walls there were old-fashioned wooden print drawers. Peck went to one drawer, withdrew several drawings and took them to the large metal-and-glass light table that dominated the center of the room. He chose two from the sheaf of drawings and laid them out flat. It showed a profile view of the Vatican Administration Building. The center section was five stories tall and topped by a small dome. The south and north wings were four stories tall and plain. There was a park in front of the building and an ornate circular driveway, while at the rear of the building was Saint Anne's Chapel. Peck withdrew the first drawing and put down the second. This showed a main floor plan for the south end of the build-

ing. There was a short hall leading to a rectangu-
lar freight elevator.

The old man pointed down at the elevator
marked on the diagram. "This is the only way
those crates and boxes could be taken to the basement."

"Where did you find all this stuff?" asked Holliday.

"There was a major renovation done on the
building in the late thirties. Years later, the chief
contractor of the job asked if I wanted to buy
them, so I did." The old man lit his pipe again
and spoke. "I've always had an interest in documents of one kind or another about the Vatican.
There seems to be a great number of people in
the public who have the same inclination. The
Catholic Church and the Vatican have had more
exotic theories, countertheories, conspiracies and
outright criminal behavior attached to them than
any other organization in the world. I have documents here going back to the Borgias. Some of it
is of quite a secret nature, but I have had a very
hard time finding out whatever happened to Huff's
contribution to the papal treasury."

"How easy would it be to get into the building?" Holliday asked.

"If you simply wished to enter the building, it
would probably be quite easy to go in through

the front door. Getting in through the side entrance and onto that freight elevator would be a different kettle of fish altogether."

"But it is possible?" Holliday said.

"As long as you were willing to take an enormous risk," said Peck.

Peck looked at the other two men in the room. "You're not planning on robbing the Vatican, are you?"

"We thought we'd give it a try." Lazarus smiled.

8

The Vatican Administration Building looked like a cross between an old Hilton Hotel, Versailles and a wedding cake. The two priests, each carrying a plain attaché case, climbed a set of wide steps to a broad patio. They crossed the patio until they reached a narrower set of stairs between a pair of columns leading to the ornately decorated front door.

They pulled open one of the large doors and stepped inside the building. It was laid out in a long, wide cross, one passage leading in all four directions of the compass. The place was swarming with people, most of them dressed like the two priests, others in ordinary business suits, and some nuns scuttling about. The two priests with briefcases turned left and moved down the hallway. Reaching the end, they came to a door that read *"VIETATO L'INGRESSO"*—No Admittance.

Ignoring the instruction, the two priests pushed through and found themselves at the far end of the building's south wing. There was a large door, a narrow set of stairs and a freight elevator. They pressed the down button for the elevator, which soon arrived, its large door sliding open. The two men stepped inside, at which point one of them turned and pressed the stop button to keep the elevator from going anywhere.

"We've got about thirty seconds," said Holliday, stripping off his vestments and leaning down to open the briefcase. He pulled out a brown workman's boiler suit with a papal patch on the chest. He climbed into it, pushed the vestments into the now empty briefcase and closed it up again. When he stood and turned, he discovered that Lazarus had done the same thing.

"The shoes are wrong, but we can live with that," said Lazarus.

"We'll have to ditch the briefcases as soon as we can. I don't want to go through all of this in reverse on our way out," Holliday said.

Holliday hit the stop button again and then the down button. The freight elevator lumbered downward and came to a jarring halt. The doors grumbled back and the two men stepped out. They faced a broad corridor between heavy pipes, boilers, generators and all the other machinery necessary for running a large building.

Interestingly, there were two narrow-gauge rails set into the concrete of the floor, like the railroads used in old coal and tin mines. They ran off into the distance without a break. Holliday and Lazarus found a dark space at the foot of one of the boilers and shoved their briefcases out of sight.

"I guess we should follow the yellow brick road," said Lazarus, nodding down at the rails on the floor.

"Well, we sure as shit aren't in Kansas any-more." Holliday laughed.

Freed of their priestly burden, the two men walked down the main passageway surrounded by the sounds of machinery.

Both the priests' vestments and the papal boiler suits had been easy enough to come by. They had all been purchased at Barbiconi, a reli-gious department store only a few blocks from the Vatican.

The two men walked past half a dozen or so similarly dressed workers, who ignored them com-pletely. Holliday saw a clipboard resting on a set of valves and scooped it up; there was nothing like a clipboard to make you look official. They finally reached the end of the broad alleyway and came to a stop in front of yet another door marked "No Admittance." They ignored the warning once again and stepped through the door.

This time they could quickly see that they were out of place. A small room on the left with windows on three sides contained several banks of closed-circuit TV monitors. At the far end of the passageway was an area guarded by what looked like steel bars. The railway tracks went under the steel bars and ran farther on. A security guard sat in a folding chair eating a Quarter Pounder with bacon and cheese and a supersized bag of fries. A giant paper cup stood at his feet. He had neatly made a bib out of a paper napkin and that had only marginally succeeded. There was food in a Niagara of special sauce, ketchup and bacon bits spilling over his large belly.

"Ventilatore," said Holliday, waving the clipboard vaguely in the direction of the area behind the bars and stretching his Italian vocabulary to the absolute maximum. The guard grunted something with his mouth full toward the television monitor room. There was a clanging noise and the gates popped open. Holliday and Lazarus stepped through the barred gate into what appeared to be the outer chamber of a bank vault. Walls of safety-deposit boxes rose to the ceiling

on either wall and directly in front of them were two massive doors, each fitted with a large combination lock. Holliday waved his clipboard at the single large vent in the ceiling and Lazarus nodded in agreement. In fact, both men were focused on the two massive doors and their large locks. The doors had the scrolling escutcheon of Chubb & Sons. Each of the doors had its own turning wheel and combination dial. It looked as though it had been made sometime in the 1920s.

"How the hell are we expected to get into that?" whispered Lazarus.

"I don't have the slightest idea. I guess we should ask your friend Saxon Peck."

Holliday and Lazarus made their way back down the basement hallway, got into the elevator and made their way out, walking past a tall gray-haired man in what appeared to be an extremely expensive suit. Accompanying him were two tall, burly priests who looked more like bodyguards than clerics. Lazarus frowned as they passed.

"Something wrong?" Holliday asked.

"Yes, but I can't quite put my finger on it," Lazarus said.

They eventually made their way to Saint Peter's Square and crossed it, heading back to the antiquarian bookstore.

"Shit!" Lazarus said. "Now I know what was bugging me."

"What was it? Something to do with those two bully boys we passed in the corridor back there?"

"Yes, and the man they were guarding—Eric Bingham. He owns the biggest auction gallery in Palm Beach and he's run more than one scam in the art world. What the hell is he doing here?"

"What kind of scams?" Holliday asked.

"A painting would be sold in a New York auction to a telephone bidder. The telephone bidder would then put the painting on permanent loan to a fictitious municipal gallery in the Midwest. Meanwhile, the painting would be sold under a different name to a different Midwestern gallery. And then it would be sent to the Miami branch of the Bingham Gallery, where it would actually be sold. A large and prominent art expert in New York would give bona fides to all the versions of the paintings. That way the two 'owners' of the painting got substantial tax write-offs. All the paperwork was handled by the Bingham Gallery in Palm Beach. He escaped prosecution by going to the FBI and providing evidence for the criminal prosecution of several major smugglers of art, ancient artifacts and stolen jewelry. He has been a good boy ever since, but seeing him here doesn't make me trust that he's a good boy now."

"Can you see any way the Vatican could be involved with a man like this?" Holliday asked.

"The paintings and other fine art brought to the Vatican on Huff's train and the fact that the Vatican Bank has been involved in several serious scandals lately might have something to do with it, but I can't see what exactly."

"Let's get back to Peck's as quickly as possible and see if we can think this out."

Holliday, Lazarus and Peck sat around the round table at the rear of the old man's store. The table was littered with espresso cups, whiskey tumblers and a three-quarters-empty bottle of Glenlivet. After an hour of discussion, they had decided several things. Number one, the big old Chubb safe would be impossible to open by two amateurs under so much security. Number two, hiring a proper cracksman was too dangerous from a secrecy point of view. The only possible way to discover what was going on was by keeping track of what Bingham was up to—following him was going to be a lot safer than breaking into the safes.

"Well, I can tell you one thing about Bingham: he never goes second-class. And that means we'll find him in the most expensive hotel in Rome."

"That would be the Hotel de Russie on Via del Babuino," said Peck. "These days it's considered to be the place where the Hollywood A-list goes."

It took two phone calls to confirm that Bingham was in residence there.

"Now what do we do?" Holliday asked.

"Pay him a visit, I suppose," replied Lazarus.

Rusty Smart sat in the Fort Myer Drive safe house control room, a satellite phone to his ear.

"Were our suspicions correct?" he asked.

"He went to the Vatican and came out empty-handed," said Tom Harris, the leader of the group, who had been sent to keep track of Holliday and Lazarus's movements.

"Where is Bingham now?" Smart asked.

"He's in the Hotel de Russie but he's scheduled to be on a train to Paris by ten o'clock tomorrow morning. He'll arrive at eleven thirty the following day and will take the morning Chunnel train to London."

"I want you to get somone to fly to Paris and another person to fly to London to meet both trains. Harris, you'll follow him directly from Rome."

"Okay, boss, but what do we do about Holliday?"

"Somehow I have a suspicion that Holliday isn't going to be too far away from any of this, so keep your eyes open."

Smart turned off the encrypted satellite phone and idly watched the screens in the control room. Something was wrong. He could smell it from a mile away. If he wasn't absolutely careful, the whole damn project would come crashing down and more than likely take the entire CIA with it.

Holliday and Lazarus stood in the plain but luxurious lobby of the Hotel de Russie. Holliday stood by one of the house phones while Lazarus stood at the reservation desk talking to the man behind the counter. Holliday checked his watch, then dialed the number of the hotel. He could see the man picking up the phone behind the reception desk as Lazarus removed a rather cumbersome cell phone from his jacket pocket and flipped it open below the eye level of the receptionist. Simultaneously the man at reception connected with Holliday.

"Hotel de Russie," said the receptionist politely.

"I'd like to speak with Mr. Bingham. Is he in?" Holliday asked.

"I'll ring," replied the receptionist. The call went through with the strange triple ring of most Italian telephones and by the fifth ring it was clear that nobody was going to answer.

"I'm afraid he doesn't seem to be in," said the receptionist.

"Perhaps I'll call him again later," said Holliday.

Lazarus and Holliday meandered into the Stravinskij Bar and both of them ordered mineral water.

"Did it work?" Holliday asked.

"Like clockwork," said Lazarus, taking the phone from his jacket pocket and looking at the small screen. The device was called a phone cloner. By standing close enough to a phone the cloning device could then "steal" the other phone's signal. "Bingham is in a penthouse suite. Room 509."

"Excellent," said Holliday. "Let's go see what Bingham and his two thugs took out of the Vatican."

"Won't that be illegal?" Lazarus said with a wink.

"Frankly, I couldn't give a shit."

The hallway on the fifth floor of the hotel was empty. Like most hotel rooms these days, it had an electronic card lock. Holliday bypassed it with the heel of his shoe. The door banged open.

"We've got maybe three minutes before security comes to the rescue," said Lazarus.

"More than enough time," said Holliday.

They began to search. At the one minute, forty second mark Lazarus withdrew a red plastic mailing tube out of the closet. It was sealed at both top and bottom with a cap.

"Shall we open it?" Lazarus asked.

"Why not?" replied Holliday.

"Here," said Lazarus, handing over the long red case. "The honor is yours."

Holliday took the tube, snapped off one of the caps and shook the contents onto the bed. There were two rolled canvases and a brown envelope folded outside them, everything held together with a rubber band. Holliday slipped off the rubber band and Lazarus came closer. He rolled the paintings open while Holliday picked up the envelope.

"Dear God in heaven!" Lazarus said, looking down at the two paintings lying side by side on the bed below him.

"What is it?" said Holliday.

"The one on the left is *The Stone Breakers* by Gustave Courbet and the other one is Caravaggio's *Saint Matthew and the Angel*."

"What's so special about them?" Holliday asked. "You sound like you popped a heart valve."

"Because neither one of these paintings exists anymore. They were both destroyed during World War II bombings."

"Shall we keep 'em or take 'em?" Holliday said.

"Leave them," Lazarus said. "I'd like to see where this trail goes."

Holliday held up the brown envelope. "I'll tell you one thing," said Holliday. "Miss Hannah Kruger of 104 Jasmine Street in Southfield, Wisconsin, can tell us a thing or two, but for now let's get the hell out of here."

PART TWO

CRAQUELURE

9

Hannah Kruger, once known as Hannah Kru-gerovich Alevsky, headed out of the fine arts build-ing of Caldwell College, went around the Gould Library and cut across the Bald Spot, then took a shortcut between the Laird Stadium and the resi-dences. She checked for traffic, crossed the road and stepped onto the narrow footbridge across Cannon Creek to the residential side of the town. A few minutes later, she was on tree-lined Jasmine Street, turning through the open gates of the door in the low stone wall that went around her small saltbox house.

As she opened the door, she could smell tur-pentine and shellac. She smiled, went through into the kitchen, flipped on the coffeemaker and headed to the rear of the house and into her stu-dio. She stared at the painting on the easel, smiled again and went back for her coffee. Sipping the strong, harsh brew, she returned to the studio and sat down.

She looked at the painting again. It was a twelve-by-fourteen-inch watercolor of palmetto leaves in the sun. She had taken the necessary photograph of it during her vacation last winter in case anybody ever asked any questions. It was a perfect copy of John Singer Sargent's *Palmettos*, which had last sold to the Metropolitan Museum of Art for $7.5 million. The one on her easel would be sold to somebody in Europe for half that amount. One way or the other, the painting was hers.

Hannah had been born June 11, 1968, in Moscow. She attended the Moscow Art Institute until she was eighteen, then gained an internship at the Hermitage as an apprentice in the restoration department. In 1988, she began a brief affair with a much older man named Pytor Novestev, a midlevel official at the USSR Department of Immigration, who made good on his promise to allow her and her parents to emigrate to Israel. They stayed briefly—just enough time to get their Israeli passports—and then traveled to New York. Over the next few years, Hannah attended NYU, Columbia and the Canadian Conservation Institute in Ottawa, an institution renowned for producing some of the greatest art conservators in the world. She worked for several years at the Guggenheim and was finally coerced into taking an appointment as head of the fine arts department at Caldwell College.

Pytor Novestev had also been a high-level KGB officer looking for potential sleepers in the United States. There had already been a plot to quietly sell off the Hermitage's lesser-known works, and several years later the KGB, now reformed as the FSB, began to develop the idea. Over time contacts were made with less than loyal members of MI6, the French DGSE, the BND in Germany and, most important, the CIA. It was the BND with its incredible record keeping that had discovered Huff's train and the complete inventory of its contents.

It was in this way that the Vatican had become involved. By the time Pope Benedict had been hired for the top job in the Catholic Church, the Vatican Bank was already in trouble, not to mention its other problems and scandals about priestly pedophilia and the enormous lawsuits that resulted from it. All in all, Vatican City was tipping into bankruptcy. With the election of the Argentinian Pope Francis, bankruptcy was inevitable. Being a practical man, as well as a Jesuit, Francis agreed to liquidate the world's art assets. The conspiracy was called Operation Leonardo, named after the most famous artist in the world, Leonardo da Vinci.

Hanna Kruger was a small but vital part of the project. It was her job as a master copier and forger to re-create masterpieces that would replace the real artworks in museums all over the world. The real artworks would be deaccessioned and sold on the open market.

On the surface the plan was perfect, but in reality it went one step further. After announcing the upcoming sale of the work in question, one of Hannah's near perfect forgeries would go on the auction block instead. The original gallery or museum got to keep the original and Operation Leonardo got the cash. This worked especially well with the tens of thousands of works that had been looted from Germany, Poland and other soon to be Soviet countries that were then sent back to the Hermitage, never to be seen again. It also worked extremely well with the contents of Huff's train, in which the only inventory of the contents rested with the Vatican and the British secret police. It was really nothing more than a card player dealing from the bottom of the deck.

The planning committee of Operation Leonardo met at Bolton House, which they rented from the National Trust. Bolton House was a beautiful and majestic country estate built of stone—the epitome of English country living. It was located in Lincolnshire and the house itself was surrounded by a thousand acres with three or four wooded areas plus its own lake. It was about as private as you could get.

The individual members of Leonardo and their personal security teams began trickling in early in the day. By evening the members, dressed for dinner, met in the dining room with its magnificent table capable of seating eighteen. The meeting began with a sumptuous catered dinner that included oysters with champagne vinegar mignonette, celery soup, fig and Stilton salad with port wine dressing, venison tenderloin with Madeira wine peppercorn sauce, Yorkshire pudding, shepherd's pie, floating islands with lemon custard sauce and raspberries, and English Eccles cake.

It was almost nine o'clock before the remains of the meal were removed and the men around the table were comfortably smoking cigars and drinking brandy. Finally Sir Henry Maxim, director of operations for MI6, tapped a spoon against his brandy snifter and called the meeting to order.

"Although most of us already know each other well, for the sake of our new guests I thought proper introductions should be made. On my left, representing the CIA, is Russell J. Smart. Beside him is His Eminence Cardinal Secretary of State of the Vatican Arturo Ruffino, followed by Pytor Novestev, our Russian friend from the FSB; beside him, Dieter Rhine of the BND; and, last but not least, Thierry Grenier of France's DGSE.

"Together on my right are the new members of our organization. Representing India, Kota Raman of the well-known Raman family, Abraham Ivankov from Russian organized crime, from the Unione Corse Dominique Venturi. And from Japan, Katsu Giri, head of the Yamaguchi-gumi yakuza group. Thank you all for being here. I'll now turn the meeting over to Russell Smart from the CIA."

"My friends," Smart began, "over the past few years we have all come to the same conclusion. The entire world is rapidly approaching what the astronomers refer to as a singularity. In astronomical terms, a star becomes so heavy it falls in on itself, thus creating a black hole. In our own singularity, the entire world has come to the point where money has no true reality. Banks create invisible and meaningless things to sell to each other; entire countries are imploding. China has now become the inevitable snake eating its own tail. It has almost inflated itself out of business by lending more money to the markets than they can possibly repay, thus losing those markets to sell to. India is on a bold upward curve based on low labor costs and virtually no environmental controls, and their government is totally corruptible and the perfect nesting site for capitalists from the West. At the same time India is literally killing itself as its freshwater supply dries up due to bad hygiene, creating pockets of plague that will eventually cover the entire country.

"In my own country, bailing out companies that can no longer survive has become a farce, yet the United States still believes itself to be the world's greatest country. Our biggest industries revolve around the military, but at the same time we start wars that we cannot hope to win. The whole world has gone crazy. The only way for us to succeed as a group is to develop our own economy. One of the ways we intend to do that is with Operation Leonardo. Our new member from Japan, Mr. Katsu Giri, has expressed an interest in our new 'criminally' oriented members. I'll let him speak for himself and those other new members of Leonardo."

Giri, a short, slim man with iron gray hair, took a short sip of brandy. His English was perfect, though slightly accented. He nodded formally and began to speak. "My dear friends, the most common difficulty in the transfer of money from one place to another is its size and weight. Billions of dollars in currency are lost every year due to vermin infestations in the basements where it is hidden. The simple fact that a billion dollars in American currency weighs nine tons is an enormous problem. It's extremely risky to transport it in any of the ordinary commercial ways. Thus our proposal is this: Fine art is simple, compact and easy to move in any number of ways. In fact, international trade in such works of art can be done perfectly legally and with no customs necessary. By calculating the value of each work of art using an objective scale, the art held in a central bank or vault could then be used as currency. Ergo, one organization owes another organization a billion dollars. The first organization has a theoretical deposit in the bank of art and therefore pays the other organization in the value of X number of artworks that it has on deposit. In point of fact art has been used this way on a smaller scale for years. The art simply becomes a different form of currency. Our suggestion is that the banking institutions or vaults be located in countries not involved with Leonardo. There are several of these, but obviously Switzerland would be the simplest and most central option."

Cardinal Secretary of State Arturo Ruffino spoke up. "Why not the Vatican?" he said. "We already hold much of the art in our own vaults."

Russell Smart laughed derisively. "I don't mean to be blasphemous, Your Eminence, but that would be rather like taking all the gold from Fort Knox and storing it in Sing Sing Penitentiary instead. You know as well as I do that the Vatican, particularly the Vatican Bank, has more corruption in it than a giant block of Swiss cheese. I agree with Mr. Giri. Set it up in Switzerland."

For a moment there was a great deal of chatter around the table. After letting various people vent their opinions, Sir Henry Maxim rapped his knuckles on the linen tablecloth.

"Gentlemen, shall we vote on the subject? All those in favor of setting up their own bank or vault in Switzerland, raise your hands. Those against it and in favor of continuing the discussion on the subject, remain as you are." Every hand was raised except for Ruffino's and Pytor Novestev's of the FSB.

"We appear to have a majority. It seems that Leonardo is going into the business of Swiss banking."

*   *   *

Holliday sat in the window seat of the direct Air France flight to Nassau in the Bahamas and looked out the window into the dead black night. Beside him Peter Lazarus breathed evenly as he slept. The L-1011 was cruising at over thirty-eight thousand feet and the dark clouds rolling off into infinity mimicked the Atlantic so far below them.

He realized the feeling that had been slowly creeping over him, perhaps for years now. It was the soft breaking of his heart. How long had it been now since Amy's death? All he knew was that she had been gone longer than he had been with her. His memories of the good times had been eroded by the time he had lived without her. He could remember the sound of her voice, the feel of her skin and the look of her smile, but it gave him nothing now. Age had come upon him silently and with it a deep, weary loneliness.

To make it worse, his cousin Peggy and her archaeologist husband, Rafi, had been brutally murdered in the sands of Israel. And now Eddie, as noble a warrior as he had been a friend, had been murdered too. The people he'd treasured had vanished and all that was left was this never-ending quest that had begun almost a thousand years before in the heart of France.

The question was, did he care anymore or did he just want to do what soldiers always did—simply fade away? Once upon a time, he had loved nothing better than his life with Amy, his teaching at West Point and the book he was writing on the history of armor. All of that was long past. The future ahead was no more than the infinite nothingness of the skies outside his window. The search begun by his uncle was a noble one. But monks, martyrs and mythology had finally turned to what they inevitably had to become: money.

"Penny for them," said Lazarus.

Holliday turned to his companion. "Gloom and doom, I suppose," he responded.

There was a pause and then Lazarus spoke again. "Can I ask you a question?"

"Sure," said Holliday.

"What does a bunch of looted art have to do with the Templars? I thought you were chasing the Dead Sea Scroll that is supposed to be the Gospel of Jesus."

"My cousin Peggy and her husband died for that scroll and the message it contained. If it was ever discovered and publicized, it would rock the very foundations of the Church and perhaps shake the faith of half the world."

"Then why look through the artwork on Huff's

train and whatever else was held in that old vault?"

"Because I think the scroll was in that vault. The Vatican Bank is in such serious trouble now that they'll even risk putting the scroll on the market. After all, the buyer who purchased it would need years to properly open it and translate it. And even if they went to that extreme, the Church could always deny its authenticity. The value of the scroll is ephemeral. Its worth is in the eyes of whoever owns it."

"Well, if it's reason enough for you, it's reason enough for me."

10

Holliday and Lazarus drove their rental car down Jasmine Street and parked a few houses down from Hannah Kruger's. They'd spent most of the previous day hopscotching on airplanes and the night at the local Best Western hadn't done much for their jet lag.

"Pretty," said Lazarus.

"Quiet too," replied Holliday. "It's hard to believe their master forger lives here. Not a place where you'd expect to find knockoff Vermeers."

"There is only one way to find out," said Lazarus. "Let's drop in on Hannah while she's giving her 'Age of the Romantics' lecture to the girls and boys enrolled in her art appreciation class."

They climbed out of the car and walked casually down the street to the little house behind the low stone wall. They went up to the front door, with Lazarus in the lead. He took a four-inch strip of credit card plastic and slipped it into the simple lock. The door opened and they stepped inside. "I can do the same thing with dead bolts. It just takes a little longer."

"You certainly have skills," said Holliday as they stood in the gloomy vestibule of the house.

"Anybody home?" Lazarus called out. There was no reply. The two men made their way to the back of the house, casually checking the rooms on either side of them. They finally came to the studio in the rear.

"My, my," said Lazarus. "The lady's a purist." He pointed to a large table with a dozen or more mortars and pestles on it as well as a set of storage shelves against the wall full of jars of brightly colored powders, clumps of mineral and unidentifiable things that looked like pieces of wood. On a second table were stacks of thin wood planking of indeterminate age, as well as a pile of very old canvas that had been scraped of any painted surface. Opposite was a large light table and on it an eighteen-by-twenty-inch transparency of the Caravaggio they'd seen in Rome; a jeweler's loupe rested beside it. Between the tables the studio was dominated by an immense easel. A canvas placed on it could be clamped to a central mechanism and moved in any conceiv-

118

able direction or position. At the moment a canvas—the exact size of the small painting they'd seen in Italy—was suspended on the easel.

"She makes her own paint, uses canvas or wood from the correct era—definitely a professional. If you look around at the far end of the studio, you'll probably find a chemistry set fully outfitted with all sorts of chemicals and witches' brews used to make a painting authentic, or at least look that way."

Somewhere there was the sound of a door opening and closing and then footsteps approaching the studio.

"Shit!" said Lazarus.

A moment later Hannah Kruger came through the open doorway. Her face took on an expression of horror as she saw the two men standing there.

"Oh, God," she said. "You don't know what you've done. You've killed them."

"Killed who?" said Holliday.

"My mother and my father and me. That's who."

"You haven't even asked us who we are," said Lazarus, "or what we are doing here."

"It doesn't matter. Cop, crook, whatever. We're all dead."

"Maybe you might want to explain that," said

Holliday. "Just to get things clear before we're all killed. And by the way, his name is Lazarus and he's an Interpol art cop and my name is Holliday and I'm just along for the ride."

"Fine," said Hannah. "Now I'll know who signed my parents' death warrant as well as mine and yours. Under other circumstances, maybe I'd offer to make you a cup of tea, but right now somebody is coming and he's carrying a gun."

"You're under surveillance?" Holliday asked urgently.

"Of course I'm under surveillance," said Hannah. "All of us are."

"All of us?" Lazarus asked.

"You obviously know what I'm doing here and the kind of people I'm connected to. You *must* know that I'm not the only one doing this. I deal with the eighteenth-century paintings back through the Renaissance and specializing in Dutch masters, Italians and the Baroque school. There are other people for other periods. As far as I know they are located all over the world. We even have three or four hidden Web sites where we exchange information and find materials we need."

"You're talking about a very big organization," said Lazarus. "Do you know anything about the people who run it?"

"In my case, it's a bastard named Pytor Novestev from the FSB. We don't have time for any more of this—" She shook her head angrily. "We've got to get out of here. *Now*."

"She's right," Holliday said to Lazarus. He turned back to Hannah. "Do you have any kind of weapon?"

"Yes, give me a minute." The woman ran out of the room. She was back a few moments later with a small black automatic pistol in one hand and a box of 9-millimeter ammunition in the other. She also had a bulging backpack slung over one shoulder.

Holliday looked at the gun. "A Beretta M1934. Seven rounds in the magazine and one in the breech make eight. Not much, but it'll have to do."

"Why should I give it to you?" said Hannah belligerently.

"Do you know how to use it?" Holliday asked.

"Not really," Hannah answered. "The man at the gun show where I bought it said it was just point and shoot."

"It's a little more complicated than that," said Holliday.

"Believe me, Ms. Kruger," said Lazarus. "He was a colonel in the U.S. Army. If somebody needs shooting, he's your man."

Hannah tentatively handed over the gun and

the box of ammunition. Holliday opened the box and the entire contents into his left-hand jacket pocket.

"What's with the backpack?" Lazarus asked.

"I knew this day would come and I wanted to be ready for it. I call it my 'go bag.'"

"Do you have a car?" Holliday asked.

"No. The town is no bigger than a postage stamp. You can walk anywhere."

"Have you seen the surveillance?" Holliday asked.

"I've spotted the same car parked at the end of the block several times," she answered.

"Is there a back way out of here?"

"There's a side door at the end of the studio that leads into the garden."

"Who's your neighbor at the back?"

"I have no idea"

"Fence?"

"Just a picket one."

"Let's get out of here."

There was a crash as the front door of the house was kicked in.

"Too late!" Lazarus said.

"The two of you get going," said Holliday. "I'll be right behind you."

As Hannah and Lazarus turned and ran, a man appeared in the shadows of the hallway. The intruder was tall and heavy-set, like a bouncer. He was carrying a small boxlike MP5 submachine gun with the long tube of a silencer screwed onto the muzzle.

In the split second he had to make a decision, Holliday threw away every instinct and rule the army had ever taught him and aimed for the head rather than the easier target of the man's chest and center mass. The first shot had to be a kill shot. As he raised the little Beretta, Holliday's thumb flipped up the safety and he fired. His finger squeezed the trigger again and again until the magazine was empty. The man's face disappeared in a spray of gore and the machine gun dropped out of his nerveless fingers. He stood for a moment, the last spasms of life rushing through the rest of his body, and then fell backward like a toppled tree. A voice yelled out from the far end of the hall.

"Max? You okay?"

Max was definitely not okay. Holliday scooped up the MP5 and rummaged through the man's pockets, finding three more of the long, sticklike magazines. Then he ran like hell.

He met with the other two on the next street over.

"What now?" Lazarus asked.

Holliday looked up and down the quiet street.

So far the gunfire inside Kruger's house hadn't attracted any attention. Directly in front of Holliday, parked in the neighbor's driveway, was a late-model Mercedes minivan with the driver's-side window wide-open.

"Go ring the doorbell," Holliday told Hannah. Meanwhile, he popped open the door and slid behind the driver's seat. He checked under the visor, but there was nothing. He leaned down and felt under the seat. Nothing there either. He got out of the car and felt inside the front wheel well. He was rewarded with a small metal box: a magnetic Hide-A-Key. Hannah came down the steps of the house.

"Nobody home," she said.

"Good," Holliday replied. He squeezed the key fob and the doors popped open.

"Climb in." Holliday backed out of the driveway and drove slowly down the tree-lined street, the mayhem of a few seconds earlier vanishing behind them.

They found the interstate and drove south toward Madison.

"You must have a contact," said Holliday, pulling into the middle lane, his foot on the gas keeping their speed at a resolute fifty-five miles per hour. "Somebody other than this Novestev character."

Hannah Kruger was riding in the front passenger seat. She turned to Holliday. The shock of the last few minutes was still clear in her expression.

"I only had dealings with one person. A man named Rupert Sheridan. He's a curator or something in the fine art division at Blackthorn and Cole."

11

According to the research Lazarus had done while they were making their way to New York, Blackthorn and Cole, although not the largest auction house in England or the United States, was definitely the richest and by far the most discreet. The original two partners, George Blackthorn and Isaac Cole, had shared a seat at Lloyd's. Both had been furniture manufacturers and had a fondness for antiquities. They decided to consolidate their interests and leave the dreary ledgers and tolling bells of the insurance business to establish the firm of auctioneers that still bore their name.

Since the establishment of Blackthorn and Cole coincided with the huge speculative losses in the American land bubble and the resulting crisis in the British monetary system, the two men had no difficulty finding antiquities. Blackthorn coined what was to become the firm's dark and unwritten motto: "We prosper on the desperate tears and broken dreams of others."

Apparently, while they prospered on other people's desperate situations, they developed a long-standing reputation for discretion. If anyone employed by the firm was ever caught whispering about the sudden sale of a duke's gold-plated candelabras, for instance, he was immediately terminated. Rumor and gossip had no place at Blackthorn and Cole.

With the rise of Hitler and the blossoming of the Third Reich, their respective grandsons saw the handwriting on the wall and an opportunity to prosper even more. David Blackthorn arrived in New York in late 1934 and immediately purchased a large plain brownstone office building on Madison Avenue. From 1934 to 1941 Blackthorn's representatives began purchasing from a variety of auctions and sales in Switzerland, France and Germany. Most of what they purchased either had been from Jewish dealers fleeing and trying to liquidate their inventory or had been outright plundered by Hitler's Rosenberg brigades. Tens of millions of dollars exchanged hands. Buying almost up to America's entrance into the war in December 1942, the New York division shipped out the last purchases within a few days of the attack on Pearl Harbor.

When the shipments arrived, they had nothing more than coded labels on the crates containing the paintings, sculptures and other precious objects. They disappeared into the basement storage rooms of the building on Madison Avenue and did not appear on any inventory lists. The artworks simply ceased to exist.

Shortly after the arrival of the last shipment, Michael Cole left England on a Swissair diplomatic flight to Lisbon. He then took a Pan American flying boat to New York, stopping once to refuel in Bermuda. Cole and Blackthorn greeted each other at the LaGuardia Marine Air Terminal. They shook hands warmly, but the sadness in their expressions told the true story: they had plundered the past and defiled a people to mortgage their own future. Both men felt like grave robbers, which was exactly what they turned out to be.

Holliday, Lazarus and Kruger traveled south to Madison, where they dropped the minivan in one of the university parking lots and took an Amtrak bus to Chicago. From there they took the Lake

Paul Christopher

Shore Limited into New York and got a room at the Fifty-seventh Street Holiday Inn. With the stolen minivan and a dead body behind them, traveling by bus and train offered the smallest security risk. At the hotel, Doc Holliday used one of his inexhaustible credit cards and paid for all three rooms.

Late the next morning they stood at the hot dog stand in front of the Whitney Museum.

"How do we approach this?" Holliday asked.

"I called after breakfast and asked for Rupert Sheridan. It turns out he's one of their top appraisers," Lazarus said. "I told him I had a Rubens I wanted to sell and asked if he'd give me some help. He said that as long as we sold it through Blackthorn and Cole he'd have no problem. We have a meeting in five minutes."

"What do we do while you're having your meeting?" Holliday asked. "I thought there might be some shock value in confronting him with Hannah."

"I'm the copier, remember?" Lazarus said. "We keep Hannah in reserve. Bring her in now and they'll just shut down everything. This way, we may get them to panic a little."

Lazarus walked down the street to the corner, crossed and walked back up to the facade of Blackthorn and Cole. He went up a short flight of steps

130

and through the front door. The interior was an only slightly updated version of the original building. A broad set of granite stairs leading up to the mezzanine's main auction rooms flanked a wrought-iron cage of an old-fashioned elevator. At the reception desk was an attractive woman in a maroon blazer whose name tag read "Julia Anderson." There was a modern multiline telephone to her right. Lazarus approached her.

"My name is Peter Lazarus. I have an appointment with Rupert Sheridan."

Ms. Anderson picked up the telephone receiver, punched a few buttons and waited.

"Mr. Sheridan? I have a Mr. Peter Lazarus in reception for you." There was a moment's pause and she hung up. She looked up at Lazarus. "Mr. Sheridan will see you now." She smiled. "He's on the fifth floor. Just turn right as you get off the elevator."

Lazarus pushed back the scissored door to the old elevator and climbed in. He closed the door and hit the ivory button marked "Five," then rode up with an almost majestic and equally tedious slowness. When he eventually he reached the fifth floor, he turned right down a broad modern corridor. At the far end on the left there was a small waiting room with a reproduction of Miró's *The Farm* on one wall. Another receptionist sat behind a small desk; she too wore a maroon blazer.

"May I help you?"

"My name's Lazarus."

"You can go right in."

Lazarus gave the maroon blazer a nod and went through the doorway leading to the inner office. The room was large, the floor covered with a variety of Persian and Afghan carpets. The desk was some kind of sixties Swedish thing. The man standing behind the desk was a tall, blond, narrow-faced figure with cheeks that were perfectly shaved. He wore bright blue bifocal half frames and an Armani suit. He held out a hand. There was a Harvard "Veritas" ring on his pinky finger. Lazarus shook the extended hand. Mr. Sheridan's grip was just a little too soft for Lazarus's taste and he held for just a little too long. Sheridan motioned toward an Eames-style chair in front of his desk. Lazarus sat.

"I'm very pleased to meet you," said the appraiser. "Might I ask which Rubens you wish to sell?"

"I lied," said Lazarus with a broad smile. "There is no Rubens."

Sheridan looked only slightly startled. "If there is no Rubens, then why are you here?"

Lazarus reached into the inner pocket of his

jacket. He took out his Interpol ID wallet and flipped it open on Rupert Sheridan's desk. "What can you tell me about your involvement with Hannah Kruger?"

"Who?" Sheridan asked.

"You know," said Lazarus. "The woman who forges Caravaggios and Da Vincis for you."

"We haven't handled a Da Vinci or a Caravaggio at Blackthorn and Cole for a number of years. Real or otherwise."

"Your pupils just expanded, there's sweat at your temples, the blood is going out of your lips and your cheeks look like you're wearing rouge," said Lazarus.

"Perhaps that's because I find myself confronted by some sort of schizophrenic. I know of no Hannah Kruger or for that matter anyone else who forges paintings for this firm. Please leave immediately."

Lazarus stood, scooped up his ID and gave Sheridan another smile. "I'll be back."

He found Holliday and Hannah Kruger on the third floor of the Whitney contemplating Edward Hopper's dreamlike *Woman in the Sun*.

"Did you get it?" Holliday asked.

"The cat's among the pigeons," said Lazarus, taking the phone-cloning device they'd used in Rome out of his jacket pocket.

*   *   *

Rupert Sheridan was on the phone before Lazarus reached the elevators. "I need to see Mr. Blackthorn immediately. We have a problem."

Michael Cole, grandson of founder Isaac Cole, had died unmarried and with no heir in 1962. Under the terms of the original partnership agreement, in such a situation the living partner left inherited his share. David Blackthorn had one child, Harrison. The elder Blackthorn and his wife, Sylvia, had died together in a plane crash from Charles de Gaulle to JFK, leaving Harrison as the sole owner of Blackthorn and Cole.

Harrison Blackthorn kept the same small office on the third floor that his father had used, with the same elegant furnishings. There was a narrow window behind the Georgian desk and a beautiful old coal-burning fireplace on the far wall. The office had dark oak wainscoting and worn silk wallpaper above. The wallpaper had most likely originally been a dark red, but time had faded it to a pale pinkish hue. To some people entering the office, it was like looking into another time.

Harrison Blackthorn was a somewhat severe-looking man in his mid-fifties. His crisply cut short hair was graying at the temples. He had his father's hawklike nose and deep creases on either side of his large mouth. He was broad shouldered and thickening with age but he had obviously been a strong and active man in his youth.

When Rupert Sheridan burst into Harrison Blackthorn's office, the older man immediately stood up and went to the small bar made from a converted writing desk. He poured the flustered appraiser two inches of vodka and handed it to him.

"Sit down, drink this and pull yourself together." Sheridan drained the glass in a single swallow.

"You said we had a problem," said Blackthorn. "What it's all about?"

Sheridan spent the next ten minutes explaining the Interpol agent's sudden appearance and his use of Hannah Kruger's name.

"Did he say anything about anyone else?" Blackthorn asked.

"No," said Sheridan. "But if he knows about the Kruger woman, he must know everything."

"Not necessarily," said Blackthorn. "But we'll have to take a few precautions. We'll have to talk to Bingham in Palm Beach and Scott in Miami. Call them now and tell them that I expect them in this office by ten tomorrow morning."

"What about the Leonardo committee?" Sheridan asked.

"I'll deal with them myself," said Blackthorn. He stood up, went to the bar and poured himself a glass of Scotch, dropping two ice cubes into the glass. He lifted the vodka bottle, gesturing toward Sheridan. "A little more?"

12

At precisely nine thirty the next morning Rupert Sheridan, Eric Bingham and his partner William Scott, who operated the Miami branch of the Bingham Gallery, sat in Harrison Blackthorn's office on Madison Avenue.

"I have been in touch with Leonardo and they are not pleased with the situation. On the other hand, we have a little more information to work with now. Lazarus is in fact an Interpol investigator. He was recently in Paris and is connected to Colonel John Holliday. There is a further connection in Rome that leads to Hannah Kruger. The result is that the whole arrangement— the entire existence of Leonardo as well as our own—is now in jeopardy."

"Do we have any options?" Bingham asked.

"In the first place, all movement of our 'special' inventory is to cease immediately. In the second place, records of the inventory must be either destroyed or removed from your premises. So far only the East Coast seems to be involved. The rest of the country is still in operation. However, in the interim, that will be closed down as well. Paul Roth's operation in Chicago was the only one in the Midwest who actually used the Kruger woman. If we can contain it, we may be able to save ourselves."

Eric Bingham coughed into a small pink fist, then cleared his throat. "And precisely how is our salvation going to come about?"

"Agent Lazarus and Colonel Holliday must be removed from the playing field."

"And just who is going to do that?" William Scott said.

"I thought that would be obvious," said Harrison Blackthorn. "We hire someone to kill them both."

Later that afternoon, Harrison Blackthorn sat on a bench overlooking the reservoir. Beside him was a large manila envelope. He was smoking an illicit Montecristo Cuban cigar, inhaling the soft aromatic smoke and then exhaling. He waited patiently, staring out at the water. There was a slight breeze, and the leaves on the trees sighed pleasantly. Blackthorn rarely had time for such quiet moments and he was thoroughly enjoying this one. A few joggers thumped past, their feet crunching on the gravel pathway. No one paid him the slightest attention. Five minutes later another man sat down on the bench. He looked like an accountant— medium height, a little potbelly, dressed in an off-the-rack suit from Barneys. The shoes were Florsheim brogues.

Without turning from his view of the reservoir, Blackthorn spoke.

"You're Mr. Snow?"

"That's right," the man replied in a faintly Irish accent.

"You come highly recommended," said Blackthorn.

"Our mutual friend said you were a discreet sort of person. If you have me under any sort of surveillance or if you're wearing a wire, I'd advise you to get up and leave this place immediately. Do we have an understanding?" Snow's voice never rose above a calm conversational level.

"We have an understanding," said Blackthorn equally calmly.

"So, now, what would you have me do for you?"

"I need several people eradicated."

"Let's not be coy. You want me to kill some-one, yes?"

"Actually several people," said Blackthorn. "A woman in particular. She has information that could have disastrous consequences if it were made public."

"By several, exactly how many do you mean?"

"Three," answered Blackthorn.

"Do you have any idea where these people are at the moment?"

"Most likely at a hotel in Manhattan, regis-tered under the name John Holliday."

"One *l* in Holliday or two?" Snow asked.

"Two," Blackthorn answered. "All the infor-mation you need is in the envelope."

"All right," said Snow. "The price will be five million dollars. Half now and half on comple-tion. Our mutual friend will handle the details."

"How do I get in touch with you?" said Black-thorn.

"You don't," said Snow.

"I'll have to know what sort of progress you are making," said Blackthorn. "A great many people are dependent upon your success or fail-ure.

Standing up, Snow picked up the envelope, tucked it under his arm and looked down at Blackthorn. "If I discover that you have discussed anything we have said in this conversation," said Snow with a cold, sinister tone in his voice, the Irish accent very pronounced now, "I'll kill everyone you've ever talked to. I'll kill your family, your family's family—I'll kill your dog. Do we have an understanding?"

There was a long pause. "I understand."

"See that you do." The assassin turned on his heel and walked away from the bench. The breeze had fallen and the trees were silent.

Holliday and Alexander "Zits" Mitchell walked across the Plain to Thayer Hall. As Holliday had predicted long before, the zits were all gone but his widow's peak had turned into complete baldness. He was still bony, but he had thickened up some. Holliday had come to West Point on his own, leaving Lazarus and Kruger back at the hotel.

"If it wasn't you, Colonel Holliday," said Zits Mitchell, "I'd put you under arrest and throw you into the stockade."

"But it is me and I wouldn't ask if it wasn't very important," Holliday said.

"What kind of important?" asked Mitchell. "You're asking me to break every rule in the book."

"People are trying to kill me and my friends."

"Why are they trying to kill you?" Mitchell asked.

"It's complicated," said Holliday. "The less you know, the better. I don't really want you involved in this."

"You want me involved enough to risk my career," said Mitchell. "You were the one who wanted me to teach, so I think I deserve to know why I would throw away the job I love."

"You're right," said Holliday. "I can tell you this much: it involves organized crime, art the Nazis looted and the Vatican. That enough for you?"

"Maybe I should take you to the hospital instead of the stockade," said Mitchell. "You sound crazier than shit, Colonel."

"Maybe I am, but it's the truth. You'll just have to trust me. Maybe we can sit down and talk about it over a Scotch when the whole damn thing is over."

The young major sighed. "All right. What exactly do you need?"

"Three automatics—hopefully nothing as bulky as a Colt—and maybe a small automatic weapon or two."

"Jesus," said Mitchell. "Why don't you ask me for the moon as well?"

"Can you do it?" Holliday said urgently.

"Yeah, I can do it," said Mitchell, sighing again. "Where are you staying?"

"Hotel Thayer. Room 406. North wing."

"I'll try to be there by ten o'clock, unless you hear from me. By midnight, it will be me in the stockade," said Mitchell.

Mitchell met him in the hotel well before ten. He brought three hammerless Smith & Wesson Chief Specials and two boxy Heckler and Koch UMP45s.

"Good enough for you?" Holliday's old student asked.

"Couldn't ask for better," said Holliday. "You were a good student, Mitchell, and I'll bet you're an even better teacher. Thanks a lot. You make an old man proud."

"Not so old, sir." Mitchell grinned.

Cardinal Arturo Ruffino sat behind his desk in his office, staring at his computer screen. Mario Tosca, his friend and head of Vatican secret police, entered the room without knocking and sat down opposite him.

"We have a serious problem," said Tosca.

"You're going to tell me that Holliday knows about the Huff train? I already know."

"It's not that," said Tosca. "What he knows goes far beyond that. As you are aware, he was searching for the lost scroll when our people tried to kill him a year ago. He now knows that it was retrieved by us and that we once had it in the Vatican. And he knows it's for sale to the highest bidder. If he manages to find out who that highest bidder is, it could destroy the Church."

"How did he find all that out?" Ruffino asked.

"Apparently he and his friend were recently in Rome. Somehow Holliday also enlisted the aid of an Interpol agent. Believe it or not, he and the agent were in the storage area here and almost reached the vault. His friend, the Cuban, was killed by some unknown faction, but Holliday and Lazarus managed to get out of Rome unharmed. And somehow in all this mess they managed to find out about Bingham, the Caravaggio and the Courbet. They also found out about someone named Hannah Kruger. They're back in the United States and now they're after the whole Leonardo operation."

"Useful information, but not particularly drastic," said Ruffino. Although he was angry that Holliday and this Lazarus man had been able to breach the Vatican itself.

"I was just getting to the real problem," said

Tosca. "My men found out who killed the Cuban. It wasn't your friends and it wasn't us. As far as we can tell, it was somebody on the inside. It looks like there's a mole in Leonardo and whoever that mole is wants to take everything."

13

Vijay Sen ran through the dark empty streets to the shipyards. He was short and very thin, dressed in ragged sweatpants, a David Bowie T-shirt and a knockoff New York Yankees baseball cap. His feet were bare. He was fourteen years old. His only weapon was an eight-inch ceremonial kirpan he'd stolen the previous year from a wealthy Sikh's house, which was enclosed by a makeshift cardboard sheath threaded through the drawstring of his sweatpants.

He had been a thief for as long as he could remember. He had been born in the Dharavi slums, which was where he had first begun his criminal career. He had stolen pots from pot makers, embroidery from the embroiderers and cookware from anyone who was foolish enough to leave it unguarded. His mother had died when he was five, his father was completely unknown to him and he was the youngest of ten. He had been raised alone, his nine other siblings having either died of various diseases or escaped long ago to some other fate. For two years he had lived with his grandmother, also a resident of the slum, but then she too had died. From the age of seven he had lived on his own, adding the theft of food to his list of crimes.

For a few years he had survived as a beggar on the richer streets of the city's center. Eventually he had joined a gang of pickpockets. But he had been discovered shortchanging the man he worked for and once again was on his own. His next criminal escalation was stealing a tea boy's uniform from the Taj Mahal Palace Hotel. Wearing the white-turbaned uniform, he would wander the long hall-ways of the hotel checking doors. There would inevitably be one or two doors left unlocked. Often he came up with nothing, but sometimes there would be valuables left behind: a watch, a pair of expensive earrings, once an American tourist's wallet stuffed with American money and credit cards. As young as he was, he knew who to sell the credit cards to and kept the money for himself. But just as inevitably as the occasional open door, Vijay had been caught red-handed once. He'd been arrested, tried and convicted, then sent to Arthur Road Jail. He did not fare well in the notorious prison and it was only by sheer luck that he did not contract tuberculosis or become forcibly infected with HIV. On release, any trace of Vijay's childhood had vanished. At fourteen he would do anything to survive.

He was used to the darkness. His large dark eyes gathered up whatever light there was. The rest of his senses were equally tuned in to his environment. A dog barking could be just that— or perhaps a warning to its master. The sound of footsteps could mean nothing at all or it could mean imminent danger. The air carrying the scent of tobacco could announce that he wasn't alone. Vijay knew, perhaps better than anyone else, that while Mumbai was one of the fastest-growing, richest cities in the world, it was also one of the most dangerous.

He reached his destination, a high wooden wall surrounding a scrapyard of which he knew two things. There was a rotted section of the fence he could easily squeeze through and the interior was guarded by an enormous black Rajapalayam hound. Once he would have been frightened—but not now.

He found the rotted planks in the darkness, pushed in the boards, and squeezed through. Vi-

Paul Christopher

jay knew the dog was chained during the day but set loose after the scrapyard closed each evening. Occasionally a night watchman would occupy the small tin hut that served as an office, but Vijay knew the dog was the more dangerous of obstacles he faced tonight. He slipped the dagger out of its cardboard sheath and waited.

He was surrounded by scrap metal of every kind. Piles of indeterminate junk from demolished buildings, including window frames, rebar, broken-down air conditioners and pipes of every kind. Across the yard there were piles of old engine blocks and entire automobiles. All the junk was centered on an enormous shredding machine. Great scoops of metal dropped into it from a crane mounted on a large flatbed trailer at the far end of the scrapyard, where several massive dump trucks would take the shredded metal to local foundries to be melted down into useful ingots for its future incarnation. Vijay listened and sniffed the slight breeze. Nothing.

He moved forward, heading toward the main gate of the scrapyard. He had one job tonight: unlock the gate and leave. The keys to the three enormous padlocks on the gate were in the pocket of his sweatpants and had been given to him by the man he was working for. Halfway to the gate, Vijay tensed, the hair on his arms and the nape of his neck rising.

He turned. The giant guard dog was pounding toward him like something out of hell itself. Vijay could see the bared fangs and huge muscles as the creature leaped toward him. The young man waited until the creature had committed itself, its rear haunches pushing it into the air. With all four of the dog's powerful legs off the ground, Vijay dropped onto his back, and as the dog descended he thrust the kirpan into the dog's throat, letting the dog's own momentum carry the knife down to the chest and belly. Its guts poured like a warm pile of offal onto Vijay's chest and face. He gagged and rolled out from under the eviscerated corpse, scraping the guts and blood away from his face and eyes and turning to vomit. He stood up, his hands on his knees, and waited for his breath to return.

The dog's attack and his response had taken less than fifteen seconds but would be imprinted in Vijay's mind for eternity. In that split second he had seen Death approaching, but somehow he had managed to elude it.

Still covered in filth from the dog, Vijay walked toward the gate. He turned again at the sound of lumbering footsteps. The night watchman was approaching, flashlight in hand. He was an obese man wearing a filthy shirt and dhoti. His lime green flip-flops slapped the dirt as he chugged forward. The beam of his flashlight found the ruins of the dog and then turned and found Vijay, the dagger still in his hand.

"What have you done to Raji? You've murdered him." The fat man charged at Vijay, his arms extended. The young man ducked under the grasping arms and slid the kirpan into the night watchman's belly without hesitation. He fell to his knees, gasping and holding his stomach as blood began to stain his shirt in a wide circle. Vijay stepped toward the helpless man and without any thought of remorse drew the sharp blade of the dagger across the man's throat. The fat night watchman fell forward, still on his knees. Vijay wiped the kirpan on the back of the man's shirt and slid it back into its sheath.

Silently the fourteen-year-old murderer padded toward the gates and used his keys to unlock them. He threw the gates open and then walked silently into the darkness.

Kota Raman sat in the gaudy, lavishly decorated dining room of his equally lavish mansion in South Mumbai. His breakfast was anything but traditional. The head of the largest gangster family in India had adopted the eating habits of English lords and ladies. He breakfasted on an assortment of dishes including eggs, bacon, toast from a silver toast rack, some sort of fish dish usually with a sweet sauce and an endless supply of stewed fruit. All of this was provided by an executive chef he'd hired away from the Mumbai Palace Hotel.

Today he ate alone. The compound, surrounded by a large stone wall topped with broken glass, contained three other houses—one for his eldest son, one for his mother, his mother-in-law and his grandmother, and one for his security staff. His youngest children—two teenage boys and a teenage girl—had been sent away to expensive boarding schools in England.

His breakfast finished, one of the kitchen boys cleared the serving plates and dishes while another served the bitter coffee that Raman preferred. He continued reading the newspaper for a few minutes more and then got up and went to his large office in the rear of the house. The room was large and modern, a single large window with a perforated wooden screen letting in the cool morning air. A sixty-inch plasma screen was turned on on the wall across from his desk. It was tuned to one of Mumbai's business channels, a scrolling list of companies and their stock prices reeling across the bottom of the screen. He watched the screen for a moment, waiting. Eventually his second in command, Ali Kapoor, entered the office.

"What is this I hear about the scrapyard last night?" Raman inquired.

"Someone unlocked the gate and let them in. They also killed the guard dog and the night watchman," Kapoor answered.

"Who is 'they'?" Raman asked.

"We're thinking it was Vijay Sen," Kapoor said.

"Any way we can find out for sure?"

"We're rounding up as many of his little slumdogs as we can lay our hands on. Someone will know something about what went on last night."

"Make it quick," said Raman. "The fat bastard is making me look bad. You steal from my property, you steal from me. This will not be tolerated."

Holliday, Lazarus and Kruger reached Palm Beach after driving through the night. They sat in a Denny's on South Congress Avenue waiting for the Bingham Gallery to open.

"Do you two have some sort of plan? It seems

like we're leaping into the lion's den," Hannah said.

"One of us has to go in there and check the lay of the land. The only way we're going to put these people away is by finding evidence of what they're doing."

"We've got a problem," said Lazarus. "They almost certainly know what I look like. I guarantee you Blackthorn and Cole has cameras everywhere."

"Frankly, that applies to all of us," said Holliday. "If these people are as powerful as we suspect, they'll have file pictures of all of us. We've got to take the chance that Bingham is still in New York. Hopefully there won't be anybody in the gallery able to identify us."

"So who goes in?" Lazarus said.

"I do," said Holliday. "I'm the one who got us into this." He smiled. "Now, finish your Grand Slams, and we'll get out of here. I want you guys to back me up with a getaway car."

The Bingham Gallery was located on Worth Avenue, the Rodeo Drive of Palm Beach. It was a square two-story building with a windowless facade. The entry was through a pair of heavy glass doors. To the left of the doors was a simple brass plate that read "The Bingham Gallery. Established 1972." Holliday pulled open the glass door and stepped inside. The interior of the gallery was remarkable. The walls, approximately twenty feet high, were done in claret red. Above the walls there was a curved ceiling containing dozens of lighting fixtures running on tracks. In the center of the gallery was a gigantic misshapen desk made from a slice of marble. At the very far end of the gallery was a doorway in the middle of the rear wall most likely leading to an office and perhaps a storage area for paintings. The paintings on view were a variety of canvases from the seventeenth, eighteenth and nineteenth centuries, each one ornately framed and hanging from a gallery rail high above.

Seated behind the desk was an extraordinarily beautiful woman with long blond hair, high cheekbones and model's figure draped in a black dress. Holliday approached her.

"Is Mr. Bingham here?"

"I'm afraid not, sir. He's out of the city at the moment."

"How long is he gone for?"

"I'm not sure. Is there anything I can help you with?"

"Perhaps I'll just look around," Holliday replied.

The blond woman handed Holliday a glossy four-color catalog. The cover had a photograph of James McNeill Whistler's *Nocturne*, a peaceful evening riverscape of the Thames looking toward Chelsea.

Holliday tucked the catalog under his arm and wandered through the gallery, pausing briefly in front of each painting. Every one of them had been created by an artist Holliday knew. Everything from Gainsborough to Guérin and Rembrandt to Renoir. It was an amazing collection to be seen in one room, and Holliday smiled quietly to himself wondering how many of them had really been painted by Hannah Kruger or one her colleagues working for the Leonardo group.

As he reached the end wall of the gallery he peaked through the open doorway. There was very little to see except an industrial metal stairway leading up to the second floor. As he continued his survey of the paintings, he was now looking for signs of any kind of security system or surveillance cameras. He saw none, but as he reached the front entrance he spotted a Chubb alarm system panel. He briefly noted that there were settings for pressure alarm, motion sensor and heat. He turned back to the blond woman, returned the catalog, thanked her, then left the gallery. He crossed the street to where the rental car was waiting, Lazarus behind the wheel. He climbed in on the passenger side and sat down.

"It's wired like a bank vault. We're going to have our work cut out for us."

14

Enoch Snow slipped his master key card into the lock on Holliday's door in the Best Western on Palm Beach Lakes Boulevard. The lock clicked, the light turned green and the door opened. Snow stepped inside and walked to the sitting room of the suite. It was like any other high-end suite—bland, yet well proportioned and well laid out. Matching small tables flanked the couch. There were two lamps and two matching paintings above the sofa. Beside the couch there was an oversized club chair. Behind it was a wooden desk. The whole room was dominated by a large plasma-screen TV. The carpet was a neutral gray broadloom.

Snow crossed the room and put the small black suitcase he was carrying onto the desk. He looked around the room, trying to imagine how it would be.

Finding Holliday, Lazarus and Kruger had been a relatively easy task in Manhattan. Snow was on good terms with the young woman in the main Visa offices and she readily gave him the tracking code he could use to follow Holliday's economic trail.

From the Holiday Inn he'd followed their car rental and their gasoline purchases all the way down to Palm Beach. Snow had been in the Denny's at the same time they were having breakfast. Finishing his cup of coffee, he made his way to their hotel. Twenty years earlier, that kind of surveillance would have been impossible for a man like him, but computers, not to mention simple greed, had made the entire process remarkably easy.

He dialed the combination on the suitcase lock and flipped it open. Inside, packed in hard foam, was a bomb maker's traveling kit. It included a kilo of Semtex sealed in a lead-lined aluminum foil pouch, making it odorless, non-gas-emitting and effectively invisible to most security procedures. Also packed was an assortment of fuses, timing devices and several untraceable cell phones. He broke the seal of the Semtex package, tore off approximately half the Plasticine-like substance and began molding it into the shape and size of a child's red rubber ball.

*   *   *

Vijay Sen, still dressed in the filthy clothes he had worn the night before and which in fact were the only clothes he owned, stood shuffling his bare feet on the thick carpet in Kota Raman's office.

"I could have you killed. You know that, don't you, slumdog?"

"Yes," mumbled Vijay.

"But you are not afraid," replied Raman. "Why is that?"

"I have nothing so I have nothing to fear," answered Vijay.

"Wise philosophy for a slumdog."

"The only one for a slumdog to have," said Vijay, a trace of a smile appearing on his lips.

"You don't deny that you broke into my yard and killed my dog and my watchman?"

"No, sir," said Vijay. "I killed them both. I broke into your yard and I opened the gates."

"Why did you do this?" Raman asked.

"Because the Bapat people paid me a thousand rupees to do so," Vijay said plainly.

The Rohit Bapat family was Raman's equal in Mumbai but their influence only reached the borders of the immense city. The Bapat had risen from the slums, the same slums that Vijay had come from, and the stain of his upbringing hung to him like inescapable chains. He was blunt, stupid and used violence rather than any kind of intelligence to achieve his goals. This was the first time in Raman's experience that Bapat had ever attacked him directly.

"Which of Bapat's people in particular came to you?" Raman asked.

"Bobby Dhaliwal."

Raman leaned back in his chair. Bobby Dhaliwal was one of Bapat's most effective soldiers. He was an old-fashioned Thuggee dressed in silks and leathers like a Bollywood film star. His trademark was a pair of giant mirrored aviator sunglasses. It was said that if Dhaliwal removed his sunglasses and you saw his eyes, it would be the last thing you ever saw. Oddly, Raman knew for a fact that Dhaliwal was a *pakoli*—that is, gay as a songbird twittering in the trees. If Bapat ever discovered this, he would lop off Dhaliwal's head.

"Interesting," said Raman. "Why are you telling me this?"

"Because when your people found me, I knew you would kill me one way or the other. Telling you or not telling you makes no difference except that if I didn't tell you you would torture me until I did and then kill me." Vijay shrugged.

Raman sat forward in his chair, his hands clasped together. "What is your name, slumdog?"

"Vijay," said the fourteen-year-old.

"How would you like to work for me?" Raman said, with his best fatherly smile.

The remaining members of the CIA's ghost unit once again sat in the safe house on Fort Myer Drive and once again Rusty Smart looked concerned.

"Kitchen is worried about a mole in Leonardo and we all know what that means. Have we heard from Blackthorn?"

Streeter shook his head. "Not a word, but the man we put on him saw somebody interesting going into the New York offices of Blackthorn and Cole. He took a photograph of him and we ran it through every database we have access to."

"Who is it?" Smart asked.

Streeter swiveled around in his chair and punched up the photograph and an identification panel beside it. "His name is Enoch Snow. Born in Belfast right at the height of the Troubles." Streeter turned back to the screen again. "At the age of fourteen he shot and killed a member of the Royal Ulster Constabulary but his pals in the IRA managed to spirit him out of Northern Ireland before the RUC tossed him into Long Kesh. Ten years later he resurfaced with the assassination of a high-ranking member of the Unione Corse. From then on he reappears with regularity as a hired assassin all over the world, sometimes bombs, sometimes shootings, with the occasional slit throat thrown in for good measure. The guy is a sociopath—a stone-cold killer."

Rusty lit a cigarette. "So presumably Blackthorn has hired him to nail Holliday and his pals. Shit." He shook his head. "One more monkey wrench into the works. Somehow we have to get to Holliday first, which means we'll have to get rid of this man Snow in the process. This whole thing is turning into a shitstorm. If we don't, the whole Leonardo project is going to be compromised, maybe even blown. The very fact that Kitchen thinks he has a mole is bad enough. But if he gets to Holliday before we do, we're dead men. And frankly, I'd like to continue living a little while longer."

Holliday, Lazarus and Kruger got off the elevator and walked down the carpeted hallway to their hotel suite. Holliday paused in front of the door, the card key poised over the lock. He stopped and crouched down, his eyes scanning the floor at the base of the door. In a variation on the old James Bond hair-in-the-crack trick, earlier that day he'd spit-glued a small black piece of paper from a magazine onto the corner of the doorframe. The paper was gone. He stood, thinking hard. He turned to Lazarus and Hannah, a finger to his lips.

"Wait," he said. He pushed the key card into the lock and went inside, leaving the door open behind him. He walked down the short hallway and stood looking into the sitting room. He let his eyes wander over the room, looking for anything that shouldn't be there or things that should be there but weren't. He scanned the room a second time and caught it. There had been a chip in the ornate frame of the picture over the left side of the couch. The chipped frame was now on the right. One thing led to another. The indentations of the legs on the couch were fractionally out of alignment. He stepped slowly backward and rejoined Lazarus and Hannah out in the hall. "Somebody's been in the room. There are a few things off-kilter. Wait here while I check it out."

"Is it Blackthorn or somebody else?" Lazarus asked.

"Hard to tell at this point," answered Holliday. "I'll let you know in minute."

Holliday went back into the sitting room once again, leaving the door open behind him. He took the painting off the right side of the wall and flipped it over. He immediately saw a small black box and a six-inch dangling wire. He carefully put the painting back on the wall. He went to the left-side painting and repeated the process. Another transmitter and wire. He hung the painting back on the wall and looked around the room again. The only other logical place for another bug was under the table. He crossed the room, went to the table, crouched down and looked beneath it. There was no transmitter. Smiling, he pulled out the chair and there it was: the third bug.

The room had been thoroughly bugged. But why? Anybody on his trail already had all the information they needed. There had to be something else going on. He stood and turned around. Why had the couch been moved?

He crossed to it and carefully lifted off the pillows. Nothing. Then he noticed a surgical split in the fabric covering the springs. He peered inside and saw the familiar shape of a small plastic pressure plate, its wires leading down to a spot underneath the couch. He found an identical switch in the fabric under the other pillow.

Walking with extreme care, Holliday backed away. He went down the hallway again and motioned for Lazarus to join him, then whispered as softly as he could into his ear, "Pressure switch. Bugs."

Lazarus nodded.

The two men stepped into the room. Holliday pointed toward the couch and Lazarus nodded again. They stepped forward and Holliday pointed out the familiar switches he'd seen so many times in Iraq and Afghanistan.

Holliday leaned forward and grabbed the back of the couch on the right side while Lazarus stepped up and grabbed the left. Very gently they eased the couch forward so that it was lying on its back. On the floor directly below the couch, where the couch had stood, there was a lump of plastic explosive wired to both the pressure switches and a cell phone.

Holliday motioned for Lazarus to step back. The two men eased their way out of the room and went out into the hallway yet again.

"Are you carrying a cell phone?" Holliday asked.

"Yes," Lazarus said.

"Is the GPS turned on?"

"Certainly not." Lazarus seemed a little angry.

"Good," said Holliday. "Crack it open and give me the chip."

"What are you going to do?"

"I'm going to take apart the bomb," replied Holliday.

"I'm going with you," said Lazarus.

"No, you're not," said Holliday. "It's far too dangerous."

"If I don't come with you, you don't get the chip."

"This is not the time for goddamn heroics," said Holliday. "Don't be an idiot."

"I'm not trying to be a hero and I'm not an idiot. It just makes good sense. You may need an extra hand in there."

Holliday thought for a moment. Lazarus was probably right. "All right. Let's go."

"So I'm supposed to stand here in the hall singing German beer hall songs?" Hannah said.

"You're more important than either of us. You know more about this whole business than we do. If that thing in there goes off, you run like hell to the nearest FBI office and spill your guts."

Hannah didn't look happy about it, but she nodded.

The two men went back in the room.

"Good luck," Hannah whispered.

The two men reached the end of the short hallway and Holliday paused again. He slipped off his shoes and Lazarus followed suit. Once again he gestured for silence. He had now figured out why the room had been bugged. Whoever was after them needed to know that they were all in the same room together before he triggered the bomb. The killer was clearly a very careful man. The pressure plates would have been enough, but he had a fallback trigger with the cell phone. If they made too much noise and alerted the killer, he would dial the cell phone. The tiny current from the ringtone would be enough to set off the explosive. They were going to have to do this very quickly.

Using a thumbnail, thick and calloused by his many years of being a soldier, Holliday began to crack open the lethal cell phone. Out of nowhere came the bellowing, screaming siren of a fire engine followed immediately by the electric wail of an ambulance. Holliday froze for an instant, the faceplate of the cell phone half open and half closed above the mechanism below. He took a deep breath, waited until the sound had faded and then removed the faceplate. He immediately pulled the chip and replaced it with the one Lazarus had given him. As he did so, he gestured to his companion to simultaneously pull the wires leading from the pressure plates. Holliday grabbed the now inert ball of plastic explosive in his hand and stood up.

He spoke loudly, "I spy with my little eye a

bomb that doesn't work anymore. Whoever you are, you screwed up big time." Holliday took the ball of explosive to the desk, flipped over the chair and removed the transmitter. He stuffed it into his pocket and crossed to the two paintings and removed both of the transmitters. With the other two transmitters in his hand, he went through to the suite's bathroom, ripped the wires out and flushed all three transmitters down the toilet. He went back into the sitting room.

"That was interesting," said Lazarus. "I thought I was going to wet my pants there for a moment. How many of those things have you defused?"

"Actually," said Holliday, "that was my first time. We had a course on it behind the wall in Baghdad, but that's about it."

"Mother of God," Lazarus whispered.

15

It took Holliday and his companions exactly seven and a half minutes to check out of the Best Western; Holliday timed it with his wristwatch. Driving the rental, they headed toward the restored Spanish colonial Amtrak station on Tamarind Street. Holliday made a stop along the way at a Chase Bank to get twenty-five thousand dollars off his American Express Centurion card.

As with all of his credit cards, he had received the Centurion card using the old notebook he'd been given by the monk Rodrigues. The manager of the bank, a Mr. Harold Bloom, although quite used to platinum cards, had never seen one of the rare black cards when he came out to do Holliday's banking for him.

"Are you enjoying our little town?" Bloom asked.

"A bit hot for me," Holliday answered.

"May I inquire why you need such a large amount of cash?" Bloom asked. He kept smiling, but that kind of cash usually went along with either drugs or money laundering, and carrying this kind of transaction on his books might very easily tinkle a few federal bells he didn't want tinkled. Bloom wasn't so much a stickler for rigid banking practices as he was for keeping some of his wealthy but less than palatable clients happy.

"Sure." Holliday smiled pleasantly. He knew exactly what the bank manager was thinking. "I'm going to a particular destination that doesn't take credit cards of any kind."

Bloom nodded. Cuba. Now it made sense. "I see," said the bank manager. "I'd be happy to get the cash for you myself."

"I'd love to come with you," said Holliday. "I've never really seen the inside of a bank vault before." The only way to ensure that Bloom didn't run off to make a phone call to the local FBI was by accompanying him.

"I'm sure that's not true," said Bloom coyly, "but by all means, follow me."

They went to the vault in the basement of the bank and Bloom chose two banded ten-thousand-dollar bricks and broke the band on a third brick, then counted out another five thousand dollars from it. The manager found a bank envelope and slipped the money inside. They went back up-stairs, where Holliday signed the requisite forms and Bloom finally handed him the money. Their cat-and-mouse game over, Holliday shook hands with Bloom and left the bank.

They carried on to the large pink-stuccoed train station surrounded by large beautiful palm trees and went inside. Holliday bought three tick-ets for the short trip to Miami. They went to the waiting room and sat down.

"Now what?" said Hannah.

"Yes, now what?" Lazarus said.

"I've got a plan," said Holliday.

"Do tell," said Lazarus.

Enoch Snow was furious. Holliday had out-thought him at every point along the way. He'd listened to Holliday's teasing on the FM receiver. He waited in his room three floors above and thought furiously. He'd clearly made some kind of mistake that had alerted Holliday or one of his companions and now he was paying for it. He went to his suitcase, took out a Beretta 92FS and screwed a suppressor onto the tapped muzzle. He popped the magazine, checked that it was loaded and slammed it back into the grip. He pumped the slide once, ensuring that there was a cartridge up the spout. Snow left the room with the pistol held in his right hand and hidden under his jacket. He walked down the hallway to the stairwell and made his way carefully down the three flights that would put him on Holliday's floor. He reached Holliday's suite, took out his master key card and slipped it into the lock. Snow then tapped the door slightly open with his foot. He stood, all of his well-honed senses hard at work. All he could feel was emptiness behind and failure beyond the slightly opened door. Using the splayed fingers of his left hand, he pushed the door fully open and stepped inside, but he was already sure it was too late. He took the silenced pistol from under the coat and with a two-handed grip he moved quietly down the little hallway. He stepped into the sitting room and took in the overturned couch and the paintings lying on the floor. He had failed and now it was too late.

"Fecking hell," said Enoch Snow.

It was eight twenty in the evening, dusk quickly turning to full night. Holliday, Lazarus and Kruger sat in the rental car directly across from the Bingham Gallery. Holliday took the ball of Semtex out of his pocket and tore it in half. He sniffed. It was odd that the bomber had chosen such an exotic plastic explosive. The Czech-made explosive was usually confined to use in Eastern Europe and sometimes by terrorists in Paris and London. The only thing this told Holliday was that the bomber in the hotel room was probably European. An American killer would more likely have used C-4 or any one of the dozens of DuPont products, all of which were readily available on the black market.

Holliday formed half of the Semtex ball into a palm-sized pancake roughly half an inch thick. He took the assassin's jury-rigged cell phone trigger, inserted a small wire into the pancake and folded the plastic explosive up around the phone. He casually climbed out of the rental, walked across the street and slapped his little package just above the lock on the front door. Just as casually he turned around and walked back to the car and sat down. He took his own cell phone out of his pocket and handed it to Lazarus, who was beside him in the passenger seat.

"Dial yourself," said Holliday.

"What then?" asked Hannah, sitting in the back.

"Duck," said Holliday. "But roll down your window first." With all four windows lowered Lazarus dialed his own phone number, its chip now in the assassin's trigger mechanism. They all ducked. The response to his call took as long as it took for the signal to bounce up to the nearest cell tower and down again to the object on the Bingham Gallery door.

The shock wave of the Semtex's detonation was enough to lift the left side wheels of the rental car a foot into the air and set off every car alarm for blocks. As the rental car rocked back to an upright position, there was a furious fireball that reached out to the middle of the street before it back-drafted into the interior of the gallery.

"Go!" Holliday ordered, his voice booming. They all tumbled from the car and ran toward the cavernous opening where the doorway to the Bingham Gallery had once been.

Holliday's plan had been simple and direct. It was unlikely that the West Palm Beach Police Department had either a bomb squad or anything else capable of dealing with a large explosion. They'd probably spend time talking to public works about gas mains before dispatching a fire truck and a squad car or two. He prayed that the cops' response time would leave them a window to get in and out of the Bingham Gallery and back to the train station before all hell broke loose.

Ignoring the ruined interior of the gallery, all three of them headed for the now shattered glass door leading to the stairway up to the office area. They worked as quickly as they could, gathering up paperwork and ledgers. Holliday used his foot to smash in a locked fire drawer in what had to be Bingham's desk and scooped up two long, slim ledgers.

"I think this is it," he said. "Time's up."

He gathered up the ledgers and pushed Lazarus and Hannah toward the stairway, following close behind. As they stumbled over the debris in the gallery, Holliday could hear the distant sound of sirens. They raced out of the gallery, crossed the street and jumped back in the car, dropping everything onto the floor. Holliday eased out of the parking spot and drove away.

His name was Jean-Pierre Devaux, his surname attached to the Templar Order for the better part of a thousand years. A Devaux had been one of the founding members of the order and there had been a Devaux instrumental in the discovery of the Dead Sea Scrolls, one of which lay partially open on the table in his laboratory.

Devaux's laboratory was his own. He had no connection to any university, and he would never have called himself a scholar. In fact, Devaux was an archaeologist for hire, a profession that was becoming more and more common in these modern times. Private archaeologists were thriving, giving developers clearance from any possible connection to Indian tribes, sacred burial grounds or any other historical reason for a large development to be stalled. Devaux's part of that professional circle was an elite one: he verified and authenticated stolen historical artifacts from around the world. And for this, he was remarkably well paid.

His laboratory was in his home, a large apartment on Avenue de Wagram, one block from the Arc de Triomphe, seven stories above a bar with the unlikely name of Le Paradis du Fruit.

It had taken him almost a year to unroll the scroll, which revealed four pages of the faint Aramaic script. As any archaeologist would, he photographed every tiny section of the scroll as it was revealed with a regular digital camera and an ultraviolet fluorescent camera. By the time a large section had been unrolled, he had brought over his portable X-ray unit and filmed it a third time. As the sections were unrolled, a long, absolutely smooth plate of Plexiglas moved on rollers on the table immediately covering and protecting each new section. It was a tedious business, but it was Devaux's philosophy that things should be done well or not at all.

He stood up, arched his back and sighed. He

was getting too old for this kind of thing. Although never a professor, he did have a professorial look about him. He was a thin man in his late fifties, and his graying brown hair was balding into a large half-moon above his forehead. He wore old-fashioned wire-rimmed spectacles that continually slipped down his nose until he'd begun to wear a small piece of white adhesive tape as a brake. He had never married and had never been tempted.

Life for Jean-Pierre Devaux was a never-ending series of projects. He took two vacations a year: one to the Costa del Sol in Spain and one to Las Vegas. On the Costa del Sol, he tanned himself on the beaches and enjoyed the spectacular food. In Las Vegas, he enjoyed the spectacular women, as many as he could absorb in a ten-day visit. Refreshed in both cases, he would return to work, his true passion.

The scroll in front of him was certainly authentic enough, although not terribly revealing. The four pages so far were nothing but a long-winded, elaborate introduction to the real meat of the scroll that was promised to come. On the other hand, the mention on several occasions of Yeshua ben Yosef, which translated to "Jesus, son of Joseph"—now commonly known as Jesus Christ—was certainly interesting. He had also uncovered the line "The King of the Jews is dead. The Messiah is risen in the East."

One of the most fascinating things about the quotation was that the present owner of the scroll came from India, a man named Kota Raman. Having done a great deal of research, as he did for all his clients, buyer or seller, he knew that Raman almost certainly had not obtained the scroll in any legitimate way. Devaux, of course, couldn't have given a damn either way. His entire career had teetered on the edge of crime for almost three decades and he was used to walking the razor's edge.

The scroll was in limbo. The group trying to purchase it had made an offer that he had passed on to Raman for consideration. The price offered had been almost beyond comprehension. But how much would you expect to pay for a Dead Sea Scroll, especially one that mentioned Christ and the Messiah rising in the East? It didn't matter to Devaux. What mattered was that if he authenticated and brokered the scroll to its new owner, his commission of ten percent would keep him in the lap of luxury for the rest of his life. Even more important to Devaux was the fact that his part in selling such a marvelous artifact would make him a piece of history. He smiled, staring down at the stitched piece of two-thousand-year-old cured, scraped sheepskin parchment in front of him. It did wonders for one's ego.

Unlike Raman, Rohit Bapat never stayed in one place for more than one or two nights. He could have occupied any of the high-rise apartment buildings in Mumbai, but he chose not to—and for good reason. A great deal of the Bapats' revenue came from their control of the building industry. The family had long before infiltrated the tradesmen union, the construction unions and even the loose organization of monkey boys who ran up and down the frighteningly high bamboo scaffolding that was used instead of cranes. The monkey boys hauled everything up by hand, floor after floor. Bapat would no more live in the penthouse apartment of any of these buildings than walk across Niagara Falls on a tightrope. Bapat of all people knew that the Mumbai building codes were covered in the dust of bad cement, bribes, subgrade materials of all kinds and general neglect. Architects on file were generally fictitious and the engineers involved in putting the buildings up were often educated only in a technical college, if that.

Instead Bapat and his entourage of bodyguards and family members would rove through Mumbai occupying a variety of houses, small family hotels and other residences, all of which they owned and operated. Bapat's most deeply held philosophy was to build his riches in small increments, one rupee at a time, just like the monkey boys and their buckets. It was an intelligent enough way to think in a city of twenty million. But Bapat had what could be called a fatal flaw. He was terribly envious. He envied Kota Raman's wealth and status among the crime families of India, and was wildly jealous of the man's enormous international reach. Somewhere in his small mind he knew that he could never quite attain such heights, but he knew he could destroy him. This was the reason for his first small attack on Raman.

Today's location for the Bapat traveling headquarters was in a small tumbledown hotel in central Mumbai. Bapat now generally used the building as a storage locker for stolen electronic goods, but today he'd taken it over for his own personal use. He sat in what had once been a Raj-style dining room, eating a meal of a Bombay sandwich, butter chicken and several Kingfisher lagers. Bobby Dhaliwal entered the room in all his glittering glory, which included a vastly oversized red leather jacket. He had Vijay Sen by the scruff of his neck.

Bapat wiped his lips and chin with a large linen

napkin that was tucked into the top button of his shirt. He took a swig of beer, wiped his lips again and gave an enormous closed-mouth belch, which Vijay thought sounded like he was choking to death. Bapat's small eyes squinted. He was near-sighted but refused to admit it.

"Who's this, Bobby? Looks like a piece of rubbish you picked up off the streets," Bapat said.

"His name is Vijay Sen, sir. He was the one who killed the night watchman and opened the gates at the scrapyard last night."

Bapat took a bite of his sandwich and spooned up some of the butter chicken. He ate noisily, then swallowed. He drained the bottle in front of him and flipped the cap off a new one, then drank deeply. He put the bottle down and leaned forward, trying to get a better look at the little creature standing on the other side of the table.

"Has he not been paid?"

"Yes, sir," said Dhaliwal.

"Does he want more?" Bapat asked. In point of fact the street urchin deserved far more than he had been given. Not only had the attack on the scrapyard been a small dagger in Raman's thigh, but Bapat had also managed to remove three excavators and four dump trucks from the yard. He was sorry the dog had been killed. He liked dogs, especially big ones.

"Then why is he here?" asked Bapat.

"He came on his own," said Dhaliwal. "He said he had something to tell you."

"And what would that be?"

Vijay shook himself free of Dhaliwal's grip and stepped forward. "I came to tell you that Mr. Kota Raman has paid me ten thousand rupees to spy on you."

Bapat eased himself against the back of his chair, the street urchin's face a blur in front of him. His mind twisted through all the implications of the child's simple statement. Was the child just trying to extort more money from them? Was he telling the truth or was he telling him what Raman had told him to say? It was all very confusing. Bapat sat forward and grabbed his bottle of beer. He took a long, thoughtful swallow and then sat forward again.

"You're a liar!" Bapat yelled.

Vijay held his ground. "I am not lying."

"Prove it," said Bapat.

Vijay pulled a thin folded wad of well-circulated orange-and-red thousand-rupee notes from somewhere inside his pants and placed it carefully on the desk in front of him. Bapat reached out and picked up the greasy packet of notes and counted them. "There are only nine here," said Bapat.

"I put one of the notes in a safe place on the chance that you might take it all."

"Why do you tell me all this?" Bapat asked.

"Because I thought it was important for you to know."

"And why is that?"

"Because everyone knows that you have now grown stronger than Raman. I want to be on the winning side in this great battle."

Bapat's heart swelled at the little slumdog's statement. If street thieves now thought of him as the stronger, then perhaps it was time to truly put himself at war with the Raman family. Why should he be content with what he had when he could have it all?

"So what can you do for me?" Bapat asked Vijay.

"I can spy on Raman's movements and tell you his intentions."

"And how much would you like to be paid for these services?"

Vijay shrugged. "Mr. Raman paid me ten thousand rupees," Vijay said, an unassuming tone in his voice.

Bapat sat back in his chair and bellowed with laughter.

"This little thief will go far in this world," Bapat said to the man in the red leather jacket and sunglasses.

Dhaliwal frowned. Praise received by another was praise not received by him.

"Would fifteen thousand rupees do?" Bapat asked.

"I suppose," Vijay said, sighing.

"All right, then—twenty thousand a month. Good enough?"

"A week," said Vijay firmly.

"Every two weeks," said Bapat.

"Every ten days," Vijay countered.

"Done!" Bapat said and let out a huge laugh.

16

Holliday and his companions gathered yet again in a hotel suite, this one in the Miami Hilton. The living room of the suite was pleasant, a mixture of classic and modern: the inevitable flat-screen TV sitting above a large black credenza, the walls golden yellow, the couch a long blue rectangle, the carpeting matching the walls. It was all very nice. There were papers strewn everywhere, the booty they'd mined from their assault on the Bingham Gallery. Holliday, Lazarus and Kruger were each working their way through separate piles of paper. In Holliday's case, that meant the two ledgers.

"It's crazy," said Holliday. "Bingham is dealing with hundreds of millions of dollars but none of it seems to stick for very long. It comes in and it goes out. There are inventory codes that probably match individual works of art. The same numbers are paired on the opposite page with amounts of money, but the inventory numbers show that the works of art are moving along another chain of buyers and sellers. If a forensic accountant ever saw these, he'd have a field day."

Lazarus held a bundle of pages in his hand. "There seem to be two major sellers, one named Fone and another one called Leonardo. Together they sold more than half a billion dollars of art in the last eighteen months alone. What the hell does 'Fone' mean?"

"I think I have a pretty good idea," said Holliday. "It's not 'Fone'; it's 'F One.'"

"Which means?" Lazarus asked.

Holliday smiled grimly. "F One: Francis the First. It's these people's code for the Vatican."

"And Leonardo is those *sukiny deti* who've been running me," Hannah said, her face a black scowl.

Holliday sat back on the boxy blue couch and tried to see the big picture. It came to him relatively easily. "It's a gigantic money-laundering scheme," he said thoughtfully. "They're running around buying and selling and legitimizing everything through Blackthorn and Cole."

"If that's the case," said Hannah, "what do they need me or any of the other forgers for?"

"Because you provide the real cash. Your paint-

ings replace the real ones thus allowing the orig-
inals to be sold on the black market. Without you
and your friends, the scheme wouldn't work."

"Ohooiet!" Hannah snarled. Holy fuck!

"It also answers a question that's been bothering me for the last two years," said Lazarus.
"I've been noticing a gradual decline down to
almost nothing at all in the independent smuggling market. I'll bet the small guys are frightened of getting knackered by this juggernaut.
It's beginning to make sense."

"Food for thought," said Holliday, slapping
his knees and standing up. "I'm hungry. Let's
get something from room service."

Both Holliday and Lazarus had giant sirloin
cheeseburgers with fries, while Hannah settled
on a small Cobb salad.

"I don't want to be walking down the street
one day and watch my arteries explode in front
of my eyes," she said, eyeing the large, dripping
pieces of meat skeptically.

"It's the American way of death," said Holliday, speaking around a forkful of thick-cut French
fries.

"We must all follow our own appetites," said
Lazarus happily, crunching his way through one
of the burger's pickle slices.

They got back to it and by midafternoon the

whole process didn't seem to be getting ahead at all. At just after three Lazarus paused and looked up. "Doesn't this ring a bell?" he said. " 'The King of the Jews is dead. The Messiah is risen in the East.' "

"That was on the wall of the cave at Qumran where Peggy and Rafi died," said Holliday, his voice tensing.

"Well, it's in the letter here," said Lazarus. "It refers to 'our friend in Mumbai' and gives a final offer of sixty-five million U.S. dollars. The letter is from Jean-Pierre Devaux, Poste Restante, Paris Twelve, France."

"Who is the recipient?"

"Post Office Box 3829, Crystal City, Virginia."

Holliday went to the minibar, got another can of Red Bull and took a swallow. "They're talking about the scroll," said Holliday. "Bingham is playing middleman to the people who actually have it. Crystal City sounds like it might be someone or some interior organization within the CIA. I know for a fact they maintain all sorts of covert operations and safe houses there."

Crystal City was a forest of modern, bright white high-rise buildings sprouting on Jefferson Davis Highway, close to the Pentagon and Washington D.C. It was also just a short hop to Ronald Reagan Airport. Its office buildings and its maze of tunnels weren't solely the province of the CIA. The Department of Defense, Defense Intelligence, off-site Pentagon offices, defense contractors and off-site offices of the National Security Agency also occupied the anonymous collection of buildings. It might as well have been called Acronym City.

"There is something a bit off there," said Hannah Kruger. "If you assume that the owner of the Crystal City post office box is the seller and 'our friend in Mumbai' is the buyer, then who is the person in Paris? If Bingham is brokering the deal, how does Jean-Pierre Devaux come into the whole thing?"

"I hadn't thought of that," said Holliday. "It's like playing a shell game or three-card monte."

"So where is the damn scroll?" Lazarus asked.

"Give me the letter," said Holliday, holding out his hand.

Lazarus handed it over and Holliday looked at it. The letter was on ordinary paper, typed and printed on a laser printer. The salutation was "My dear friend" and the closing was "Hopefully, Yours." In other words, it was absolutely anonymous. "It doesn't tell us much."

"It's got a lot number," said Lazarus. "Ergo, it's an auction."

Holliday shook his head. "Not a lot number

191

that's carried on either Bingham or Blackthorn and Cole's books."

"So which one do we go after?" Hannah asked.

Holliday pinched the bridge of his nose, closed his good eye and leaned back into the couch. A few moments passed. He sat forward and nodded to himself.

"Let's think this through logically," said Holliday. "Mr. Mumbai is making an offer, so he doesn't have it. Mr. Crystal City has mentioned that the Frenchman has just come up with the line 'The King of the Jews is dead. The Messiah is risen in the East.' I'd say we go after the Frenchman."

They drove the rental down to Key West, into the parking lot of the somewhat pompously named Key West International Airport. They chartered a Vulcanair P68 twin-engine high-winged monoplane. From Key West they flew to Lynden Pindling Airport in Nassau and from there flew to London Heathrow on British Airways. From Heathrow they flew a final leg to Geneva via a Swiss shuttle flight.

They checked into the Kempinski Hotel, ate a little and then all had a good night's sleep. In the almost ten years since Holliday had discovered the hidden Templar sword he'd been on long treks like this many times, but neither Lazarus nor Hannah was used to it. He let them sleep in and when they finally woke early in the afternoon he gave them their instructions. They were to disguise themselves by changing their hair color and purchasing plain cosmetic eyeglasses.

While they were busy with that, Holliday went to one of several private banks he used in Geneva. He retrieved one hundred thousand euros in large denominations and took four blank passports, all current, from the stack in his safety-deposit box. Holliday returned to the hotel. They all had their passport photos taken; then Hannah and Lazarus returned to their rooms at the Kempinski.

Holliday took the passport blanks to a man he had used several times before. All Holliday really knew about the man was that his name was Marcel and he was remarkably discreet. Marcel worked out of a small set of basement rooms beside a backstreet garage. The sign above his door read "Photo Marcel" and nothing else.

Holliday went down three steps and knocked on the heavy, slightly pitted dark green metal door. There was a peephole in the door and Holliday knew that he was being watched. A few seconds later the door opened. A small elfin figure appeared with a broad smile on his face. Marcel looked remarkably like a garden gnome. He was short with a round face and red cheeks, a round belly and short legs. His hair was snow white and cut overly long. He wore a very old suit, long out of style, and bedroom slippers on his feet. Around his head was a metal band with a swing-up optical loupe attached to it.

"Ah, Mr. Smith," said Marcel, his voice quiet and pleasant. "Do come in." He stepped back and let Holliday into his little lair. The outer room was surrounded by dozens of filing cabinets. There was a small desk for doing business with a high magnifying lamp clamped to one end. Marcel sat down behind the desk and Holliday seated himself in front of it.

"You're looking well, Marcel," Holliday said.

"Gerta tells me I drink too much schnapps, but I get along."

Without saying anything, Holliday took out the four passport blanks and the passport photographs.

"British, German, Canadian."

"Which is which?" asked Marcel, holding up the strips of photographs.

"I'm the German. My name is Max Shulmann. The British goes with the other man, whose name is Paul Andrews, and the Canadian goes for the woman, whose name is Helen Manning. I'm a businessman returning to my French office after an eye operation. Paul Andrews is a travel writer and Helen Manning is a university professor."

Marcel nodded, making notes, and then inserted the strips of passport photos into the appropriate blanks.

"Are you going to have trouble with mine?" Holliday asked.

"Not at all," said Marcel, smiling. "As you know, passport photographs are all digitized. I will simply digitize yours, take the left side and flip it over to join with the right side, and your face will be perfect. Presumably you will have a large bandage on your bad eye."

"That's what I was thinking," said Holliday. He paused. "What about the plastic veneer?"

Marcel smiled again. "These days passport photographs are printed directly onto the passport, which is exactly what I will do. I then add a two-micron-thick secondary veneer, which the scanners won't pick up. It's really quite simple."

Holliday reached into the inside pocket of his jacket and brought out the money he'd taken from his safety-deposit box. He counted out fifty thousand euros and placed it on Marcel's desk. Marcel watched, his small, thin lips moving silently as he counted along with Holliday.

"Half now, half later?" Holliday asked.

"Perfect," said Marcel. "When do you want them?"

"Is tomorrow too difficult?"

"Not at all," said Marcel. "Come in the early afternoon."

Holliday shook hands with the little man, then turned and left the studio. Instead of flagging down a taxi on one of the main streets, he decided to walk back to the hotel.

As he walked, he thought about Peggy and Rafi but mostly he thought about Eddie. He had wondered ever since his friend's death whether that had been some sort of sign that his own time was drawing near. Now there were two others he had taken into his very dangerous way of life. There was no doubt in his mind that the deaths of Peggy, Rafi and Eddie were all his responsibility. Perhaps even the old monk Rodrigues, when you got right down to it. If he hadn't been following the endless trail his uncle's sword had started him on, would Rodrigues be dead? If he hadn't gone to that tiny island in the middle of the Atlantic, would he have still watched as Rodrigues's blood seeped out onto rain-spattered ground? Would he have taken the notebook from the dying man, spurring him even farther along the road to where he was now?

He found himself thinking, once again, that with Eddie's death perhaps he should stop this seemingly endless adventure. But somewhere deep within his true heart he heard Amy's soft voice from long ago saying to him: "Of course you can't, sweetheart; you must keep on going to the end."

A single line of tears flowed down his cheek as he made his way back to the Kempinski Hotel.

They booked a flight to Orly. Orly, being almost entirely a domestic European facility, had considerably less stringent security in place, and was much less risky than Charles de Gaulle.

They arrived at Geneva's Cointrin Airport an hour ahead of time and lined up in front of the EasyJet ticket desk. They had separated by this time, with Holliday somewhere between Hannah and Lazarus. Holliday watched Hannah reach the head of the line and offer up her passport and her ticket. The girl behind the counter tapped out a few things on her computer, turned, smiled and handed Hannah back her passport, ticket and boarding pass. Hannah turned away from the counter.

Out of the corner of his eye Holliday saw a nondescript man wearing a raincoat with his hands in his pockets striding forward quickly.

He felt the hairs on the back of his neck rise, but he was too late. The man ran into Hannah and then quickly turned away, losing himself in the crowds of the busy airport. Hannah looked stunned and Holliday saw a huge spreading flower of blood on the chest of her blouse. She fell to her knees. Holliday bolted out of line and ran to her. The blade was still in her chest. It looked like a Fairbairn-Sykes commando knife and the stab was a fatal one. Holliday saw her eyes widen and the life drain out of them.

She spoke.

"Get away from me," she whispered. "We're not supposed to know each other."

And then she slumped over dead onto the floor.

With his heart pounding but sticking to his role, Holliday yelled, *"Rufen Sie einen Kranken-wagen!"*

The line in front of the EasyJet counter had fallen back in horror. Holliday moved away from Hannah's body and took his place again as security police, airport medical staff and stretcher bearers arrived and took Hannah away. By that time Holliday and Lazarus had passed through the line, and with boarding passes in hand they headed to their flight. They took their separate seats on the Airbus A320 and stonily endured the flight to Paris, where all of this had begun.

17

Holliday and Lazarus checked into the Hôtel Meurice on the Rue de Rivoli, once the head-quarters for the Nazi high command in Paris. They went up to their adjoining rooms, showered and rejoined each other in the restaurant Le Dalí, where Holliday ordered an Angus rib steak and Lazarus predictably ordered fish and chips. Holliday chose a Merlot, Lazarus a Chardonnay, and they talked as they ate.

"I can't believe Hannah is gone," Lazarus said sadly.

"It's the most terrible thing in the world. I've had it happen a hundred times before. Buddies dying beside you in battle—alive one minute, dead in an instant. It's something you think you'd get used to after a while, but you never do."

In his mind Holliday saw Hannah as the man approached and slid the dagger up between her ribs. The man was totally nondescript. A nothing in a raincoat. His thoughts jumped again, this time to Eddie and then to Peggy and Rafi, their lives so violently wasted in a single instant.

"No, you never do," he repeated.

They ate in silence for a moment; then Lazarus spoke, a forkful of perfect French fries poised in front of him. "How are we going to get at this Devaux person?"

"Either we figure out a way into Devaux's apartment or we stake out the poste restante."

Holliday sliced into his steak and thought. "Or even better. We could deliver something to him."

Lazarus cracked open the light tempura batter on a piece of fish, then dipped it in the adjoining dish of tartar sauce. "Sounds good to me," he said.

"We'll need to make a few preparations," Holliday said, "but I think we'll be ready by late tomorrow."

"What are we looking for?" Lazarus asked.

"A gun, a weapon, a pair of dark blue workman's coveralls, a tennis ball, a screwdriver and a butane lighter."

"Very mysterious," said Lazarus.

"No," said Holliday. "Necessary."

The weapon was the easiest. Holliday had long before purchased safety-deposit boxes in most major cities. Here it was in the BNP on the Champs-Élysées. He went to the box, opened it and took out a small Walther PPK and two extra magazines. He locked the box again, rejoined Lazarus and they went off to make their various purchases.

By nine o'clock the following morning they were standing in front of a DHL office on a side street close to the Place de l'Opéra. Holliday was wearing a pair of blue workman's coveralls and carrying a toolbox. Lazarus was dressed in a suit a carrying a large parcel that they had put together the previous night.

"I want you to go in there and send that parcel to yourself," Holliday said. "You keep the clerk busy and I'll slip around the counter into the back. When you're finished with the package, go around the block and I'll be waiting."

Lazarus went across the street and through the door of the small DHL office. Holliday counted to fifty to give Lazarus and the clerk time to get fully involved in their transaction. It had been easy enough to see through the window that there were no other clients in the store. Holliday crossed the street and opened the door into the office.

Lazarus was having a conversation with the clerk, and without stopping Holliday went behind the counter and went through a doorway into a large room. Parcels were stacked on wire racks and behind the packages was a row of lockers. Holliday opened the lockers one by one and found two yellow-and-red DHL uniforms. He scooped them up, stuffed them into his empty toolbox and proceeded out the back door. He found himself in a small lot with half a dozen parked DHL vans. He first went and slid back the gate on its rollers, then chose a DHL van at random.

The previous night they had used the butane lighter to heat up the screwdriver, punching it through the tennis ball, leaving behind a slit in the ball approximately three-quarters of an inch long. In the DHL parking lot he took the customized tennis ball out of his pocket and slipped it over the lock of the driver's side of the van. He held the ball in place with two fingers of his left hand and with the palm of his right hand slammed the tennis ball hard.

Almost magically the door unlocked, the pressure of the air from the tennis ball forcing the lock button up. He opened the door, slid behind the wheel, reached beneath the dashboard and quickly hot-wired the van. With the engine running, he went into the back of the empty truck, climbed out of the overalls and put on one of the

DHL uniforms. He got behind the wheel again and calmly drove out of the lot.

At the corner Holliday, spotted the waiting Lazarus. Lazarus climbed in. "Any trouble?"

"Not a bit," said Holliday. "Climb into the back and put on your uniform." He waited for Lazarus to change, then headed for Avenue de Wagram and the residence of Jean-Pierre Devaux.

Fifteen minutes later they parked in front of Le Paradis du Fruit, went through the side door and up to the top floor.

"Package for Mr. Devaux," said Lazarus, his French perfect.

There was no answer. Lazarus knocked harder and repeated his statement, standing directly in front of the peephole in the center of the door. There was still no response. Holliday slipped the Walther PPK out of his uniform pocket and held it tightly along his thigh. He gestured for Lazarus to try the latch. The latch gave under Lazarus's thumb and the door opened slightly.

Holliday toed the door open even more and stepped inside, the automatic pistol raised in his hand. He found himself facing a tall man who was either Indian or Pakistani. His hair was slicked back with oil and he wore large mirrored sunglasses. He had a mailing tube slung over his left shoulder and an old MAB Model D in his right hand. The man's first and only shot splintered the doorframe.

Holliday fired back, hitting the other man in the meat of his upper arm. The man dropped the old semiautomatic, then charged forward, bullying his way past both Holliday and Lazarus and bolting down the stairs.

"Follow him!" Holliday yelled, tossing the Walther toward Lazarus. The Interpol agent deftly caught the weapon and headed after the fleeing man.

Holliday closed the door and stepped forward, going through a series of rooms until he reached Devaux's compact laboratory. Devaux was on the floor, shot once in the belly and once in the upper chest. He was still breathing.

Holliday went back into the sitting room, found a pillow and returned to Devaux. He placed the pillow under the dying man's head and knelt down beside him.

"Who was it?" Holliday asked.

"He took the scroll."

"Who took the scroll?"

"I don't know, never saw him before," Devaux mumbled, his breath coming hard now.

"Was it your friend in Mumbai?" Holliday asked,

remembering the letter they had taken from the Bingham Gallery.

"No. The scroll belonged to him."

"What's his name?" Holliday asked.

"Raman," said Devaux. "Kota Raman." He took one heaving breath and then Holliday watched as the life drained out of his eyes. He used his finger and thumb to close them and then stood up.

Holliday stared down at Devaux's light table. The man with the oily hair and sunglasses had been a thug. Without bothering to lift the Plexiglas off the table, he'd simply torn off the scroll, leaving the four unrolled pages behind. He'd clearly purchased the mailing tube beforehand to stuff the scroll into it.

Holliday looked around the laboratory. There were digital photographs, ultraviolet photographs and X-ray plates everywhere, all concentrating on the exposed pages of the script. The only thing that Holliday knew for sure was that the writing was Aramaic. In fact, he'd seen almost the exact same setup in Rafi's laboratory in Jerusalem. He looked around and saw several flat leather portfolios. He picked the largest and began carefully putting all the photographs and X-rays into it. That left only the four pages of the scroll under the Plexiglas, which he knew he could not remove or transport, so he simply left it where it was.

There were no filing cabinets or any addresses that Holliday could see. There was, however, a laptop computer. Holliday took it, put it into the portfolio, zipped the container up and left the laboratory.

He returned to the Meurice, first stripping off the DHL uniform in a narrow alley beside the bar.

He met up with Lazarus almost three hours later. "Where the hell have you been?" Holliday asked. "I was starting to get worried."

"Our man in the sunglasses led me on a long chase," Lazarus explained. "His first stop was a pharmacy. He was obviously buying something to dress his wound with. After that, he went down to a Métro station, where he went into the men's room. Five minutes later he was out again and I think he knew he was being tailed. We went all over the city until he finally went down into an RER station and took an express train to Charles de Gaulle. I managed to board it as well. I lost him in all those plastic tubes and escalators, but I checked the departures board and discovered there was only one flight leaving for Mumbai. I could see him through the glass into the security lounge and there wasn't a damn thing I could do about it. The flight took off an hour and a half later. I waved my Interpol ID around at the Air India desk and they finally gave me the man's name. His passport identified him as Ranjit Dhaliwal."

Rusty Smart sat alone in the Arlington safe house brooding. Elliot Foster, the Ghost Squad's man in Paris, had recently contacted him via coded e-mail. The scroll they had been bidding on had been stolen and Devaux was dead. Somehow Holliday had become involved along the way. The last time Holliday had been spotted was in New York and now here he was booked into the Hôtel Meurice in Paris under the name of a German tourist. Also with him now was the Interpol agent Peter Lazarus.

According to Foster's contact at Interpol, Lazarus was a loner and prone to disappearing for weeks at a time before reappearing with a vanished piece of art and a grin on his face. That morning Lazarus and Holliday had booked a direct flight to Mumbai and by now they were almost certainly on their way. The son of a bitch Holliday was as relentless as an avenging angel sent down from the heavens to destroy him and the ghostly empire it had taken him so long to build.

Smart knew that he had only two choices now: either collapse the empire he had built and make a run for it, or try one last time to save it.

Russell J. Smart thought briefly about taking his own life but shook off the thought as quickly as it had come. He stared down at the Yale ring on his right hand. Beneath it he knew there was engraved a small pirate's skull and bones. He rubbed the ring with a finger of his other hand. "Bonesmen forever," he whispered to himself, and then began to cry.

He couldn't fail. It simply wasn't an option—no matter how you looked at it.

18

Holliday and Lazarus arrived at the Grand Sarovar after an hour's drive through the stupefying, slightly nauseating atmosphere and traffic. By all appearances every single human being smoked. So did a thousand chimneys from a thousand factories, working relentlessly to mass-produce consumer goods for pennies that would magically turn to dollars as soon as they hit the shelves in Walmart and a hundred other companies that took advantage of India's incredibly low labor costs and the country's willingness to let its people toil under appalling working conditions.

The Grand Sarovar was a salute to Mumbai's new prosperity, a towering modern building, slightly cantilevered on the upper floors and bathed in spotlights that would force any occupant to close its curtains tightly if you wanted to get a good night's sleep. They walked into the lobby look-

ing ragged from the ten-hour flight and inappro-
priately dressed for arrival in the fetid air of the
Indian city. Both men needed a shave and shower
at the very least.

The man behind the counter wore a turban,
had a marvelously sculpted mustache and carried
the unsurprising name "Raj" on the breast pocket
of his uniform. He looked at Holliday and Lazarus
skeptically, but his skepticism turned to utter
obsequiousness when he saw Holliday's black
American Express card.

"I'd like a two-bedroom suite," said Holliday.

"Absolutely and immediately, sir. We will provide you with our most wonderful executive suites,
one beside the other, to provide you with the two-
bedroom accommodation which you require. There
is an adjoining door and every possible amenity
the hotel can provide for you within seconds of
your request. Is that good enough, most excellent sir?"

"I guess it'll do," Holliday said blandly.

Raj snapped his fingers and out of nowhere
three tiny Goanese bellhops appeared. Not one
of them was over five feet tall and they looked
slightly absurd in their ornate uniforms. There
was no way of figuring out how old they were,
but from their seamed faces and weary eyes they
could easily be in their fifties or sixties.

"Nikel, Paullu and Pedro would be most happy to carry your bags, sir," said Raj, smiling so broadly his white teeth glowed and the tips of his mustache almost reached to his cheekbones.

"Thanks, but that won't be necessary," Holliday said, indicating their two overnight bags and the portfolio full of material from Devaux's laboratory.

"Nikel, Paullu and Pedro would be most upset if you do not let them take your bags, excellent sirs. It is their only source of income."

Lazarus looked appalled. "You don't pay these people a wage?"

"Certainly not, sirs," said Raj with a slight note of disdain in his voice. "They pay us for the jobs. It is a great honor for one of their people to be chosen to work at this grand hotel."

The tips, of course, thought Lazarus. They handed one piece of luggage to each of the three bellhops.

Raj handed Holliday and Lazarus two key cards each and then said in an imperious voice, "Suites 1109 and 1108."

The bellhops scuttled off ahead of them, and they all rode the elevator happily up to the eleventh floor. There was slight confusion as to which person was occupying which suite, but they finally got it all sorted out and the men tipped each of the bellhops lavishly. The three Goans took the American dollars, their eyes almost popping from their heads, and bowed their way out of the room.

"The world turned upside down," said Lazarus. "A hotel where the employees pay the employers."

"I think we may find the whole country is that way," Holliday replied.

They had spent most of their time on the flight from Paris going over the possible ways to approach the man named Kota Raman and had decided that the direct approach was most probably the best.

"So how do we do that?" Lazarus had said as they flew over the Indian Ocean.

"He's a big-time criminal in a giant city. That means he probably controls everything from gambling to whorehouses to the black market."

"Which of those do we start with?" Lazarus had asked.

"I was going to ask you the same question," Holliday had said.

"I've only been to a casino once. I've never been to a brothel. So I guess it better be the black market. It's more my cup of tea anyway."

The next morning they shrugged off what they could of the jet lag and returned to the lobby to find Raj the Sikh still on duty.

"Do you remember us?" Holliday asked.

"Most definitely, excellent sir. I must say that my bellhops and I were most grateful for your esteemed generosity."

"Dear Lord," said Lazarus. "Do you take a kickback from the bellhops?"

"Of course, sir," said Raj. "It is necessary for them to retain their employment. It is all part of the system, sir."

"Where do I find the black market for ivory?" Holliday asked bluntly.

"I beg your pardon, sir?"

"Black market. Ivory," repeated Holliday.

"I have no idea what you are talking about, sir. I am merely a humble night manager."

"If I understand this system of yours, this should do something to change your mind." Holliday took out his wallet and placed a single hundred-dollar bill on the marble counter. It disappeared in the blink of an eye.

"Well?" Holliday said.

"Bakshi's Antiquities on Mutton Street in the bazaar. Would you like a cab, sir? They all know the way."

"Sure."

"I shall fetch one immediately."

The old black-and-yellow taxicab was a knock-off of a 1962 Peugeot, decorated with pompoms, decals, curlicues, swastikas and artificial flowers glued to the roof above the door posts and the windshield.

Reaching Mutton Street and turning into it was like trying to swim upriver in a current of honking cars and wandering merchants festooned in wristwatches, long bolts of cloth and anything else that could be pinned, hung or draped around necks or arms. Tuk-tuks raced in all directions, chased by scooters and 50cc motorcycles. Cymbals clanged, horns honked, people pitched their wares in loud voices and once more smoke stood like soup above them in the thick humid air.

Eventually forcing its way to the sidewalk, the old cab pulled up in front of a shop with the name "Bakshi's Antiquities" written in faded paint on an old board. Above the shop, like everywhere else on the street, grotesque apartment blocks hung over everything. Here and there banners had been strung across the street bearing inscrutable messages and in the middle distance a train groaned its way across an overpass. Holliday paid the driver with a fistful of bills and he and Lazarus exited onto the crowded sidewalk. The air was redolent with spices and cigarette smoke.

They pushed through a dozen people yelling and thrusting their goods in front of them and finally reached the door of Bakshi's.

They went inside, slammed the door shut and stood for a moment enjoying the relative quiet and semidarkness.

"It's the Old Curiosity Shop," whispered Lazarus, eyes wide as he gazed around the small room, its every shelf, counter and display case bearing strange treasures from another age and another world. Rattan chairs of indeterminate age hung from hooks on the ceiling, along with lanterns, incense burners, three brass monkeys dangling from chains. There were books, boxes of wood and ivory, figurines carved in jade, Buddhas in various sizes and made from various materials, from weathered sandalwood and brass to copper and stone, and one small one looked as though it might have been made of gold. There were Victorian mirrors, piles of rugs, one complete Bombay regiment Sepoy uniform draped on a mannequin. At the back of the store a very old man, his long white hair tied in a rough quoit at the back of his head and wearing a long white silk sherwani and thin linen trousers, sat on a high stool watching them.

Holliday and Lazarus stepped carefully down an aisle of treasures and approached him.

"May I help you?" the old man said, his hands coming together in the classic prayerful greeting. His face was kind and gentle. His dark eyes glittered intelligently from behind a pair of gold-rim spectacles that might easily have been an item for sale in his store.

"We're interested in ivory," said Lazarus.

"I have an old chess set from the early 1800s you might be interested in," said the man.

"You are Mr. Bakshi, I suppose." Lazarus smiled.

"I am, sir." The old man nodded.

"Well, sir, we're interested in more ivory than a chess set."

"I think I may have a piece of scrimshaw done on a whale's tooth by a seaman from a royal West Indian merchant ship from the same period as the chess set," said Bakshi.

"Larger than a whale's tooth, I think, Mr. Bakshi."

Bakshi continued staring at them pleasantly, but Holliday saw the old man's right hand drifting under the counter.

"Gentlemen, I fear you are saying less than you mean to say."

"You'd be right," said Lazarus.

"Then perhaps you'd tell me exactly what you are looking for."

"Well, if we're going to be exact," said Lazarus,

"let's say we want exactly sixty kilos of ivory—or even more, if you have access to it."

"Trafficking in ivory of that quantity is both expensive and illegal."

"How expensive?"

"Approximately three thousand per kilo, American currency."

"So sixty kilos would cost me a hundred and eighty thousand dollars?" Lazarus said.

"It would cost you that or slightly more if I had it to sell, but, being a law-abiding citizen, I don't deal in such exotic or illegal sales."

"We heard that you did," said Holliday, keeping his eye on the man's right arm as it inched forward under the counter.

"And who did you hear this lie from?" Bakshi asked quietly.

"A friend of yours," said Lazarus.

"And what friend would that be?" asked Bakshi.

"A close one," said Holliday. "His name is Kota Raman."

The man's right arm jerked forward under the counter. Holliday had been ready for the move and reached over, gripping the man's thin wrist as it reappeared. The hand below the wrist held a massive and very old Webley service revolver. Had he managed to fire it, the .455 caliber cartridge would have blown a hole in him the size of a golf ball. Holliday used his free hand to pry the weapon out of the old man's grip.

"Now, now," said Lazarus, staring at the huge pistol. "There's no need for violence."

Holliday slipped the pistol into the pocket of his jacket. He'd noticed that the weapon was an original 1888 model, which made it even older than Bakshi.

"We're not really looking for ivory, Mr. Bakshi," said Holliday. "We're looking for Kota Raman. Perhaps you could tell us where to find him."

Bakshi, somewhat deflated, sank down on his stool again. He sighed. "I know of no such man."

"Of course you do," said Lazarus. "If you didn't know him, why did you pull that great ugly thing out from under the counter at the mere mention of his name?"

Bakshi carefully took off his spectacles and placed them on the counter, his hand shaking. He took a linen handkerchief from the breast pocket of his long coat and polished the lenses of the glasses, buying time to assemble his thoughts. Finally he replaced the spectacles and the handkerchief back where they belonged and spoke. "I know of the man," he said. "He is not someone to be taken lightly."

"All we want to know is where to find him."

"I'm afraid I cannot tell you," said Bakshi. "It is worth my life and the life of my family to give you that information."

"Put it this way," said Lazarus brightly. "Whether you tell us or not, we will eventually find Mr. Raman, and when we do, we'll tell him that it was you who led us to him and he'll kill you and your family anyway. So why not tell us now and save ourselves all a great deal of time and effort?"

"If I tell you," said Bakshi wearily, "will you give me your promise that you will not tell him that it was me who told you?"

"I guarantee it," Holliday said.

"All right," said Bakshi. "I will tell you."

And he did.

19

"So we've got his address," said Lazarus as they rode a tuk-tuk away from Bakshi's and back to the hotel. "What do we do with it now?"

They rode through the stunning chaos of Mumbai streets. Holliday was deep in thought. Seated facing backward, looking at the city scene as it unraveled behind them, Holliday tried to concentrate on a single vehicle and follow its path. It was almost impossible.

"It's a matter of urban camouflage. Unless Raman has eyes in the back of his head, it shouldn't be too hard to follow him around for a few days until we get a feel for him."

The tuk-tuk reached the hotel and deposited them in front of the main door.

"I can't see how it's possible," said Lazarus. "A man like him will be in a big car with lots of bodyguards. We could get stuck in traffic any-time and lose him easily."

"That would be true. We could try to follow him in a cab or a car or even a tuk-tuk, but what I'm suggesting is a little bit different."

Rohit Bapat sat in the rear of a workingman's restaurant he owned, eating deep-fried onion balls and a fiery curry, which he scooped up with chunks of naan, occasionally dipping the bread into a bowl of raita to cool off his mouth and tongue. Bobby Dhaliwal, dressed in one of his exotic Bollywood outfits, sat across from his boss, with the plastic mailing tube on his lap. He had a beer in front of him, which he occasionally sipped.

"Is that it?" Bapat asked, curry dripping down his chin and onto the napkin tucked into his shirt.

"Yes, boss. I had to kill him to get it."

"No matter," said Bapat. "He was no longer useful anyway." He dipped his bread into the raita and bit a chunk off, swallowing noisily. Using his hands, he picked up one of the deep-fried onions balls, dipped it into the raita as well and shoved half of it into his mouth, biting down hard. He dropped what was left of the onion ball onto the side of his plate, belched and wiped his hands on a napkin. "Let me see it," he ordered.

Dhaliwal uncapped the mailing tube and slid out the scroll. He held it up carefully for Bapat to see.

"It looks like a piece of goat shit," said Bapat skeptically. "You're telling me this thing is priceless? How can a piece of petrified goat shit be priceless?"

"It is a scroll, boss. It was made by monks almost two thousand years ago. From what I understand, the Vatican would do anything to get their hands on it, if only to keep it away from the Jews."

"What does this fucking goat turd have to do with the Jews?"

"The Jews own all the Dead Sea Scrolls that were ever discovered—all except this one."

Bapat turned in his chair and gestured for a beer. A man brought it to him unopened, bowed and placed it on the table. The fat gangster used his thumb to flip it open. He took a long swallow and belched again, then shook his head. "How can these goat turds everyone wants be so valuable?"

"I'm not an expert," said Dhaliwal, "but I

found a piece of paper in the Frenchman's office offering five hundred million dollars in U.S. funds."

"Then this is indeed a great goat turd that you have brought me. If what you say is true, you have brought me the single weapon I need to bring down Raman and to fulfill my destiny." He paused and shook his head again. "Imagine that. Kota Raman and his empire brought down by a goat turd."

The first thing Holliday and Lazarus did once they had formulated their plan was to go out and purchase the cheapest, most garish, obviously touristy clothes they could.

Their next stop was a garage that sold motorcycles and scooters. Holliday, who was more accustomed to motorcycles, chose an olive green Royal Enfield Bullet that looked as though it might have been driven by a dispatch rider in World War II. Lazarus, having never driven anything besides a car, chose a battered bright red Vespa scooter. Both men bought helmets with heavily tinted visors. Holliday's helmet was a garishly striped red and green, while Lazarus's was robin's egg blue with an amateurish flame job painted on both sides.

"You realize we look like complete bloody idiots," Lazarus said, looking at Holliday in full gear on the old motorcycle.

"That's the general idea," answered Holliday, his voice muffled by the visor.

They spent the next three days following Kota Raman's large black Mercedes around the city. His trips were erratic—some short, some long. The locations ranged from tall office buildings to small confectionaries, storefronts to gigantic factories.

There was one thing each day had in common. Toward late afternoon the Mercedes would inevitably drive up the Mumbai peninsula to Shivaji Park, a large green sanctuary full of children's play areas, gardens of peace and meditation for the elderly, and what Raman clearly came for: the cricket fields. It didn't seem to matter who was playing on the large training pitch in the park; Raman seemed to enjoy them all. Without fail, he would set up a folding chair and table and a white-jacketed servant would appear out of nowhere bearing a silver service of tea and biscuits. Raman was never alone, but usually when watching the cricket matches he had only his second in command and one burly bodyguard accompanying him.

On the fourth day Lazarus and Holliday decided to act. They had one of the hotel cars take them to Shivaji Park an hour ahead of the time Raman usually arrived. There, they waited until he had set himself up with his table and tea, and then they approached him slowly. They were dressed in light business suits, and Lazarus carried the portfolio of items from Devaux's laboratory in Paris. The second in command and the bodyguard reacted quickly. Spotting Holliday and Lazarus approaching their boss, the two men intercepted them when they were still fifty feet away from the cricket pitch.

"My name is Ali Kapoor. Do you have business here?" Kapoor was tall, broad shouldered and looked as though he might have been a wrestler in his prime. He was impeccably dressed in an Armani suit. The bodyguard beside him was much larger and remained silent.

"We have important business with Mr. Raman and we must speak to him immediately."

"You don't mind if my friend here checks you for weapons, do you?" Kapoor said.

"Not at all," said Holliday. He lifted his arms and spread his legs slightly.

The bodyguard did a thorough pat-down and then did the same for Lazarus. The bodyguard shook his head. Holliday and Lazarus returned to a normal position.

"Follow me," said Kapoor.

Kapoor led them over to where Raman was watching the cricket match. The men on the practice field were dressed immaculately in white uniforms.

"These two men say they have business with you, boss," Kapoor said, stepping to one side.

"And who might these gentlemen be?" Raman asked, squinting up from his chair.

"My name is Colonel John Holliday. I was recently at an archaeological dig in a place called Qumran outside Jerusalem. The words 'The King of the Jews is dead. The Messiah is risen in the East' were carved into the wall of one of the caves there. The same cave where my cousin and her husband were murdered. Those words also appeared in a scroll that was recently stolen from you by a man named Ranjit Dhaliwal."

"Should I take your word for this or do you have proof?"

"My name is Peter Lazarus. I'm an agent for Interpol and here is your proof." He handed the portfolio they had removed from the apartment in Paris over to Raman.

Raman unzipped the portfolio and snapped his fingers. The white-coated servant appeared and cleared off the table beside Raman. He laid the open portfolio on the table and began to go through it page by page. When he was finished, he closed the portfolio and turned back to Holliday. "How do you know it was Dhaliwal?"

"Because I shot him high in the right arm as he was going out the door and because Mr. Lazarus here used his connections to find out who he was and where he was from."

"Interesting," said Raman. He continued speaking. "You gentlemen have done me a great service. Surely there is more than altruism involved here."

"I wish to know where you got the scroll from originally," said Holliday.

"Why should that be of interest to you?"

"I would have thought it was obvious," said Holliday. "When I find out who it was, I intend to kill him just the way my cousin and her husband were killed, not to mention getting revenge for the death of my best friend."

"You are a believer in revenge, then, Colonel Holliday?"

"At one time I would have said I didn't believe in it, but apparently I'm a changed man." Holliday's voice was chilly with death.

"This is not the place to discuss such things. You will come to my house for dinner tonight and we will discuss your concerns and my interest in Mr. Dhaliwal and his employer. I am beginning to see that what I thought was a simple transaction goes much deeper than the simple buying and selling of an artifact. Dismiss your driver and come with me. You will be perfectly safe."

"Why should we trust you?" Lazarus asked.

"Because unlike Mr. Dhaliwal and his employer, I am a man of honor. If I guarantee your safety, I will die myself to secure it. Now come along."

A 1956 Ford one-ton pickup, its color scraped off almost to the bare metal, sat at the end of a narrow makeshift airfield. In the rear of the truck a .50 caliber heavy machine gun was mounted. It was manned by a figure wearing a filthy shirt and torn trousers along with a hastily wrapped half turban on his head. The man in the cab of the truck, seated behind the wheel, was heavy-set, muscular and dressed entirely in white, except for his neatly wrapped turban, which was jet black.

The light gray Piper Meridian turboprop appeared out of nowhere, its coloring as vague as the Afghan sky. It hit a tiny runway at the extreme end, its single prop reversing almost immediately. By the time it reached the pickup truck it was rolling slowly. It came to a full stop within thirty feet of the truck. Two men climbed down from the aircraft. One was Ranjit Dhaliwal. The other was Rohit Bapat.

As Bapat's sandaled feet touched solid ground,

he fell to his knees and then to his hands in an attitude of prayer. Bapat, who had foolishly gorged himself before flight, vomited. He was always a nervous flier under the best of circumstances, but having had such a large meal accompanied by at least half a dozen bottles of beer was asking for disaster.

Dhaliwal left his boss for a minute and climbed back into the plane. He returned a moment later with a bottle of water. He helped his boss to his feet and handed him the bottle. Bapat accepted it gratefully, and he took a long swig, filling his mouth, then spit it out onto the dusty ground. He took another long draw of the water, swallowing it this time, then handed the rest back to Dhaliwal. Dhaliwal recapped the bottle and slipped it into the pocket of his light linen jacket. Bapat delicately stepped around the pool of vomit and headed toward the pickup truck, the twin barrels of the .50 caliber machine gun following him as he moved. Behind them the single-engine turboprop turned and went hurtling down the runway. It rose into the late-afternoon sky, disappearing in the haze. Bapat reached the passenger side of the truck and pulled open the stiff, resistant door. He sat down beside the driver.

"Your friend rides in the back," said the man in the black turban.

"There's room enough for him beside me," said Bapat.

"He rides in the back," repeated the black-turbaned man.

Bapat turned to Dhaliwal and shrugged.

Without a word Dhaliwal went to the rear of the truck, boosted himself over the transom and sat down on a bench directly behind the machine gunner. Without another word the man in the black turban turned on the engine and threw the old truck into gear, and they turned away from the small airfield.

Three hundred yards away they found a two-lane highway and followed it for about an hour. A side road to the right presented itself and the truck turned, heading toward a low range of hills in the distance. Turning off the side road, they followed a pair of rutted tracks for perhaps fifteen miles before eventually reaching a small compound that looked completely abandoned. They turned in through the gate in the wall and quickly parked.

"Get out," said the man in the black turban. Bapat did so. He went to the rear of the truck and told Dhaliwal to join him. The truck moved toward the smaller of the two buildings. The smaller building was fitted with two large doors. As the truck approached, the black-turbaned man honked his horn. Immediately the two doors of the building opened and the truck drove in.

"We must get inside at once," said the man in the turban. "The drone is due to pass over us in five minutes."

He pushed Bapat and Dhaliwal toward the simple wooden door. He knocked twice and the door was opened by what appeared to be a low-level servant. The three men stepped inside and the door was closed behind them.

"Take off your shoes," the turbaned man said. He led them down a carpeted passageway to a small room. There was a single man in it. He was on his knees, moving up and down and muttering prayers under his breath while he touched his chest, lips and closed eyes with his bare hands. He did this for a few moments and then stood.

Bapat bowed deeply and then stood up again and smiled.

It was the man he'd come to see, the most infamous Taliban terrorist in the world and without a doubt the most powerful man in Afghanistan, a man who owned almost one hundred percent of the opium crop in the country and who, despite his power, was almost certainly certifiably insane.

"Mullah Omar," said Bapat, smiling at the tall bearded man with his right eye sown shut.

20

Holliday and Lazarus sat in Raman's dining room. It was a simple enough place, a long table made of teak and chairs upholstered in dark blue silk. A breeze blew through the ornately carved shutters and a single stick of sandalwood incense burned on a sideboard on the far side of the room. Above them a pair of four-bladed fans turned gently.

The food was as simple as the room and was brought to the table by several white-jacketed servants. There was rice, dal, pakora, cauliflower mixed with exotic spices, chapatis, a main dish of curried lamb and a jug of mango lassi. For dessert there was cardamom barfi, a rich, sweet confection made from condensed milk.

"You lay an excellent table, Mr. Raman," said Peter Lazarus.

Holliday smiled. "I don't know much about Indian food at all, but this was really good. It was kind of you to offer us dinner at such notice."

"It was my pleasure, Colonel Holliday. In my business I rarely meet with people I can have a decent conversation with."

"Eventually we're going to have to get down to brass tacks, however," said Lazarus.

"Allow me a moment or two to pretend that I'm not what I am." Raman smiled wistfully. "You know, I am the only man in my family to have graduated university. I managed to get quite a good first in history at Oxford. My father wanted me to become something more elevated than head of a criminal empire. That was to be for my older brother, Nadir. Unfortunately, Nadir was both impetuous and stupid. Not a useful combination. He died in a knife fight over the affections of a girl in a nightclub. As the second son it was required of me to take his place."

"And if that hadn't happened?" Holliday asked.

Raman shrugged. "In India we believe that everything is foretold and that you cannot escape the fate assigned to you. Had Nadir not died that night, he would have been killed eventually for some useless reason. Before I left for Oxford I knew that I would be returning and I think my father did as well. I think my father was very sad for me that day because he wanted me to be so much more."

"Why not simply stop?" Holliday asked.

"Because I have sisters, cousins, hundreds of people under my employ whose families depend on me. Because I am at the center of a horde of people, a horde of people I must take care of. I am father to them all."

"I've heard that rationale before," said Holliday. "Michael Corleone used it over and over and over to justify his actions. He could have simply walked away from it all right from the start, turned his back with his beautiful bride-to-be and never returned."

"Yet you, Colonel Holliday, search out the people who killed your cousin. You're as much a hypocrite as Corleone or myself, whatever you think. At the end of your life your family is everything."

"Who did you purchase the scroll from?" Holliday asked, a bitter tone in his voice.

"From a thief who offered it to me."

"What would the thief's name be?"

"He never told me his name, only that the scroll could be very valuable in my negotiations with an important man I hope to deal with in Afghanistan."

At that moment Ali Kapoor entered the room and whispered in Raman's ear. Raman thought for a moment and replied to Kapoor concisely. Kapoor left the room and Raman turned back to his guests.

Raman smiled pleasantly. "It looks like our good friends Mr. Bapat and Mr. Dhaliwal have stolen the march on us."

"How so?" asked Holliday.

"Apparently Mr. Bapat and Mr. Dhaliwal flew into Afghanistan today and met with the very man I had hoped to do business with. I'm afraid Mr. Bapat's intention is the same as mine, to offer the man in Afghanistan the scroll for what he has to offer."

"Who is he?" asked Lazarus.

"His name is Mullah Omar. I'm sure you've heard of him, Colonel Holliday."

"Yes, I've heard of him. He's the most powerful Taliban leader in Afghanistan. There's even word of him being offered the presidency of the country once the Americans have gone for good."

"Do you know how he got that way?" Raman asked.

"He gained popularity during the Russian occupation and he was even backed by the CIA to foment as much sabotage and discontent as he could. They paid him a great deal of money to do it."

"That's only part of the story," said Raman. "Most of the money wasn't spent the way the CIA intended. Opium has been cultivated in Afghanistan since 300 BC and it is so fundamental to the Afghan economy that the country would fall apart without it. Regardless of American attempts to eradicate the opium crop, Afghanistan is now the largest manufacturer of opium in the world."

"You're saying that's where Mullah Omar spent the money?" Holliday said.

"Certainly," said Raman. "He went from village to village buying their opium crop and was seen as being a patriot for supporting hundreds of small villages that would have suffered first under the Russians and then under the Americans. The more opium he purchased, the more he sold. The more he sold, the richer he got. The richer he got, the more opium he could buy. Omar now owns at least half the entire opium crop in Afghanistan and pays the individual growers in advance. Now that's political and economic clout for you."

"And that was your plan? To buy all this opium from Omar?"

"Yes, but not the same way Bapat is planning to do it. Bapat will buy as much opium as he can and sell it immediately on the wholesale market, making a quick profit. My intention was two-fold. First, I would purchase as much of Omar's crop as possible. And secondly, rather than sell-ing it at once, I would warehouse it and wait for the market to rise."

"Which it would inevitably do as the sources dried up," said Lazarus.

"Precisely," said Raman. "Eventually I would put Omar out of business."

"How would such a plan put him out of busi-ness?" Lazarus asked.

"Because if I hold three-quarters of his crop and the people in the world of drug trading know it, he will have no one else to sell to. This does two things: I become the benefactor of the Af-ghan farmers, and as a result the Taliban's power is impotent. Imagine how appreciative your gov-ernment will be about that, Colonel Holliday. They will let me market my opium anywhere I want, except in the United States. A perfectly eq-uitable deal, as far as I'm concerned."

"You sound pretty sure of yourself," said Hol-liday. "Do you really think the United States gov-ernment would agree to all of that?"

Raman smiled. "They already have."

"You've got it all worked out, don't you?"

"Most of it."

"Except for the fact that you don't have the scroll. Bapat does."

"Bapat is a pig but he is a cunning pig," said Raman. "He will not have taken the scroll with him on this journey—only some small evidence that it exists and that it is in his possession."

"So what do you do now?"

"Take it back from him."

Cardinal Secretary of State Arturo Ruffino sat at the edge of Bruno Orsini's swimming pool at his villa in Tuscany. Beside the cardinal there was a table loaded down with assorted fruits and cheeses and two tall sweating glasses of lemonade. Ruffino had been watching Orsini swim laps for almost fifteen minutes now. According to his wife, this was some sort of midafternoon ritual.

With his exercise finally ended, the man climbed out of the pool. Orsini was of medium height with a potbelly and so much body hair that it was almost obscene. The burly man rubbed his hair with a towel, threw on a robe that was lying at the edge of the pool and draped himself in it. He sat down across the table from Ruffino, stabbed a slab of Asiago cheese and popped it into his mouth.

"So, Your Eminence, what brings you so far from your holy roost in Rome?"

"We have a serious problem, Signore Orsini."

"And what can P2 do to help?" Orsini replied.

"P2" stood for Propaganda Due, a semifascist Masonic Lodge springing from Mussolini and his jackbooted Blackshirts. Even after Italy fell to the Americans, the British P2 continued to stockpile weapons of all kinds for what they assumed would be a new revolutionary battle for Italy. They became deeply involved with the CIA, and in the early fifties and sixties there were even plans for a CIA-backed coup of the communist government then in power. After being banned in 1976, Propaganda Due went underground once again. Since that time its activities were mainly criminal, although still closely associated with the Vatican.

Orsini picked up a ripe peach and bit into it, the juice running down his chin. He chewed and swallowed, then wiped his face and lips with a napkin.

"Usually when you come to us these days it's to kill someone who's causing you scandals and problems."

"I'm afraid it's not that simple this time," said Ruffino. He took a small sip of the lemonade. "This time Propaganda Due may well be the cause of the problem at hand."

"You came all this way just to insult me?" Orsini said coldly.

"It is hardly an insult, my dear Orsini. As I understand it, your organization purchases more opium than anyone else in Europe. You ship that opium from Italy to Marseille, where it is then turned into heroin. The bulk of that heroin winds up in the United States, with a small portion going to England."

"What does that have to do with you or your church?" The anger was clear in Orsini's voice now.

"It has everything to do with the Church and your association with it. The Holy See is being blackmailed. Either we underwrite your purchases of opium in much larger quantities than you now purchase or an artifact will be made public that would almost certainly destroy the Holy Church's credibility around the world."

"Why does that involve us? Nobody's trying to blackmail Propaganda Due."

"What your criminal organization does is of little interest to me," said Ruffino. "But now we have been tied together in a relationship almost as bad as the blackmail we now find ourselves fighting."

"I still don't see what you want me to do," said Orsini.

"I want you and your thugs to do what they do best. I want them to find the blackmailer, find the scroll, find anybody else involved and wipe them off the face of the earth."

The young lieutenant sitting at the video screen was named Martin Rooney. He was five foot nine, had large feet and barely possessed the physical qualifications necessary to be in the American armed forces. He was, however, an excellent video game player and had shelves of trophies in a small apartment in Indian Springs, Nevada, to prove it.

He sat in front of a screen showing the view looking downward from a Predator 2 drone flying dangerously close to the Pakistan border. The drone had been covering the same spot for almost two hours. It was a small compound with a house and a single outbuilding, most likely a garage. The area beneath the drone looked completely unoccupied and there had been no movement for the entire time Rooney had been watching. Rooney's acute eyesight had picked up fresh tire tracks with a wheelbase that probably meant a truck had been there. The tracks led directly to the outbuilding. It was late morning in Nevada, but the sun was setting over the compound in Afghanistan. Rooney was bored. Every now and again he'd take a bite from his Subway cold cut combo and a slurp from his long-melted extra-large grape Frosty.

"An army of one, my ass," Rooney muttered under his breath. The forty other young men in the darkened room were probably all of the same opinion. Sometimes it was extremely hard to concentrate on something you knew was taking place halfway around the world. The concentration was made even more difficult by the fact that nothing ever seemed to happen.

Covert ops chief Doug Kitchen sat beside a screen operator in the Afghan desk office on the second floor of CIA headquarters. He'd asked to be pinged when any resources were called up for relay to Russell Smart, which was exactly what he was watching now. The name of the man sitting at the screen was Koppel. He was a nobody in the CIA, just like most of the Company's staff. But little nothings like Koppel helped to gather up the bits and pieces of the puzzle for important people like Kitchen to analyze.

"Mr. Smart ordered the predator run this morning. We're watching it now," said Koppel.

"What's the relay?" Kitchen asked.

"An unregistered safe house in Arlington."

"Is there any chatter?" Kitchen asked.

"Yes, sir, quite a bit. Computer and satellite telephone."

"Who's getting the chatter and where is it being sent?" Kitchen asked.

Koppel checked a second screen on his left. "It looks like Bombay."

"I want details on my desk within two hours," said Kitchen. "Every damn word that goes in and out of that place in Arlington."

"Yes, sir," said Koppel.

Kitchen stood up, patted the man's shoulder the way you would an obedient dog and went back to his solitary office on the fifth floor to think about what all this meant. He was getting a cold feeling in his fingertips.

Something was going on in the Company—something he wasn't privy to—and that would not do.

21

As soon as Koppel began monitoring the traffic between Rusty Smart and his men, most of whom were already in Mumbai, a strident alarm went off on his computer.

Automatically every screen in the safe house blacked out except for the single machine he was transmitting on. Working quickly, he gathered up any papers implicating him or any of his people in any sort of off-campus operation. He sent a single line of text to all his people simultaneously, which was encrypted in a private coding that was particular to the Ghost Squad. That done, he set a series of booby traps in the safe house and left immediately.

He went down into the garage of the building, took out two sets of keys and approached the green Range Rover that was his normal mode of transport and the only vehicle registered in his name.

Once again he set a single booby trap under the front seat of the Range Rover and locked it up. He then went down one floor in the parking garage and fobbed open the doors of a four-year-old Toyota Corolla registered in the name of Arthur Brant, a resident of New York City. Brant was also the name on one of the passports in his attaché case and the one he would be using later tonight. He opened the trunk of the car, took out a set of New York plates and exchanged them for the Maryland plates the car usually carried. He then placed the old plates into the trunk, got in behind the wheel and drove out of the parking garage, heading northwest. Driving slightly above the speed limit, he expected to be at Chicago's O'Hare International by midnight and in the air shortly thereafter.

Back at Langley, Koppel noted the relay being dropped and also the flash message being sent out from the Arlington safe house. He flagged down a clerk and told him to take the message to cryptography. Koppel himself rode the elevator up to the fifth floor, a place he almost never visited. He found Kitchen's office and told him what had happened. Kitchen dismissed him, got on the telephone and ordered a complete sweep of the Arlington safe house, telling the crew to take a demolition expert with them. It was standard tradecraft to booby-trap a facility being abandoned.

Heaving a large sigh, Kitchen stood up, left his office and then walked down the long blue-carpeted hall to tell George Abramovich the bad news.

Holliday and Lazarus sat at the dining table in a suite at the Grand Sarovar. It was early morning and instead of enjoying the local cuisine Holliday and Lazarus had decided on eggs Benedict, orange juice and strong hot coffee.

"We're not actually thinking of going along with this, are we?" Lazarus asking, taking a piece of egg and swiping it through the hollandaise.

Holliday sipped his coffee, his expression dark. "I don't give a shit one way or the other about our Oxford-educated friend Mr. Raman or his lowlife opponent Bapat. The only thing that concerns me right now is that scroll. Peggy and Rafi died because of it and I'll be damned if I'm going to let anyone use it to screw around with the opium market. All the heroin dealers and junkies in the world can go to hell. I just want the scroll."

"Easier said than done," said Lazarus. "Who do we fight? Raman or Bapat? And what do we

fight them with? These people have armies behind them."

"I can do better than an army," said Holliday.
"I've got Pat Philpot."

"Who?"

"Potsy and I go back a long, long way," said
Holliday, smiling.

Holliday had first met Patrick R. Philpot, otherwise know as Potsy, while on a Ranger operation in the Helmand Province of Afghanistan.
Potsy was an intelligence officer, one who had his
fingers in more pies than Holliday had ever seen
before. He scavenged bits of unconnected information like old ladies gathered up string. They
had run into each other again when Philpot was
climbing the ladder of success at the newly con-
structed Counterterrorism Center not far from
the Langley headquarters of the CIA. The next
time they met was shortly after Holliday and Eddie had crashed a giant snowplow through the
main entrance of the security gate of the U.S. embassy in Moscow.

After finishing their breakfast, Holliday and
Lazarus went down to the hotel's business center
and reserved a private cubicle fitted with a computer terminal, a printer and a satellite phone.

"Watch this," said Holliday. He punched out
a series of numbers on the satellite phone. There

were several buzzes and clicks and finally the ringing of a telephone.

A groggy voice answered. "What?"

"Potsy! It's John Holliday."

"Do you know what damn time it is here?"

"I thought you guys in Counterterrorism were ever vigilant."

"Vigilant, my ass. Whatever you want, the answer is no."

"Don't be that way, Potsy," Holliday said. "How many people know you've covered my ass for the snowplow thing?"

"You said you'd never tell anyone about that."

"I lied."

"You're blackmailing me?" Philpot said.

"I wouldn't call it blackmail. I'd call it a small nudge in a particular direction."

"What direction would that be?" said Philpot wearily.

"I want you to send me your latest Onyx pictures on location of the Mullah Omar."

"There is no Onyx."

"Don't be silly, Potsy. I know Onyx exists. You know Onyx exists. For God's sake Wikipedia knows Onyx exists."

"Why do you need this material?"

"Because I'm going to kill the son of a bitch," said Holliday. "I never got to kill Bin Laden, so I thought I'd try my hand as the chief honcho of the Taliban."

"You're out of your freaking mind," said Philpot.

"I'm crazy?" Holliday said. "You're the man who's pathologically obsessed with two all-beef patties, special sauce, lettuce, cheese, pickles, onions on a sesame seed bun. You don't have blood in your veins—you have McNuggets."

"Why do you always bring this down to my eating habits?" Philpot said from eight thousand miles away.

"Simple," said Holliday. "Because the very mention of a Big Mac makes your teeth rattle and we both know that there is a twenty-four-hour McDonald's exactly halfway between your apartment and the Counterterrorism Center. You send me the pictures, you go to McDonald's, you have a couple of Big Macs and then you go home to bed, nobody the wiser."

"All right," said Philpot, sighing. "Where do I send it?"

Holliday gave him the IP number and e-mail address of the terminal in front of him.

"Give me a couple of hours," said Philpot.

"An hour."

"An hour, then."

Holliday turned to Lazarus. "Put a Big Mac

on the end of a hook and that guy would follow you anywhere."

"So what do we do now?"

"We wait for the pictures and then we go back to the Old Curiosity Shop."

Hashim Bakshi's face fell as Holliday and Lazarus returned to his shop. Holliday paused as he closed the door behind him and flipped over the "Closed" sign. As they approached the counter they could see Bakshi cringing.

"Don't worry, Bakshi. We haven't told Raman or anybody else about our little conversation." Bakshi's expression brightened immediately, although there was still a wary look in his eyes.

"What can I do for you this time?" the old man said.

"Let's make one thing perfectly clear before we begin. Not all the goods in this store came here legitimately and quite a few of them are fakes. Agreed?"

Bakshi hesitated for a moment and then his shoulders sagged. "Agreed," he replied.

"How did they get here?" Lazarus asked.

"I employ a number of fabricators in Mumbai who make copies of original antique furniture."

"And the rest?" Holliday asked.

Bakshi shrugged his shoulders. "They're smuggled."

"Do you smuggle things for other people?"

"Yes," said Bakshi.

"Where do you smuggle these things from?"

"Afghanistan, Pakistan. Sometimes even from China, and occasionally from Iran."

"Do you ever smuggle people?" Holliday asked.

"Rarely," said Bakshi.

"How rare is rare?" Holliday asked.

"Four, perhaps five times a year."

"From where?"

"Afghanistan."

"How do you smuggle them?"

"I don't do it myself. I know someone who does."

"How does he do it?" Lazarus asked.

"I have never asked about his methods. He is a Pakistani gentleman named Haji Ayub Afridi."

"Where do we find Afridi?"

"Look for him at the border crossing at Chaman. He has a rice and textile exporting company on Khandari Road."

22

Rusty Smart, Paul Streeter, Tom Harris, James Black and Elliot Foster met at the rendezvous point sent by Smart in his encrypted message twenty-four hours before. It was a large apartment in Prague overlooking Old Town Square. Like many old apartments in Prague, it was high ceilinged with plaster moldings, dangling chandeliers and highly polished dark oak floors. The walls were plastered and had a faint blue tint. The windows were tall and curtained with long green velvet drapery. Most of the furniture was white neo-Baroque and heavily highlighted in gold. The seats on the couches and the cushions on the chairs were all uncomfortable, but there was very little that Rusty Smart could do about that. He'd rented the apartment furnished using money from one of the numerous slush funds operated in Europe by the Company.

The men were all gathered around the large dining room table. The drapes were drawn, even though it was only midday. Smart had swept the place for bugs upon arrival and found that the only way to hear their conversation here would be to bounce an oscillating laser transmitter against window glass, turning the glass into a microphone.

"You're sure we've been burned?" said Elliot Foster.

"I wouldn't have sent out that message if I hadn't been absolutely sure. Someone was looking over my shoulder."

"You couldn't have explained it away?" Streeter asked.

"I thought about that," said Smart. "Maybe they would have believed it for a while, but they'd watch everything I did from that moment on. The trick is to be invisible and not to make waves. They caught me red-handed."

"Fuck," said Foster. "Now we're all fugitives just because you made a stupid mistake."

Smart responded coldly, "I might have made a mistake, but so did you. You had Holliday all sewn up but he somehow got away from you. If he hadn't escaped, we wouldn't be in this situation now."

"Why don't we stop playing the blame game and come up with a solution?" said Harris. He'd been the one on Lazarus and Holliday's tail in Rome.

"I already have a solution," said Smart. "The object of this whole game has been to get that goddamn scroll. We tried buying it, but that got screwed up when that Indian fag stole it. We know the final destination is Mullah Omar and we know exactly where he is."

"Where?" Foster asked.

"Just inside the Afghan border close to Kandahar," said Smart.

"Then how the hell are we supposed to get at him?" Streeter asked.

Smart turned to Foster. "Do you still know anyone in that bunch at Camp Gecko?"

"What's Camp Gecko?" Harris asked.

Foster explained: "Camp Gecko used to be one of Bin Laden's bases near Kandahar back in the nineties. The Company used to run an operation there with the joint Canadian-American special forces group that worked out of the camp. But they dropped out of the game when the Afghan government started raising shit about the Gecko unit doing unauthorized killings for the drug lords. The prime minister began to really raise hell about them after they assassinated his baby brother. They've kind of gone underground now."

"Are they equipped?" Smart asked.

"Blackhawks, Vulcan miniguns, night vision—all the good stuff. The question is, can you get us there?"

"No. The question is, can we get Afghan tribal garb, eh?"

It had taken Holliday and Lazarus the better part of three days to reach Haji Ayub Afridi's import-export company in Chaman. The journey involved an incredibly tedious train ride from Mumbai to Ahmedabad, an equally tedious bus ride from there to Quetta and finally a shorter, dustier bus ride north to Chaman.

When they arrived at the bus terminal, a desperate building of mud bricks and aluminum siding, they found a taxi to take them to something that advertised itself as a five-star hotel—a place that wouldn't have qualified as a flophouse anywhere else. The single room had two iron beds with pillows and a single sheet with a sink against one wall and a ragged rug on the floor between the beds. They dumped their baggage, went back to the taxi and then headed off to the address Bakshi had given them.

The two men went into the building through a narrow door off to the side. Holliday noticed as they entered that three of the windows had been papered over. Inside the warehouse, they were confronted by piles of jute bags, each one looking as though it could easily carry five hundred pounds. Three trucks were being loaded with the bags, each loader carrying a single bag across his back. It looked like grueling work.

To the right was an office, and again, the windows were all papered over. Holliday knocked. A gruff voice answered in Arabic; taking that as a "Come in," Holliday and Lazarus opened the door and entered the office.

There was a single desk against the left wall with a man seated in an old-fashioned wooden swivel chair. He turned away from the ledger he had been working on and stood up, silently inspecting Holliday and Lazarus. The man was of medium height and looked to be in his early to mid-sixties, although his very dark complexion made it hard to tell. His face was narrow, his cheeks were high and he had a well-groomed mustache. His deep-set eyes were black as pitch and he wore a pale green half turban on his head.

"We are looking for Haji Ayub Afridi," said Holliday.

"Why are you looking for him?" the man asked.

"We were sent by Mr. Bakshi in Mumbai."

"A good man, Bakshi. What did he tell you about this man Afridi?"

"He told us that Mr. Afridi could get us into Afghanistan."

"You have passports, don't you? Why not just use them to cross the border as any man would."

"Two reasons," Holliday replied. "We don't wish it to be known that we are in Afghanistan, and if possible we would like to get into Afghanistan as well armed as possible."

"Weapon smuggling." The man nodded. "A dangerous business."

"Mr. Bakshi said that Mr. Afridi was a very resourceful man. He also said that Mr. Afridi did not sell his services cheaply."

"Mr. Bakshi is quite right about that. To smuggle two armed men into Afghanistan would be a very expensive proposition."

"How expensive?" Holliday asked.

The man smiled at Holliday. "Ten thousand dollars," he said. "Each."

"This is a guaranteed price?"

"I guarantee all the work that I do, Colonel Holliday."

"You're well informed, Mr. Afridi."

"Being well informed is necessary for survival in my business. You agree to the deal?"

"Not a problem," replied Holliday. "When do we go?"

"Tomorrow night," said Afridi. "Be here at nine o'clock."

At nine o'clock the following evening Holliday and Lazarus appeared at Afridi's warehouse once again.

This time there was only one truck in the loading bay. Three men waited as before while the fourth stood in the truck. Afridi greeted them and led them into his office.

"The clothes won't do," he said. "Take them off."

While Holliday and Lazarus disrobed, Afridi went out into the warehouse. He reappeared carrying a bundle of filthy clothes, several strips of equally dirty cloth and two pairs of sandals. He also had a tin coffee can, which he set down on his desk. He handed one set of clothes to Holliday and another to Lazarus.

"First of all," said Afridi, "you are much too clean." He grabbed the coffee can, dipped his hand into it and began rubbing a thin layer of grit and dirt into the men's faces, necks, hands, feet and even hair. When he was finished, the two men had been transformed. Instead of two Western men, two Afghan beggars stood in front of Afridi. He nodded and wound the cloth strips onto half turbans around their heads, pinning them securely. For the last touch he gave each man a cloth sash to wrap around his waist.

"What about the weapons?" Holliday asked.

"Already loaded," said Afridi. "What about my payment?"

Holliday reached down toward the bundle of his own clothes lying in front of him, dug around in the inner pocket of his jacket and handed Afridi two rubber-banded rolls of ten thousand dollars each.

"Good enough?" Holliday said.

"Excellent," said Afridi. "Follow me."

Afridi led Holliday and Lazarus out to the truck. A large wooden box stood on the truck bed. The box was eighteen inches high and four feet wide. Both the top and one end were missing. A piece of PVC pipe five feet high and six inches in diameter ran through the box at the head end, a large hole bored into it to let air in.

There was a small battery-driven fan that would provide air during the trip. The pipe also descended through the floor of the truck bed in case the upper pipe became covered. The bottom of the box was padded with a thick cushion of blankets. On each side of the box an AK-47 and a Llama .45 caliber semiautomatic duct taped into place. The rest of the space on the sides of the box was filled with extra magazines for the weapons.

"So now what?" Lazarus asked. "You don't really expect us to get into that, do you?"

"I'd suggest that you do," said Afridi. "I do not give refunds. If you wish to be taken into Afghanistan anonymously, this is the only way."

They climbed up onto the truck, lay down side by side in the open-ended box and waited. Afridi climbed up onto the truck bed and crouched down beside them.

"Here are some things you might need," said Afridi. He handed down two jute bags. "Each one contains a bottle of water, some bread and some cheese. There is also a sheathed shortened Khyber knife. Wear it on your sash. It's very commonly used where you're going."

He continued: "In Colonel Holliday's bag there is a Garmin GPS unit. In Mr. Lazarus's bag there is a Russian military compass just in case the batteries run out in the GPS unit. You will find strips of cloth beneath the blankets. Bind the blankets into a bedroll and hide the weapons within them. Try to travel only by night and stay as far off the roads as possible. The journey will take approximately one hour. The first stop will be at the border, so maintain absolute silence. The second stop will be your destination. I don't suppose either of you speaks Farsi or Arabic, by any chance?"

"I can get by in both," said Holliday. "I was stationed in Afghanistan for three tours. I got to know a little about the place." He smiled up at Afridi. *"As salaam alaikum."*

Afridi touched his forehead with three fingers. *"Wa alaikum salaam."*

Darkness fell as the top of the box was lowered above them. The box was nailed at each corner, as was the piece of plywood at the end. Bags were loaded over them, and within five minutes, the truck was in motion.

Inside the box was total darkness. Holliday could hear Lazarus breathing rapidly beside him. He reached down and turned on the switch, activating the fan. It began to whir, sending a flood of cool evening air into the box.

"Better," said Lazarus. "You okay?"

"Fine," Holliday answered.

Half an hour later the truck came to a labored stop. They could hear the sound of crowds moving back and forth across the border as well as trucks lining up behind them. They were vaguely aware of a conversation being held between the driver and a customs official.

With a grinding of gears, the truck moved off, the loud horn making a squawking sound as it lurched around a slow-moving vehicle. Forty minutes later the truck stopped again. Bags were unloaded and the top of the box was torn open by the driver and his loader.

Without a word Holliday and Lazarus gathered up the weapons and extra magazines, rolled everything into the blankets and tied them with the strips of cloth using a longer piece as a sling. They pushed the bread and cheese into one pocket of their shirts and the bottle of water into the other. Finally they pushed the Khyber knives through the sashes around their waists and dropped down from the rear of the truck. Within seconds the loader was heaving bags back up onto the truck bed. Lazarus and Holliday joined in, making the job that much quicker.

"Shukran," said the loader.

"You are welcome," Holliday replied in Arabic.

The loader grinned and then climbed back into the truck. The gears ground, and the truck's taillights quickly disappeared into the darkness.

Holliday looked around. Mountains reared up

like gargantuan shark's teeth on all sides. The landscape was about as welcoming as walking into a cage full of hungry Bengal tigers.

"Well, I can tell you one thing," said Lazarus.

"Don't say it," said Holliday, sighing.

"We sure aren't in Kansas anymore." Lazarus smiled.

"I told you not to say that," said Holliday.

23

Harrison Blackthorn drove his silver Bentley through the quiet streets of Bedford, New York, eventually turning up his own driveway. He parked in front of the three-car garage doors of the sprawling split-level ranch house that was his home. The house was no ordinary suburban rancher; Frank Lloyd Wright had designed it for Blackthorn's parents in 1956. The attention to detail was extraordinary. The slates on the roof were all slightly angled to suit in various rooflines as they swooped up and down around the house. Instead of drainage pipes, there were chains that dropped to the ground and fed into small channels so that the water could drain toward the street, and one of the windows had been designed in the shape of an open lotus flower.

Blackthorn stared at the house for a moment, once again noting its perfection and the fact that it was more a work of art than a house. He went up the curved flagstone walk to the front door and opened it. He stepped into the front hall and stopped.

Astrella, their Puerto Rican maid, was sprawled on the floor, a large pool of blood surrounding her from the deep slash in her throat. Feeling vomit rising in the back of his throat, Blackthorn edged around the body and headed deeper into the house.

The next horror was his dog, Prometheus, an elderly golden retriever. Its head was skewered with a butcher knife to the newel post of the stairs. The body lay below the bleeding head.

Staggering now, Blackthorn headed to the second floor. At the head of the stairs he saw that the door to his daughter Danah's room was wide-open. She was lying in bed on her stomach, the covers up around her neck. Her blond hair was marred by spatters of blood and brains from the large-caliber bullet that had ended her life.

Numb now, Blackthorn moved zombielike down the hall to the master bedroom. His wife, Julia, was sitting on the end of the bed, with Enoch Snow sitting beside her. As Blackthorn appeared in the doorway, Snow casually lifted the silenced barrel of his P9 pistol and blew the woman's head off. She flopped down to the floor, arching sideways, and landed with her ruined face and head at the foot of her dressing table.

"I hired you to kill Holliday and the other two," said Blackthorn blankly, barely fathoming the horrors he had just seen.

"Somebody paid me more to kill you," said Enoch Snow. "Said you were a loose end."

Blackthorn shook his head, still not understanding. "But—"

Snow shot him.

Russell Smart and his Ghost Squad flew from Prague to Istanbul, each traveling separately. They then took a Turkish Airlines flight to Kabul International Airport, arriving close to midnight. Still moving separately, all the men drove to the Kabul Serena Hotel and booked a room using the name on their respective false passports.

At one o'clock in the morning there was a knock on Rusty Smart's door.

"Who is it?" Smart asked through the closed door.

"Harper," replied a muffled voice.

Smart opened the door and let the man in. Harper was a large man wearing Canadian BDUs and showing the rank of major. In his left hand he carried a large Samsonite suitcase. Without a word, he brushed past Smart and went into the room. He dropped the suitcase onto the bed, unlocked it and flipped it open. Inside were half a dozen more Canadian camouflage uniforms. Harper took them all out, then reached into the large pocket in the top of the suitcase and pulled out six sets of military IDs and six high-power FN 9-millimeter semiautomatic pistols.

"Hand these out to your men. Meet me in the lobby at nine a.m. tomorrow and I'll have transport waiting to take you where you want to go. Any questions?"

"No," said Smart.

At nine o'clock the following morning Harper was waiting and guided them through the security apparatus out of the hotel. A Ford minivan was waiting in the driveway. Harper got behind the wheel. Smart and his men climbed in through the sliding door, and a few moments later, they were moving out of Kabul heading west.

At six that evening they reached the city of Kandahar and drove straight to the military base there. Harper showed his ID and was immediately let through the gates. They drove along a long dirt road until they reached a parked Blackhawk helicopter, its door already open. Harper,

Smart and the rest of them climbed out of the minivan. A black-bereted man in U.S. Special Forces BDUs jumped down from the helicopter. Harper introduced him.

"This is Ivan Simons, one of the Camp Gecko people."

"Pleased to meet you," said Simons. He was a rangy man with big-knuckled hands, freckled cheekbones and a big pair of aviator sunglasses.

"He'll be your pilot," said Harper.

"Good enough," said Smart.

Harper stood by and watched as Smart and the others climbed into the helicopter. A few seconds later the rotors thundered into life, the big turbines rising to a wailing scream. The Blackhawk slid into the air, heading slightly south.

In the Blackhawk, Smart looked out the window from his jump seat position. He'd always enjoyed flying in helicopters; they gave him an almost erotic sense of power. Below him the ground looked like the craters on the moon. People had been fighting for possession of this destitute landscape since the time of Alexander. The British had fought two wars here, the Russians had fought for it too, and finally the Americans were giving it a try.

But none of them had been able to tame the warlord mentality of the scattered tribes and families in the barren country. There was talk of oil and precious minerals, but it had never really been about that at all. Ever since Kabul had been one of the major trading stops on the Silk Road, it had always been about opium.

They reached Camp Gecko an hour later. There were four other Blackhawks lined up outside a fenced-in area that held several Quonset huts and a few smaller prefab buildings. Beyond the wired area, they could see what appeared to be the remains of some sort of ancient walled compound. The helicopter landed and the men stepped out into the terrible heat. An American sergeant led them to one of the prefab buildings and ushered them inside. There was a desk, an air-conditioning unit, a Coca-Cola machine and various pieces of communication equipment along one wall. The man sitting behind the desk was a full-bird colonel with iron gray hair clipped very short. His face was thick and ruddy, and he had the look of a man who had spent too much time in the desert.

"My name is Marshall," the colonel said. "I'll be your watchdog for this operation and I'll be the one cleaning up all the messes. Which one of you is Smart?"

"I am." Smart stepped forward.

"We've had a directive about you and your boys here. It says you're a unit gone rogue. What do you have to say about that?"

"Deniability, sir," said Smart. "If the shit hits the fan, they'll have somebody to throw under the bus."

"And your objective?" Marshall asked.

"We're here to take out the Mullah Omar and bring him back here for rendition. If he doesn't come peacefully, we kill him."

"All right," said Marshall. "Let's come up with a proper plan, even though you don't really exist. Any of you guys want a Coke before we begin?"

It had taken Holliday and Lazarus the better part of three days to reach Mullah Omar's compound. They lay at the summit of a small ridge a quarter of a mile away from the compound. They had been there for an hour and had seen nothing. Dusk was falling and soon it would be night.

Using the binoculars, Holliday surveyed the compound once again. As he watched, the garage doors opened and a pickup truck with a mounted .50 caliber machine gun appeared. Holliday followed it with his binoculars. It went to the end of an almost invisible airstrip and waited. Suddenly there was the droning of a single-engine airplane.

"Keep down flat," whispered Holliday. He and Lazarus flattened themselves just below the ridgeline, making sure their silhouettes did not break the normal line of the ridge.

The plane came in for its approach, touched down in a cloud of dust and rolled forward, spinning fifty feet to a stop before it reached the armed pickup truck. Two men climbed out of the airplane.

"It's Dhaliwal," said Holliday quietly. "The other one must be Bapat. He's carrying an attaché case."

As the two men reached the truck, a man climbed out of the passenger seat and greeted them.

"It's Mullah Omar himself," said Holliday.

As he spoke the mullah took what appeared to be an old-fashioned revolver and fired point-blank at Bapat and Dhaliwal. Both men dropped to the dusty ground.

The mullah called out an order and the man behind the wheel climbed out from the truck while the figure operating the machine gun dropped to the ground. The two men dragged Bapat and Dhaliwal back to the airplane and loaded both of them through the passenger door. The man behind the wheel had a hurried conversation with the pilot. The pilot nodded. The figure that had been standing at the machine gun slammed the door and the two men then headed back to the truck. The pilot proceeded to turn the plane around, pausing for a moment as the engine worked up to full throttle. He then released the brakes and the small turboprop hurtled down the runway and into the air.

The mullah picked up the attaché case and climbed back into the truck. A few seconds later the truck turned back through the gates of the compound and dropped the mullah in front of the large fortified building that occupied the center of the compound. The mullah disappeared inside and the truck returned to the garage.

"Cutting down on the competition," said Holliday.

"You, English, stand up."

The voice came from directly behind them. Holliday and Lazarus rolled over and found themselves facing the muzzles of two AK-47s. They had been captured.

Geronimo Caserio stood in the small living room of the twentieth-floor apartment he had chosen. The owner of the apartment, a man named Jamal

Qudri, had taught geography at a nearby high school. He now lay dead, seated on the toilet in his bathroom. He no longer had a left eye. The back of the toilet was sprayed with blood and brains.

Caserio opened the long Hardcase container and laid it out on the dining room table, which had been pulled up to the window to overlook Shivaji Park. He withdrew the various components from the case, which fit together to become a Barrett .50 caliber sniper rifle. It had a tripod instead of the usual bipod front rest. The stock rested on a heavy sand-filled leather bag. The weapon had a twenty-power Unertl telescopic sight.

Using a range-finder monocular, he stared down into the park. The range was twenty-two hundred yards, or about a mile and a quarter. The cricketers were already at play, but his target had yet to arrive. He took a small leather case from his jacket pocket, which contained an ordinary glass cutter and a large wad of putty. He laid the putty on the glass, then scored a rough circle around it. He tapped the scored area with two knuckles and the glass snapped. He pulled it back into the apartment, using the knob of putty in the center.

With that done, he began the arduous task of

lowering the weapon on his tripod rest until he had the angle absolutely perfect. He adjusted for wind, basing his calculations on the movement of the trees near the entrance to the park, and adjusted a second time for the distance. It was roughly the same setup he'd used to kill the Israeli and his wife, except that he was now in an air-conditioned apartment and not a windblown desert.

Geronimo had worked for P2 for more than twenty years and always followed his orders without question He had killed policemen, ministers of parliament, housewives, doctors, several priests and even an archbishop. He was a religious man and believed with absolute certainty that his soul would burn in hell. On the other hand, there had been a reason for every person he had killed.

He checked through the telescopic sight and saw that his target had reached the cricket pitch. He slid a single round into the breech of the weapon, took in a deep breath and let it out slowly. The target was a little more than a mile away and wouldn't hear the sharp crack of the approaching bullet. Caserio kept his eyes to the telescopic sight and watched as the man's head completely disappeared. His job done, he methodically packed up everything and left the apartment.

Down in the park Kota Raman's bodyguards

were looking in all directions, stunned by their boss's death. Within a few seconds people began to gather around the dead man and it was all his bodyguards could do to pick up their dead master and carry him back to his expensive car. They drove off as police sirens began to wail.

24

Kate Rogers interviewed Professor Spencer Maxwell Boatman in his apartment on Boulevard Saint-Michel. The man's study was filled with books and piles of paper. The furniture was old and the Persian carpet on the floor was so thin in some places you could see the floorboards beneath it. Boatman sat behind the large plain table that acted as a desk and it was as littered with books and stacks of paper as anywhere else in the room.

"I'm not exactly sure what you want me to tell you," said Boatman. "Or what authority you have asking me your questions in the first place. You are with the CIA and I'm British."

Kate Rogers smiled at the handsome man across from her. "I'm CIA, you're British, and you're living in Paris. I can make things very difficult for you."

"Why on earth are you threatening me?" Boatman asked. "I teach mathematics at the Sorbonne. I'm not a spy nor do I know any spies."

"You know Colonel John Holliday."

"I met him for coffee on one occasion."

"What did you talk about?"

"Very little," said Boatman. "We barely had time to talk about anything until he fled."

"Why did he flee?"

"He got a phone call."

"You're full of shit, Professor. You talked to him about the so-called Jesus Scroll, the one that describes Christ's travels in the East after his crucifixion. On the open market it's invaluable. The Israelis are furious that they don't have it and the Vatican is terrified about the revelations it might contain. We think Holliday either has it or knows where it is."

"What can I say?" Boatman shrugged. "I spent five minutes with him and you sent him somewhere, didn't you?"

Kate Rogers didn't answer his question. "Since your conversation with him, we know that he's partnered up with a man named Peter Lazarus, an art cop who works for Interpol."

"I know Peter. He's an old friend. We went to university together. I have no idea what relationship he might have with this Holliday fellow you seem so interested in."

"The local police and French counterintelligence have you on tape leaving here five minutes after a full-blown order went out to capture Holliday. The waiter at the café where you and Holliday met each other recognizes both of you. They wanted to bring you in for questioning, but I got to you before they could act. I assure you, Mr. Boatman, your job at the Sorbonne no longer exists, and if I were you, I'd leave France at the next available opportunity."

"I'll bear that in mind," said Boatman. "Now perhaps you could leave. I have papers to mark."

Kate stood up. She rapped a single knuckle against the wooden table as she looked down at Boatman. "I'm sure we'll be seeing each other again quite soon." She turned on her heel and left the apartment.

Alexander Mitchell—Zits—flew to Washington D.C., arriving a little after ten o'clock in the morning. From Ronald Reagan Airport, he took a short cab ride to the Pentagon. Standing in the outer ring, dressed in his best army greens, he inquired after Major General Thomas Beach. Luckily

Beach was in, and they sent an adjutant to fetch him. They made their way through the maze of corridors and hallways to the fifth ring, which overlooked the Pentagon courtyard. Beach was one of those rare people who worked at the Pentagon who actually had a window.

Beach was a year or two older than Mitchell and he'd done tours in Iraq, Afghanistan and Somalia. He wore an "Airborne" patch on his shoulders and had a long angular scar through his right temple over his nose and down to his left jaw.

"You've seen a bit of action since we were at West Point together."

"No offense, Zits, but it doesn't look like you've seen any at all."

"I teach history at the Point," said Mitchell.

"You want some coffee?" Beach offered.

"No, sir."

"I'm a busy man, Zits, so why don't we get to the point?"

"It's not Zits, sir. It's Lieutenant Alex Mitchell."

"Sorry about that. That's all I've ever really known you as. But surely you didn't come here to talk about old times?"

"No, sir. I came to talk about Colonel John Holliday."

"What about him?"

Mitchell told his story and by the time he'd finished Beach was leaning back in his chair with a strange look on his face.

"Do you know what I do here?" Beach asked Mitchell.

"You are a deputy director in the intelligence agency."

"How the hell did you know that?"

"I keep tabs on everybody I ever knew at West Point," Mitchell replied. "I figure that one day the information might come in handy. Do you know what Holliday is doing these days?"

"No, sir. He just popped out of nowhere." Beach leaned forward and made a brief phone call. "There is somebody you've got to talk to now." Beach stood up.

Mitchell followed suit. "Who?"

"My boss. Follow me."

They went back through the confusing puzzle of corridors and hallways, finally reaching the south entrance. Two marine MPs stepped out. The two men gripped Mitchell by the arms and led him out into the daylight.

A Blackhawk helicopter, its rotors already whirring, was sitting in the south parking lot. The two MPs marched Zits Mitchell over to the waiting machine and assisted him inside. Beach climbed in and slid the big door shut. Ten seconds later the helicopter rose and swooped away, heading across the Potomac River.

Fifteen minutes later it landed at Joint Base Anacostia-Bolling. A Humvee was waiting. Mitchell and Beach climbed into the rear of the vehicle, which drove halfway around the thousand-acre base and dropped them in front of an anonymous building made of black glass and steel. They made their way inside. Beach flashed his ID at a guard, who then handed Mitchell a visitor's pass on a chain. Mitchell hung the chain around his neck and followed Beach to an elevator.

The elevator was key operated. Twisting the key in the lock, Beach opened the doors, and they stepped in. There was no floor indicator in the plain elevator and it was only by the drop that Mitchell knew they were going down rather than up.

When the doors opened again they stepped out into a gigantic dark control room. The huge room reminded Mitchell of every film he'd seen about nuclear attacks.

There were catwalks everywhere with large supercomputers arranged on one side. A single giant screen in the center of one wall and dozens of smaller screens were arranged like something out of NASA launch control. Beach led Mitchell to a giant curved desk with an array of chairs and telephones on it. He pulled out a chair for him and introduced the man on his right.

"General William Taber, director of the Defense Intelligence Agency." He had wavy white hair, half-glasses and looked faintly like Henry Kissinger in a very expensive suit.

"So you're the history teacher who raided the West Point armory for John Holliday."

"Yes, sir."

"You could get ten years in Leavenworth for that, you know," Taber said.

Zits Mitchell's eyes were drawn away from the general to the huge screen dominating the wall in front of them. Apparently a drone somewhere in the Afghan desert or perhaps Pakistan had fired a missile, which was now homing in on a line of vehicles coming through a narrow pass. The missile impacted the middle of the three vehicles, demolishing it in a giant blossom of dust and flame.

"You never saw that," said the general.

"No, sir," replied Mitchell.

"We were talking about your ten years in Leavenworth. Pretty serious stuff, Lieutenant."

"Yes, sir."

"Why did you do it?" General Taber asked.

"Because I looked up to him," said Mitchell finally. "He was the man who inspired me to become a teacher at West Point."

"He was a lot more than that, you know," said the general. "As far back as Vietnam we kept on running into each other and in stranger places for years after that. I used to think he was black ops for the CIA dressed up as a soldier but I checked up on him and found out he was the real thing. All in all, I'd say he was one hell of a soldier, but something happened along the way and he changed into something else."

The general leaned over the large semicircular desk and called out to one of the technicians in the pit below him. "Give me the first one, Harry," he called out.

The screen cleared. It was replaced by a crime scene videotape of a dead body lying in a hallway.

"This is the hallway of a house rented by a woman named Hannah Kruger. She has a Russian background, but we don't think that's the point. The guy on the floor is named Eric Monkman. He *is* a black ops man for the CIA. Apparently Holliday shot him several times. He then fled with Miss Kruger."

Once again the general called down into the pit. "Let's have number two now."

The second video clip showed the interior of an artist's studio set up in something that might have once been a greenhouse.

"See the painting on the easel? It's a forged

Caravaggio. There were large-format photographs of the real thing all over the place. There were also files of photographs of other paintings, most of them eighteenth- and nineteenth-century master-pieces. By the looks of it, Miss Kruger was a forger and the CIA wanted her dead. It appears they didn't get their wish. Not then, anyway."

He called down into the pit again.

"This is Cointrin Airport in Geneva," said the general as the video image appeared. "You can see Hannah Kruger there on the left, and if you look really carefully you can see Holliday in the lineup at the right. Then you can see this guy with a hat and overcoat appear and brush past Kruger. Just enough time to slide a knife up un-der her ribs and into her heart."

Zits Mitchell stared, horrified, as the woman dropped to the ground like a puppet with its strings snipped.

"Number four, Harry."

Number four was a still photograph of a man on a mortuary table. "This is a man named Har-rison Blackthorn. He was head of one of the big-gest auction houses in New York. He was shot in the chest and head, clearly the work of a profes-sional assassin."

"Do you think Colonel Holliday had anything to do with this?"

"Not directly. But when the NYPD went through the inventory of paintings that Mr. Blackthorn had on hand, they found four paintings that didn't show up anywhere on the books. One of them was the Caravaggio that Hannah Kruger was forging when the killer showed up. Give me number five."

This time the image was of a building with its doors blown open and most of the facade destroyed.

"This is the gallery of a man closely connected to Blackthorn. When they checked, Miami Police found half a dozen paintings that weren't anywhere on his inventory. Clearly, it's all connected. The next thing you know, we have both visual and signals intelligence that Holliday and an Interpol cop named Peter Lazarus boarded an Air India flight for Mumbai. A week later we get this from our office in Mumbai."

Once again a video of a crime scene came on. A man in his sixties or seventies was on the floor of his Paris laboratory. Surrounding him was photographic equipment of several different kinds and on the light table there was a single page of some kind of Aramaic scroll.

"We had the page of the scroll checked out and it would appear that it comes from Qumran—in other words, it's one of the Dead Sea Scrolls. It looks like it was torn off its mounts and the entire scroll except this single page was carried off. We also have evidence that Holliday and his Interpol friend were there either during or shortly after the theft. In the man's apartment there was a great deal of correspondence to both Harrison Blackthorn and an Indian man named Kota Raman, the head of the large and very influential family in Mumbai."

The general leaned down into the pit. "Give us the last one."

The final image was the most gruesome of all. Another autopsy table, but this time the man lying on it was completely headless, the remains of the neck and upper spine a gory mess.

"This is Kota Raman. Do you still think your Colonel Holliday is so inspiring?" General Taber queried.

"I still don't think he would have done all of that without having pretty good goddamn reason . . . General."

"We have Holliday in Hannah Kruger's house killing a man. We have Holliday connected to the auctioneer's murder as well as to Eric Bingham in Miami. We have Holliday within twenty-five feet of the Kruger woman's murder. We have Holliday and Lazarus in the Frenchman's apartment in Paris and we have solid intelligence that

Holliday and Lazarus met with Kota Raman and that both Holliday and Raman were interested in the scroll. You really think he's not involved in all of this?"

"I still stand by him, sir," Zits Mitchell said. "He may have killed people following orders in the army, but you said it yourself—he was one hell of a soldier and soldiers don't go around murdering people."

"Loyal to the last," said the general, shaking his head. He clapped Mitchell on the shoulder. "I agree with you, Lieutenant. John Holliday is too much of a good soldier, but we know he's involved in this, and unless I miss my bet right now, he's somewhere looking for that scroll and he's in a jam. It's going to be our business to get him out of it."

General Taber grinned. "I can be loyal too, son."

25

Holliday and Lazarus were marched down the hill by the two guards, who poked them every once in a while to keep them moving. They passed through the gates of the compound and paused in front of the door. One of the guards stepped forward and gave a shave-and-a-haircut knock. Holliday smiled at the use of such an Americanism. A few seconds later the door opened and the two men were pushed inside. It was absolutely nothing like Holliday had expected.

Instead of the rough interior of an Afghan home, he saw absolutely nothing at all. The rough floors were made of wide planks, and there was no furniture anywhere. Out of the corner of his good eye Holliday saw a large explosive bundle connected to a switch midway down the door they had just come through. The doorway was booby-trapped. Their two guards led them through a series of rooms, all empty except for the final one. In the last room there were piles of bags smelling strongly of diesel fuel. Holliday knew he was looking at a gigantic ammonium nitrate bomb. If detonated, it would destroy the entire compound and anything within a few hundred yards of it.

The first guard took a long hooklike device from the pocket of his jacket and thrust it into a broken knothole in the wood, revealing an almost perfectly concealed trapdoor. There was a metal ladder against one side of the man-sized hole confronting them. The guards gestured for Holliday and Lazarus to go downward. They complied, Holliday going first, followed by Lazarus. The trapdoor slammed shut overhead, leaving them in absolute darkness.

"Alice down the rabbit hole," said Lazarus, speaking in the darkness.

"I've been in places like this before," said Holliday. "The Vietcong had miles of tunnels and bolt-holes like this around strategic areas. They even had them approaching the outskirts of Saigon."

Holliday reached the bottom of the tunnel and felt his feet hit a large wooden pad. Small low-power lightbulbs suddenly switched on in the tunnel to his left. Since going back up was not an option, he waited for Lazarus to reach the bottom of the hole and then they followed the string of lights that went down the tunnel. It was no more than four feet wide; the walls and ceiling were made from hand-hewn stone. They crunched onward for what seemed an endless amount of time.

Counting strides in his head, Holliday figured they'd traveled almost two miles before reaching the end of the tunnel and another ladder leading upward into the darkness. Since there was no other place for them to go, they climbed upward. After two hundred feet, they reached the top of the hole and climbed out.

"Unbelievable," said Lazarus.

The two men were standing in an immense cave, as wide as a football field and the ceiling a hundred feet above their heads. Stalactites hung like ancient swords above them, but the floor was clean and dry. It had been divided into a number of sections, steel poles hammered into the stone with large wool rugs dividing the areas into rooms.

There were perhaps fifty men moving around the cave. Some were piling crates of weapons and bags of food, while others were tending to some penned-up goats. Somewhere there was the sound of a generator. And there was a cable running like a snake along the floor, powering several laptops set up on a metal table. From far back in the cave, they could smell food being cooked.

Yet another man with an AK-47 pointed Holliday and Lazarus to a large cubicle on their right. The two men walked to the cubicle and pulled back the two long curtains of wool cloth that acted as doors. Seated cross-legged on several bales of cloth was Mullah Omar, reading a copy of *Scientific American*. He looked up as Holliday and Lazarus entered his lair. Seeing Holliday, he burst out laughing.

"We are twins, you and I," said the mullah. "We are each missing the same eye. It must certainly be the will of Allah that has brought us together."

"I'd hardly call us twins," replied Holliday.

"I was trying to be hospitable," said the mullah. "If you want me to act otherwise, I assure you, it could be arranged."

"Was it hospitable of you to send two men with AK-47s to kidnap us?"

"You were spying on me."

"And we saw you murder two people at point-blank range. Was that Allah's doing? Is there some excuse for murder in the Koran?"

"There are several excuses for killing in the Koran, but I wouldn't invoke them on this occasion. Dhaliwal was a liar, a thief and a pedophile, and Bapat was simply a filthy criminal whose only god was his own greed. These are people who have no purpose in this world or any other."

Holliday sighed. "There must be a reason you kept us alive. Why don't we get to the point?"

"Have you ever heard the Arabic proverb 'The enemy of my enemy is my friend,' Holliday?"

"Certainly."

"Well, that is the case here. I brought you to this place so we could discuss what to do with the Qumran scroll."

The Blackhawk helicopter landed in a small canyon about ten miles from the Mullah Omar's compound. Foster, Harris, Black, Streeter, and Smart were the first out of the chopper, followed by five men from the group based at Camp Gecko. All the men were dressed as Afghan tribesmen and each carried an AK-47. The last man off the helicopter carried an Russian-made RPG rocket launcher on his back. He also was carrying the ubiquitous Kalashnikov.

"Hang on," said Streeter. "I've forgotten my pack."

The Ghost Squad member hauled himself back into the interior of the Blackhawk. As Streeter disappeared, Foster, Harris and Smart turned on the men from Camp Gecko and unloaded the clips of their AK-47s into the small band of men. As the Gecko squad crumbled to the stony ground, Streeter reached the cockpit of the helicopter and pushed the muzzle of the gun against the base of the pilot's neck.

"Who are you fuckers?" the pilot asked.

"It doesn't really matter," said Streeter.

"How the hell are you going to get anybody to fly you out of here?" asked the pilot.

"I did two tours in Iraq flying Apaches. I think I know how to fly this thing."

And then, without any warning, he shot the man in the neck, angling the muzzle down so the bullet would pass through his body rather than his head, to avoid the splattering of blood, brains and other assorted bodily goop all over the windshield.

Gripping the pilot by the back of his jacket, he hauled him out of his seat and back through the cargo section, at which point he used his foot to roll the dead man onto the ground. Before climbing down out of the helicopter, he placed a small gray package on the floor and rammed a pencil-like device into it. He then joined the other members of the Ghost Squad.

"Helicopter all fixed?"

"If any of our Taliban friends try to use it,

they'll be dancing with their forty virgins a split second later," said Streeter.

"And what happens if the helicopter is destroyed?" Smart asked. "How do we get out of here?"

"The hard way," said Foster. "We lose the headdress, use rags for turbans and walk across the Pakistan border. What's the matter, Rusty? Not up for little hike?" Foster smiled.

Smart's expression darkened but he didn't say anything. The four men began walking north toward the far end of the canyon and into the hills beyond.

General William Taber and Lieutenant Alexander Mitchell stood in the DIA's ready room at the American embassy in Islamabad, Pakistan. The large room was deep in the bowels of the compound and contained a long table with one large screen occupying the far wall. Henry Kroninberg, the DIA station officer for Pakistan, stood to one side of the screen, manipulating the controls.

"Lights, please," he called out.

One of his junior officers jumped up and killed the lights.

"This is the center of the whole problem," said Kroninberg. An aerial film taken by a high-altitude drone showed the Mullah Omar's compound. "This compound was once occupied by Osama bin Laden and is now being used by Mullah Omar. All our sources tell us that the buildings are a cover for a complex series of tunnels and caves in the mountain you see on the right-hand side of the image."

Kroninberg flicked a switch and a bright blue overlay bisected the image.

"The compound is quite clearly in Afghan territory," he continued, "but due to long-standing issues between the Afghan and Pakistan governments, the border takes a convoluted turn to the right. Depending on exactly where the caves are located, it could be on either Afghan or Pakistani territory. If the caves are in Afghanistan, the Pakistanis won't give a damn, but if they're in Pakistan and we try to mount an operation, we'll find ourselves in a shitstorm of political trouble."

"So how do we solve the problem here?" Taber asked, looking around the table.

"I don't think it is possible," said the junior officer who had doused the lights a few moments before. "Both operations would be illegal simply because they are both launched in Afghanistan."

"You've hit the nail on the head," said Taber. "We can't launch an operation of any kind; ergo, we don't launch one at all. Somebody else must."

"Who?" Kroninberg asked, surprised.

"Does anybody around this table think that if the Afghans tried to blow up Mullah Omar, it would cause anybody any particular grief—even if it is Pakistani territory? I don't think so. The present government is worried about who's coming into power in Afghanistan, just as much as everybody else in the world is."

"So what does that mean to us?" Kroninberg asked.

"It means Smart and his creepy little Ghost Squad from the CIA have to be stopped before it's too late. Our people have to get to Holliday and Omar first—which means we move our asses right now."

Holliday, Lazarus and the Mullah Omar were sitting at the narrow entrance to the cave. The sun was setting. They were eating an aromatic goat stew out of clay bowls.

"I'm sure you are aware that I own or control more than half the opium in Afghanistan."

"So I've been told," said Holliday.

"Kota Raman told you this?"

"He told me about it, but it would appear to be general knowledge."

"And my intentions?" asked the mullah.

"You will use your control of the opium crops to gain power in Kabul?"

"Nonsense," said the mullah. "This country has been dependent on opium since the beginning of time. For my country to become anything in the world, all forms of crime, corruption and the opium trade must be done away with forever. My intention is to destroy as much of the opium crop as I can. The CIA will hate me for it, most of the people in power in Kabul will hate me for it and people like your friend Kota Raman will wither on the vine when I do it. Opium is like gangrene in my country. And like the offending limb, it must be amputated. There is no other way to bring peace to this place. When I have done this, I will vanish as though I was never here. I have no wish for personal power or personal riches. Before I left my home I was a scholar and my dearest hope is to be a scholar once more."

A guard went up to the Mullah Omar and whispered into the bearded man's ear. Omar set his bowl of stew aside and got to his feet.

"We have a problem, gentlemen. I have protectors all throughout these hills. They tell me one of your country's Blackhawk helicopters has landed and that a squad of soldiers is coming to kill me. We must prepare ourselves."

26

Cardinal Secretary of State Arturo Ruffino was wearing an exclusively cut suit made by one of Italy's best tailors. He was sitting on the couch in his suite at Claridge's in London enjoying a perfectly made cup of espresso along with a chocolate éclair. Across from him sat Sir Henry Maxim. Ruffino put down his coffee cup and dabbed the cream from his lips with a fine linen napkin.

"We are faced with a problem, Sir Henry."

"And what would that be?" asked the MI6 operations director.

"The problem is twofold," the cardinal began. "Number one, we have approximately forty thousand works of art in the Vatican vaults that we have been depending on to fund out expenses at the Vatican Bank for some time now. And two, we are not in possession of the missing Qumran scroll."

"Why are you asking me for help?" Maxim asked. "I would have thought problems like these should be presented to the whole Leonardo group."

"You are the only one who has a vested interest in seeing that the Huff train and its secrets are never revealed. The others will be like vultures around a dying animal."

"What vested interests are you talking about?" Maxim asked.

"Don't be coy," said the cardinal. "Before you got your knighthood, you were Professor Henry Maxim, one of the British contingent of the Monuments, Fine Arts, and Archives Program. You were also working for MI6, looking for any documents that might be of value to British intelligence."

"What of it?"

"You and several other members of the British program as well as half a dozen more in the American section were all art experts of one kind or another. You decided to keep a number of paintings and other pieces of fine art for yourselves, shipping them to Switzerland or the United States, where you hoarded them and let them out onto the market every two or three years. Not only that, but you also ran into Rheinhard Huff in an internment camp in southern Italy when he was trying to make his escape through the Vatican ratlines established by Pope Pius XII. How am I doing at this point?"

"There's been a lot of water under that particular bridge," said Maxim. "I could just deny everything."

"You could. But it wouldn't get you very far." The cardinal leaned down and picked up the attaché case that had been resting on the floor beside him. He placed it on the coffee table beside the remains of his chocolate éclair and snapped it open. He withdrew a thick manila file folder with the words "Top Secret" stamped on it in large red letters. "Do you know what this is?"

"I don't have the faintest idea." Maxim's eyes locked onto the folder.

"You know exactly what's in here," Ruffino said, tapping the file with his long, bony index finger. "It's the interrogation file from the internment camp, the one that took place before you arrived and took over the conversation. It also includes your interrogation, because of course you didn't speak German and the whole thing had to be translated. Huff bribed you with the location of his own private stash and told you everything about the material on the train. You used that information to get even more looted art by blackmailing Pius XII until his death in 1958."

"I had every copy of that file destroyed," said Maxim.

"Not quite every copy," said the cardinal. "The man who translated it saw the value in what he had discovered and kept one copy for himself. He knew who you were and he knew that you would kill him unless he could hold this over your head. Upon his death, his oldest daughter, a devout Catholic, sent the file to my predecessor."

"What exactly is it that you want from me, Cardinal?"

"What you've always done and done so well, Sir Henry. I want you to help me dispose of the works in our vaults by using your connections with Customs and Excise. And I want you to tell us where we can find Holliday and the missing scroll, of which I am sure you've heard."

Maxim stood. "I'll do what I can."

"No, you'll do as I say. Your reputation and perhaps even your life depend on it."

Without another word Maxim turned on his heel and left the suite. The cardinal took the last bite of his éclair and then sipped his espresso. He frowned. The coffee had gone cold.

Foster and the rest of his team reached the same ridge where Holliday and Lazarus had been captured. It was almost fully dark now, and the men could just barely make out the compound.

"This is insane," Black said, staring down at the shadowed buildings. "They could have a hundred men down there."

"But they don't," said Foster. "All the satellite intel shows this place as deserted. There were even a few drone flybys that showed no activity at all."

"Then why the hell is it there and why is it on every intel file the Company has on the mullah?"

"Because it's all we've got," said Foster. Foster turned to Streeter. "How many rounds do you have for that RPG on your back?"

"Three," said Streeter. He unslung the missile launcher and pulled a single bulbous round from his ragged backpack. He slid the small missile into the front of the launching tube and twisted once. "What am I firing at?"

"Two places," said Foster. "Do you see that small narrow dark spot in the mountain, rising up above the compound?"

"Yes," said Streeter.

"The cave is target number two. The compound is target number one. I'm pretty sure the compound is a decoy, but there is no sense in taking chances."

"You're the boss," said Streeter. He armed the trigger mechanism and fired.

The detonation of the high explosives hidden in the middle of the compound's main building was so enormous that it lit up the sky like daylight for a brief moment, and then, because of the lack of oxygen, the massive explosion sucked in on itself and blew out in concentric shock waves so strong they sent all four men on the ridge tumbling backward. They crawled back up the ridge.

Streeter fired the rocket-propelled grenade a second time, aiming at the mouth of the mountain cave. Another explosion bloomed in the darkness and then faded.

"There's no way to climb up to that cave in the mountain, so there must be a tunnel leading from the compound. If we find the tunnel, we find Omar," Foster said with a smile. "That is, if North's second shot hasn't blown him to Allah land."

The five men ran down to the compound, Foster keeping his eyes on the mouth of the cave, where small fires were still burning.

The mouth of the tunnel was remarkably easy to find. Since the epicenter of the explosion had been in the room with the trapdoor, the hole in the ground was obvious. The four men pulled glow sticks out of their backpacks, snapped them to life and then dropped them down the hole. They went down the metal ladder one after the other, then marched through the long, narrow tunnel that led to the cave. Foster called Streeter forward.

"Load your RPG and fire it straight upward."

Streeter did as he was told and the round from the RPG traveled straight upward, trailing smoke and fire. A few seconds later there was a ripping explosion that made their ears ring. They waited a few moments and then, with Foster leading, climbed up into the cave. Each man reached into the other's pack and drew out a nine-inch rubberized Maglite. They switched on the LED beams and swept them around the entrance to the cave.

The whole front section of the cave had been completely destroyed. The cubicles were nothing more than smoldering piles of cloth and the entire small herd of goats had been blown to pieces. Entrails were splashed against the floor and walls of the cave.

"Did we get 'em? Is the mullah here?" Smart asked nervously.

"I don't think so," said Foster.

"What about the scroll? We have to get the scroll," said Smart.

An object slightly smaller than a football came sailing through the air and landed at Foster's feet.

"Mother . . ." was all Foster could manage before his body turned to atoms.

Rusty Smart and the others didn't have even that much time.

At the other end of the cave, Omar and others stood together for a brief instant and then made their way down the long tunnel that led to the end of the cave. Decades, perhaps even centuries ago a pathway had been carved down the side of the mountain to a steep canyon.

Staring out of the opening, Holliday could see an old Toyota, and behind it a string of donkeys and a small herd of goats. Standing at the entrance, Omar put his hand on Holliday's shoulder.

"We are both men of great patriotism, each in our own way. But of all the men I have met who desire the scroll, you are the only honest one." He handed over the mailing tube containing the scroll and Holliday slung it over his shoulder.

"Thank you, Mullah Omar, for your trust in me."

"You have a great deal of power now," said the mullah. "Be sure you use it well. *As-salaam alaikum.*"

"Wa alaikum salaam," replied Holliday.

The mullah smiled. "Perhaps we shall meet

each other again under happier circumstances, my friend."

"I hope so," said Holliday.

They began the long trek down the side of the mountain.

27

Most members of the DGSE would have been happy to have been invited for lunch in one of the private dining rooms above Maxim's. But René Dubois knew better than that. To accept such an invitation was more like a rat being politely asked to accept the cheese in the middle of a rattrap. Dubois, however, realized that the invitation was, in fact, an order.

Dubois arrived at Maxim's ten minutes before the time requested and was escorted to the second floor by an extraordinarily polite maître d'. He was not surprised to find François Picard, the deputy foreign minister, waiting for him with lunch already ordered. It consisted of vichyssoise, trout meunière, braised oxtail with seasonal vegetables and a cheese plate. There were two bottles of wine already opened on the linen-covered table.

Dubois sat down and Picard poured him a glass of wine. The men ate in silence for a few moments. Picard put down his spoon and tapped at his lips with a napkin.

"I have the pleasure of informing you that your position within the service has been elevated to full director. You will now have a full bureau at your command."

"You do me a great honor," said Dubois. He had studied the pay grades of various positions within the DGSE and realized that he could now afford the country house he and Marguerite had dreamed about ever since their children had moved away.

They ate for a few more minutes before Picard chose to speak again.

"I am afraid you still have the problem of Colonel Holliday to deal with."

The food turned to ashes in René Dubois's mouth. He put his knife and fork down and pushed himself slightly away from the table.

"As far as I know, Colonel Holliday left France some time ago."

"True enough." Picard nodded. "Nevertheless, it is incumbent upon the government of France to find him."

"Might I ask why?"

"You may ask, but I fear you will not get a

satisfactory answer. Find Holliday and bring him to France."

Both Dubois and Picard were well aware of the so-called action teams that had been created by DGSE back in the time of De Gaulle and the Algerian crisis. They still existed, now predominantly used as antiterror commandos.

"In effect, Dubois, you are merely being requested to finish a job you left undone."

In other words, the government needed a scapegoat, and he was it.

"That's hardly fair, sir. Nobody knew about Holliday's connection with Peter Lazarus. They flew out of Paris on an Interpol flight, which, as I am sure you are aware, does not have to go through passport control or customs. If I had had the proper intelligence instead of being required to give daily reports to a collection of infighting bureaucrats, perhaps I could have captured him."

Picard sighed. He poured himself another glass of Château Latour, even though it was entirely inappropriate with the fish dish in front of him. He took a long swallow.

"I realize that you are very angry, Dubois, but I am afraid things are beyond my control. Not only do I have my own minister to deal with, but the cardinal of France is putting terrible pressure on as well."

"Might I have some vague clue of where Holliday might be?" Dubois asked.

Picard flushed. He took another long sip of wine and stared at companion, his features sagging. "I'm afraid he was last seen in Afghanistan."

"Merde," whispered Dubois.

Holliday and Lazarus continued walking for two days in a roughly easterly direction toward what they hoped was the Pakistan border. They seemed to be moving slightly downward, as though going down a long incline between the towering mountains that surrounded them. The weather also seemed slightly warmer. On the morning of the third day the skies above them darkened, threatening rain.

"We should have already crossed the border, according to the mullah's directions," said Holliday, looking down at the handheld GPS unit.

"We don't seem to be anywhere at all," said Lazarus. "Any border has got to be purely hypothetical, no more than an arbitrary line drawn on a map."

At that moment it began to rain.

"Goddamn," said Holliday.

Within minutes the rain began to fall increasingly harder, and he could see no more than a few feet in front of them. Then, as suddenly as it had begun, the rainfall stopped, leaving both men soaked to the skin. They moved on down the long, widening valley that lay before them. Within moments their feet were thick with fresh mud.

Holliday paused.

"What's wrong?" Lazarus asked.

"I'm not sure," said Holliday. All he knew was that something was not right, something at the edge of his senses. He turned to Lazarus, "Throw away everything you have that doesn't fit two peasants from the mountains. The rifle, the canteen, your knife—anything you can think of."

Within seconds the two men had thrown away everything incriminating, with the exception of the scroll hidden under Holliday's jacket. They walked on for another mile before Holliday stopped again. That strange psychic itch that had saved his life so many times before was raising the hairs at the back of his neck. Holliday reached into the pocket of his jacket, withdrew the leather strap from the mailing tube, hitched up his jacket and dropped his pants.

"Bloody hell," said Lazarus.

"Get over here," said Holliday.

He tossed Lazarus the leather strap from the mailing tube and took the scroll out of the inside of his jacket.

"Strap this to my upper thigh as high as you can and make sure it won't slip off."

Lazarus did as he was told and Holliday pulled up his pants, securing them with his fabric belt.

"Listen," said Holliday. "Do you hear that?"

"It sounds like thunder," answered Lazarus. "More rain, I suppose."

"That's not thunder," said Holliday.

The thunder became a howl and then three large Mil Mi-17 helicopters bristling with weaponry appeared around a curving rock wall in the mountain to their right. A spray of machine-gun fire hit the muddy wet ground ten feet in front of them, and Lazarus and Holliday stood stock-still. One of the big Russian helicopters landed within twenty feet of both men, who had their hands raised above their heads in surrender, while the other two Mils hovered above the one that had touched down on the ground.

Five men in Pakistani commando uniforms burst out of the helicopter and ran toward Holliday and Lazarus, gesturing that both men should drop to their knees, which they did. Three of the commandos stood by, armed with AK-47s, while the other two searched Holliday and Lazarus. The two men jerked them to their feet and pushed them through the mud toward the waiting helicopter.

The commandos climbed back into the chopper, pushing their new captives into the belly of the big dark green machine. Within seconds, they rose into the air, swung around and headed eastward down the long, wide valley.

It was Saturday, Marguerite's day to sleep in. But twenty-five years of waking at the same hour had chained René Dubois to his own internal clock. He rose quietly, dressed in a pair of old corduroys, a shirt and his favorite jacket and quietly left the apartment, his notebook in hand.

He walked up the street to La Tourelle and took a table. The flower stalls were going up in the market across the way, making the air wonderfully fragrant. By noon the whole area would be alive as people browsed through the neighborhood picking up fresh fruit, meats and flowers for the week ahead.

For now, however, it was quiet and Dubois could think in peace. Two old men sat nearby enjoying their cups of hot chocolate. Every now and again one of the men would tear a piece from a fresh baguette and dunk it in the chocolate before popping it into his mouth. Neither man spoke a word during this morning ritual. Dubois ordered himself a croissant au jambon and a café au lait. His breakfast arrived and as he chewed on the ham-filled pastry he thought about his quarry, Colonel John Holliday.

When he had originally been given the task of tracking down Holliday, the various deputy ministers, including Picard, had been vague about their real intentions. You simply did not arrest a man for owning a notebook that might lead you to an ancient treasure. As far as Dubois could see, Colonel Holliday was innocent of any crime committed in the Republic of France. The incredibly complicated manhunt in Paris, which had cost a policeman his life, had been ill-advised and poorly executed, especially since there had been a complete lack of intelligence about Peter Lazarus and his connection to Interpol.

Dubois opened up his notebook, took out a pen from his jacket, and began to make a few notes.

It was unlikely that he would find Holliday and his friend Lazarus by simply sitting in the embassy in Islamabad. The last intelligence they had concerning Holliday and Lazarus was that they had boarded a flight to Mumbai. One way or the other Holliday would have had to cross the India-Pakistan border at some point. But would they have been brazen enough to do so by flight? Would they have gone by bus, or train?

Indeed the two men would probably have approached someone capable of smuggling them across the border.

Without more information, there was no point in even leaving Paris.

The Russian helicopter thundered down the valley for about twenty minutes, twisting and turning along the edge of the mountainous terrain. It had begun to rain again, even harder than before. A few minutes later the helicopters began to drop down to the ground, and Holliday realized where they were: somewhere in the Swat Valley.

The Swat Valley had once been a tourist attraction and a place for tired bureaucrats to take their holidays. It had been a verdant district once, but all that had vanished with the coming of the Taliban. With the enforcement of their strict Sharia law, tourism had all but fled overnight and the place had become a battleground between American forces in Afghanistan and the Pakistani armed forces. No one fished its rivers or plowed its fields anymore, and its minerals lay untouched within the ground. It was nothing more now than a sea of aggression.

The helicopter carrying Holliday and Lazarus touched down on the muddy ground, followed by the other two Mils. The cargo door slid open and they were pushed out onto the ground.

Through the slashing rain, Holliday could see that they had arrived at some sort of Pakistani firebase. There was a high platform carrying a nest of old Russian antiaircraft guns, a sandbagged emplacement for a Strela 2 missile launcher and another smaller tower carrying a basic radar array. Between the weapons was a stockade enclosed with heavy wiring. There appeared to be one small gate for entrance. It was apparently unguarded.

Holliday allowed himself and Lazarus to be pushed toward the stockade. One of the men from the helicopter opened the gate and pushed them into the crowded enclosure beyond. There had to be close to a hundred people in the stockade, all of them drenched to the bone, some of them sick or starving to death.

Holliday grabbed Lazarus by his jacket and dragged him toward a relatively quiet corner. The rain kept beating down, turning the mud to a thick, soupy consistency inside the enclosure. There was nowhere to sit and barely room to stand.

"Where the hell are we?" Lazarus asked.

"Somewhere is the lower Swat Valley," replied Holliday.

"What are they going to do with us?" Lazarus asked. One of his stockade-mates crashed into him, moaning something and clawing his way into Lazarus's jacket. Holliday grabbed the man and pushed him back into the crowd surrounding them.

"It's a firebase," said Holliday.

"It's also some kind of short-stay internment camp for people they find trying to sneak into Pakistan during their patrols. They'll probably hand us and the rest of this bunch over and we'll be taken to a proper camp where we'll be questioned. We'll most likely also be searched a little more thoroughly and we can't let that happen."

"How do we avoid it?" Lazarus asked.

"I've got a plan," said Holliday. "All we have to do is wait for nightfall."

They kept their fellow stockade prisoners at bay and waited for darkness. During this time, the rain never ceased. At one point in the late evening guards brought in a cauldron of boiled rice and handed it out in clay bowls to the people inside the stockade. Holliday and Lazarus didn't even bother to get their share. They watched as a man squatted a foot or so away, spooning the thin gruel into his mouth using two fingers. They were glad that they were not partaking in dinner.

Darkness fell and lights went on surrounding

the antiaircraft platform and the radar tower. One small spotlight occasionally scanned the stockade.

"Did you ever see the movie *The Great Escape*?" Holliday asked.

"At least half a dozen times," said Lazarus. "I love escape films."

"You remember the role that Steve McQueen played?" Holliday asked.

"Sure," said Lazarus. "His name was Hilts, wasn't it?"

"That's right. Early on in the movie he and the little Scotsman Archibald 'Archie' Ives decide to make a blitz out of the camp."

"You've got to be kidding," said Lazarus.

"It's the only way," said Holliday. "This fencing probably doesn't go deeper than five or six inches. We dig down through the mud and then head outward, pushing the goop behind us."

"In the movie they had little folding metal tubes to push out into the air so they could breathe," said Lazarus. "I don't see anybody handing out little metal tubes."

"How long can you hold your breath?" Holliday grinned.

As the men around them tried to sleep in the assaulting rain, Holliday and Lazarus got down to work. Putting themselves directly beside the wire of the fencing, they dug down into the mud, piling the muck up all around them. Holliday had been right. The wire went down no more than eight inches and they dug their hole another eight inches below the wire before they made their move.

Holliday went down first, squeezing through the mud, pushing the muck from the face of the little tunnel behind him. Lazarus did the same, effectively plugging the hole behind them. After two minutes, Holliday's lungs were beginning to burn. By three minutes it had become intolerable. He pushed upward through the mud, finally reaching the surface a few seconds later. He immediately flattened and turned, extending both hands down into the hole.

As Lazarus made his way toward the surface, Holliday gripped his wrists and pulled the gasping, gagging, mud-covered man upward. Neither man said anything as they tried to regain some sort of a normal breathing pattern. They lay in the muck outside the stockade for what seemed an eternity.

At least they had made their exit without being noticed. Staying on their bellies, Holliday and Lazarus made their way into the outer darkness and disappeared.

28

Under heavily armed guard by the Vatican Police, a dozen transport trucks had left the Vatican City, driving cautiously through the streets of Rome to Fiumicino Airport, where they were briefly stored in a large warehouse. All of the trucks were under Vatican seal and the armed guard remained with the transport trucks for the next two days.

On the third day, fifty large cargo containers were delivered to the warehouse and the armed guards were dismissed, only to be replaced by a dozen men in Italian military uniforms. The seals on the trucks were cut, and using several waiting forklifts, men in soldiers' uniforms unloaded the trucks and filled the large metal cargo containers.

No one commented on the fact that each of the large wooden crates was stamped with the eagle and swastika emblem of the Third Reich. When all of the containers were loaded, they were driven out to a waiting Alitalia Boeing 777 cargo plane. Twenty minutes later the big aircraft was given the okay to take off and it lumbered into the air.

Sir Henry Maxim sat in Cardinal Secretary of State Ruffino's office. His cell phone rang and he spoke into it for a few seconds before handing it across the desk to Ruffino. Ruffino listened and snapped the phone closed and handed it back to Maxim.

"I've done everything you asked, Your Eminence," said Maxim. "Now I'd like the file."

Ruffino reached into the bottom drawer of his desk and pulled out the familiar file.

"The shipment will reach Heathrow in three hours," said Maxim. "I hope that's convenient."

"Quite convenient." The cardinal nodded. "We both have identical copies of the inventory. I will keep in touch about the materials' resale onto the open market."

"You do that," said Maxim. He picked up the file, slid it into the zippered case on his lap, then stood and left the room.

The cardinal leaned back in his chair and closed

his eyes. The threat of the Vatican being found with stolen Nazi art had finally been removed, along with the horrifying scandal that went along with it—something that had nagged at him for his entire tenure as Vatican secretary of state.

He heard small shuffling footsteps entering his office and opened his eyes, sitting forward. It was a man dressed in a priest's garb carrying a large pile of newspapers. He laid them down in front of the cardinal and backed away a step.

"I didn't ask for these," scolded Ruffino, turning his head toward the priest, who was slightly behind him. At that moment, the priest let the fully loaded syringe fall into his right hand. He plunged the needle into Ruffino's right carotid artery and emptied the contents of the syringe.

Ruffino drew a horrified breath and stared blankly at the man who had just taken his life. His last thought before the drug took him into darkness was how strangely the priest's eyes glittered behind his gold-rimmed spectacles.

Ruffino fell back against his chair, looking like a man without a care in the world, simply napping.

By the time Sir Henry Maxim's private jet reached Geneva, the Alitalia cargo plane had already been unloaded. A car took the operations director of the MI6 to the warehouses where the cargo cases were now being unloaded by his men.

Six hours later the looted art had been safely taken to the large secure vaults of a bank that Maxim had done business with for many years.

Holliday and Lazarus spent four days moving south through the lower Swat Valley and into the lowlands of central southern Pakistan. They had no sense that anyone was following them. It was more than likely that their absence had never been noticed. And even if it had been, the men at the firebase weren't willing to expend the time or the energy to recapture them. They walked for a great part of the way, but eventually they were able to catch a ride in a truck loaded with turnips. They caught another ride a hundred miles south, and two days after that they arrived again at the border city of Chaman and the warehouse of Haji Ayub Afridi. They knocked on the door and Afridi himself let them in, guiding them through the shadowy warehouse and into his office.

"I'm surprised to see you, my friends," said Afridi. "I was certain that Afghanistan or the Mullah Omar would have dealt with you by now."

"Afghanistan tried its best," said Holliday. "But Omar and I have more in common than our blind eye. In fact, he saved our lives."

"His men also make quite a good goat stew," said Lazarus.

Afridi looked the two men up and down. "Perhaps you would like a shower and new clothes?"

"What a delightful thought," said Lazarus.

Afridi took them out the rear door of his office and down a hallway to what must have been his living quarters. There was a kitchen and an iron bed, and a door leading into the bathroom. Lazarus bathed first, followed by Holliday. By the time they were finished, Afridi had found them new clothes and had even managed to get them something to eat.

As the two men dressed, Holliday was careful to keep the scroll out of Afridi's sight. He had removed it from around his thigh soon after they had escaped from the stockade, keeping it tucked away beneath his mud-crusted jacket.

Refreshed, they sat down to eat with Afridi. It was some kind of chicken and rice combination that turned out to be quite tasty.

"There is something you should know," said Afridi, mopping up a mouthful of rice with a piece of torn chapati. "People have been asking about you two."

"What kind of people?" Holliday asked.

Afridi chewed thoughtfully for a moment. "At first, it was people in my business, or on the fringes of it." He paused. "People who would not be referred to as law-abiding citizens. You understand?"

"I understand."

"I do not like people prying into my business when it is none of theirs," said Afridi. "I prefer to keep things as unobtrusive as possible."

"Did it stop there?"

"I'm afraid not," said Afridi. "In my business, it helps to have good connections of one kind or another. I got in touch with a friend in the local constabulary to see where all this interest had suddenly arisen. He told me that it was political and that the local police were being pressured from Islamabad. The man they are referring to in Islamabad is Amit Singh, who is as corrupt as any policeman in the country. He buys and sells information to anyone with the money to pay him. As it turns out, the man paying him is also a policeman—a member of French intelligence."

"French? What the hell do the French want from us now?" asked Lazarus.

"They missed us last time," said Holliday. "Maybe they're trying to make up for it now."

"Whatever it is, my friends, I suggest you get

out of Chaman as soon as you possibly can. In a few days every policeman in Pakistan will be looking for you."

"Can you offer us any transportation to the border?" Holliday asked.

"I have a shipment crossing the border at Lahore. It leaves tonight. Would that suit you?"

"Yes," said Holliday.

At nightfall, they climbed into the cab of a large old Ford stake truck and began their journey. Afridi watched them leave before closing the doors of his warehouse. He took out his cell phone and called.

"Singh?" Afridi asked.

"Speak," said a distant voice.

"They are crossing the border just below Lahore. They should reach the crossing at dawn."

René Dubois sat in the counterintelligence control room at the embassy in Islamabad. He'd heard from his contact Amit Singh, a colonel in the DGI&I—the Directorate General of Intelligence and Investigation—who had informed him that Holliday and his companion would be attempting to cross the border below Lahore in the early hours of the morning. Dawn was just breaking when Dubois's phone rang.

"Dubois."

"Colonel Singh, they outsmarted us. They must not have trusted Afridi. We had a sighting two hours ago. They're on a train bound for Mumbai. I managed to get three members of the railway police on board before they crossed the border."

"Thank you for your cooperation, Colonel Singh. It is most appreciated. I'll handle it from here."

Dubois punched in the extension for communications and ordered a diplomatic jet to take him to Mumbai as soon as humanly possible.

Holliday had slipped through Dubois's net once again.

Holliday and Lazarus, still dressed in peasant outfits, sat in their sweltering compartment on the Mumbai train surrounded by the chattering of families, the sound of chickens in open crates and the smell of everything from curry to rotting fruit.

Across from them, an extremely fat woman in a full-length dull brown sari carved chunks from a watermelon and fed them to her three grandchildren, all of whom stared a few feet across the compartment at Holliday and Lazarus. The old woman cooed at her grandchildren as she fed them. Occasionally she cut a piece of watermelon for herself, pushing the pink flesh into her mouth, grunting like an animal. When she finished with her chunk, she gathered up the seeds in her mouth and spit them on the floor at her feet. She kept a continuous smile on her face, occasionally lifting one enormous buttock off the wooden seat to exude gas.

Hospitably, she had offered Holliday and Lazarus dripping chunks of the watermelon, but, smiling, they had both shaken their heads. Above them they could hear singing and chanting and a variety of other noises from the hundreds of people unable to afford tickets for the train who had climbed onto the swaying roof of the car.

"I'm going for a walk," said Holliday, standing.

"You're not leaving me here alone, are you?"

"Come along if you'd like, but our seats will probably be gone when we get back." Holliday left the compartment, his senses swirling. He made his way through one chaotic car after another. The toilets reeked and were overflowing, the air was full of smoke from a thousand hand-rolled cigarettes and the occasional scream of the train's whistle only added to the madness of the scene.

Holliday had walked three cars down before he saw the men approaching. They stood out in the crowd like diamonds in a bag of coal, wearing shoes instead of sandals and suits instead of light-colored cotton pants and shirts. He could smell cop on them even through the stench of the train. He turned on his heel and made his way back to their compartment, aware that the two men's eyes were pinned to his form.

He sat down beside Lazarus and spoke quickly.

"Cops. Get ready, and follow my lead."

A few moments later the door to the compartment slid open and the two policemen were standing there in front of them. Both men were large and burly, obviously hired for their size and not their brains. They flashed their ID at the people across from Holliday and spoke one word in Pashto: "Out!"

The old woman and her children didn't question the order for an instant. They packed up their parcels and bags, including the remains of the watermelon, and scurried out of the compartment, their eyes wide and fearful.

The two policemen immediately stepped into the compartment. One reached into his jacket and took out a 9-millimeter automatic. But the train lurched slightly as it went around a narrow curve, and the man with the gun was forced to reach out to support himself on the doorframe. At that instant, Holliday unexpectedly slid off the seat and onto his knees, driving an uppercut hard into the man's testicles. Simultaneously, Lazarus came off his seat and hit the second policeman by slamming his back into him.

As the man with the gun doubled over in agony, Holliday brought both hands together in a single fist and drove up under the man's jaw, snapping his head back and breaking his neck in a single motion. The man Lazarus had hit was still struggling. Holliday climbed to his feet and hammered the man's Adam's apple with the blade of his hand. The second policeman began to choke and Holliday sped the process along by pinching his trachea and his vocal cords between the thumb and forefinger of his right hand. The man's eyes bulged, and a few seconds later he was dead.

Holliday climbed to his feet and pulled down the old canvas roller blinds over the windows in the door to the compartment.

"Now what?" said Lazarus.

"We strip them," answered Holliday.

They spent the next fifteen minutes stripping off both men's outer clothing, taking their shoes, guns and wallets as well. With that done, Holliday tugged hard and pulled the windows downward. One at a time they heaved the dead bodies up onto the compartment seat and pushed them through the open window. The whole thing had taken less than half an hour.

Dressed in the policemen's clothing, they then headed out into the corridor and walked through the crowded cars toward the rear of the train. There was no doubt now that they had to get off the train. If they were supposed to look like Indian policemen, there was no way they would be able to pull it off. Five cars toward the end of the train, they saw walking toward them what appeared to be the twin brothers of the two men they had just killed.

"Shit," said Holliday. "There were four of them, two at the front and two at the back."

There was nothing they could do but bluff it, or find a way to incapacitate the men in some way. Holliday had a horrible image of the four of them shooting it out in a crowded railway car. The two policemen kicked a crouching urchin out of their way and proceeded forward. As they passed the ragged boy, he reached under his filthy coat and withdrew a long, curved dagger from its cardboard sheath. Crouching, he slashed across the back of the two men's knees, slicing their tendons. Both men collapsed simultaneously, screaming as they went down to the floor. Holliday and Lazarus followed the ragged boy as he ran helter-skelter toward the rear of the train. They made it through the rear door of the last car and stood on the small platform.

"My name is Vijay, sirs. I have been waiting for your arrival for quite some time. If you will follow me, the train will slow at a junction and will wait there for the signal to proceed into the station. This is the place you will jump. If you have seen motion pictures or television of people jumping from aircraft, that is how you must land—rolling and tucking your head. Do you understand?"

Before they had time to answer, the train began to slow. Without another word, the ragged boy climbed down to the bottom of the steps and then jumped. Holliday and Lazarus weren't far behind him. As Holliday went into his tuck and roll he saw that they were in the distant suburbs of Mumbai. Then his shoulder smashed into the gravel of the old coal clinkers that lined the embankment.

Vijay was the first to jump to his feet. He dusted himself off with a laugh as Holliday and Lazarus came sliding down the embankment and gathered themselves together.

"You do that very well, Colonel Holliday. You have jumped out of airplanes before?"

"Once or twice," said Holliday. "Would you like to tell me how you knew my name?"

"I was instructed to wait at the junction at Kalyan and ride every train going into Mumbai Passenger Terminal," said Vijay. He grinned. "It was not too hard to find a tall white man with an eye patch."

"And who gave you these instructions?"

"The man I must take you to now," said Vijay.

29

Cardinal Pierre Hébert, Archbishop of France, sat in a brasserie on the Boulevard Saint-Michel with Deputy Foreign Minister François Picard. The cardinal was eating a salade niçoise, while Picard was enjoying a plate of coquilles Saint-Jacôues. They were sharing a bottle of Côtes du Rhone.

"I'm sure you realize by now that I am the acting secretary of state of the Vatican."

"Why should that interest me?" said Picard.

"Don't be foolish, Picard. You know exactly what that means. It means that I am now in control of the Vatican Bank. I know far too much about your friend Cardinal Ruffino's involvement in the so-called Operation Leonardo and it means I know about your involvement with the search for the scroll and Holliday's fortune."

"So what are you going to do with your new-found power?" said Picard, spearing a scallop and popping it into his mouth.

"It means that you and I are going to exchange information about Holliday's whereabouts or I will publicize a variety of secrets you would much rather have me keep quiet about."

"I have sent a man to find Holliday, but so far he has not reported back to me. I'll be sure to let you know when he does."

"Excellent," said Hébert with a smile.

Vijay took Holliday and Lazarus deep into Mumbai, traveling first on foot, then by bus and finally by tuk-tuk to a place called Sweeny's American Bar.

The bar looked exactly like its name. It was a long dark room with half a dozen long-blade fans thumping languorously from the ceiling. There were ten booths on the left, each with its own miniature jukebox, and an eighty-foot mahogany bar with a real brass rail and barstools. A tall muscular black man with a "Death from Above" tattoo on his forearm sat at the bar, with a rag over his shoulder and a glass in his hand that he was polishing with a second cloth. He finished polishing the glass, put it under the bar and went to the cash register. He sat down on a stool and picked up a copy of the *International Herald Tribune* from the counter beside him. Half a dozen men were scattered along the bar all drinking silently.

"This way," said Vijay, leading them into the gloomy darkness of the bar. They reached a booth where a man was sitting, leisurely drinking a bottle of Heineken. He was small with thinning red hair and heavy frown lines. His face was sagging and tanned from years spent working outside in the sun. The man looked up and saw Holliday and Lazarus. He pulled his wallet out of his back pocket and handed Vijay two fifty-dollar bills.

"Good job, Veej."

Vijay scampered off and Holliday and Lazarus sat down opposite the man.

"So you're the infamous Colonel John Holliday. Boy, have I heard a lot about you."

The barman suddenly appeared beside them. "You guys want anything?"

"This is R. B. Sweeny," said the man nursing the Heineken. "Two tours in Iraq One, another two in Iraq Two and three tours in Afghanistan. Made enough money playing craps to open this place. Hasn't been back to Detroit ever since."

"I'll have what he's having," said Holliday, nodding toward the man sitting opposite him.

"Scotch," said Lazarus. "Preferably single malt, if you have it."

"Glenfiddich okay with you?" Sweeny asked.

"Wonderful," said Lazarus.

Sweeny wandered off to fill their drink orders. Holliday turned to the man with the Heineken.

"Let's get down to brass tacks. You're not army, you're not navy and you're not special forces, so that leaves CIA."

"So how do you figure that?" the man said.

"You're too small for the army or any of the others. Your shoulders are sloped, you have no tattoos and you don't look the part."

"So that makes me CIA?"

"Yes. That makes you CIA. So quit screwing around. Who the hell are you and why are we here?"

"My name's Ridley Neil. A lifetime ago I was showing the Taliban how to shoot stingers at Russian helicopters. After that, I was showing Kurds how to shoot stinger missiles at Iraqi helicopters. After that, I was back in Afghanistan showing our troops where the Taliban was hiding in the mountains and showing them how to kill the turbaned little bastards. After that they put me on a desk in Kabul. I saw orders coming in and going out that I knew were a lie. I saw operations that I knew were going to fail even before they had begun. In

Vietnam, they were looking for body counts. In Afghanistan, all that counted was the number of operations you could put together. It was like flying bombers in World War II. You did your twenty-five missions and then you got sent home. It turned out that I was running a death machine from behind that desk, and in the end I couldn't take it anymore. I came here. I've been here ever since. I still know everybody in the game in this part of the world. I knew all about you before you even crossed the Pakistan border and I know who's looking for you now."

"Who?" asked Holliday. "And why are you being our guardian angel now?"

"I'm not your guardian angel now," said Neil. "But all the fuss about you made me start thinking hard about what's going on back at the Company. I'm not sure quite how you managed it, but it looks like you've inadvertently exposed a big rotting hole in that particular piece of cheese. I knew the men who came after you in Afghanistan and I also knew the whole operation was being done off the books. I used to be proud of what I did for my country. Now I'm ashamed. If you're going to rip the skin off this whole thing, I want to help you do it."

"How do you expect to do that?" Holliday asked.

"The Company's people in Mumbai are already looking for you. Give them long enough and they'll find you. One way or another, you're not getting out of here on any regular flight."

"What other kind is there?" Lazarus asked.

The bartender brought them their drinks and then slinked away.

"An irregular one," said Neil.

Doug Kitchen sat in his office in CIA headquarters drumming his fingers on his enormous desk. Everything that could go wrong had gone wrong. Sitting there, he could feel everything slipping away. The president had only a year left in his term, so he would probably make it that long. But once there was a new face in the White House, he'd be thrown out on his ass along with a great number of other people in the Company.

There was a knock on his door. Mark Tannis entered his office with a thick file in his hand.

"Sit down," said Kitchen.

Tannis sat.

"What have you found out?" Kitchen asked.

"Holliday and Lazarus made it out of Afghanistan. The French tried to pick him up as he was coming into Mumbai but he killed two members of the Indian railway police and maimed two more. Somewhere before the terminal, he and Lazarus managed to get off the train."

"What about the Ghost Squad that Rusty Smart was running out of here?"

"Wiped out, sir. They took an off-the-books run at the Mullah Omar as a way to cover taking out Holliday, but they got beaten at their own game."

"Do we have any idea where they are now?"

"Somehow they got to Ridley Neil. No one knows how, and now Neil, Holliday and Lazarus have disappeared."

"Neil? I didn't even know he was still alive."

"Yes, sir. Very much alive. He's an information broker."

Kitchen scowled. "Just what we need now, old mistakes coming back to haunt us." Kitchen paused for a while, his fingers going back to their drumming on the desk. Finally he spoke again. "Do you like your job, Tannis?"

"Very much, sir. I've been with the Company for more than fifteen years."

"In terms of records, you must know where a fair number of bodies are buried."

Tannis nodded. "More than a few, sir," he replied.

"What would it take for you to exhume them and then cremate them?"

"Not very much, Chief. I'd like to become director of communications and also I'd like a letter from you telling me you just ordered these files destroyed."

"You going to hang the letter over my head?" Kitchen asked.

"No, sir."

"Why?"

"Because if I did, you'd kill me."

"Then we understand each other. Get it done."

In deference to his position as the voice of God on earth, Acting Cardinal Secretary of State Hébert remained standing in front of Pope Francis's heavy oak desk in the office of his suite of rooms on the top floor of the Apostolic Palace. To put the Pope somewhat off his game, Hébert spoke to him in Italian, a language the Pope was still not completely fluent in.

"What is it you are trying to tell us, Cardinal Hébert?"

"Just what I said, Your Holiness. The Vatican Bank is virtually bankrupt."

"This is not possible," the Pope said, horror in his voice. "One of the first things I did upon ascending Peter's throne was to audit the finances of the Holy Church. The reports all confirmed that the Vatican Bank had more than wisely invested large portions of its assets and was receiving excellent dividends."

"I will explain it to Your Holiness as simply as I can. In 1944, before the Vatican Bank even existed, we came into possession of more than a billion dollars worth of looted Nazi art. It was the valuation of this art which was and has been one of the basic assets of the Vatican ever since."

"You're saying we had art that was looted by the Nazis?" the Pope asked incredulously.

"That's exactly what I'm saying," responded Hébert. "More than that, Pope Pius XII knew all about it."

"This cannot be," said Pope Francis, shaking his head.

"I'm afraid it is. And it's worse than that, I'm afraid. The art has now been removed and taken to a bank in Switzerland. If we don't get it back, the Church will fall."

"But what should we do?" asked the Pope, his face taking on a cast of appalled fear.

"Don't fret, Your Holiness. You may be the voice of God on earth, but I am his fist." Hébert turned away and left the ornate offices of the Pope.

Leaving the Apostolic Palace, Hébert telephoned for his limousine and had it take him directly to

Fiumicino Airport. His private jet was waiting on the tarmac, its engines idling. The limousine pulled up to the open doors and Hébert stepped out of the car and entered the plane.

Geronimo Caserio, the silver-haired, lean-bodied assassin, was waiting for him. The killer was drinking a Campari and soda, reading the latest edition of *La Repubblica*. Hébert sat down across from him in a comfortable leather seat. He called the male attendant, who brought in a gin and tonic. Hébert rarely drank at this early hour, but telling the Pope that his whole world was coming down around his ears had taken quite a bit out of him.

"You are well, Geronimo?"

"Well enough," said the killer. His eyes were deeply set and utterly black, his face expressionless.

"I have a job for you," said Hébert. "You've read the file on Holliday?"

"Of course," said Caserio. "He was my target once before, at Qumran."

"You missed and killed his cousin and her husband instead. Now it's time for you to finish the job."

"Where can he be found?" asked the assassin.

"It's not where he can be found now; it's where he will be in the future."

30

They drove through the crushing streets of southern Mumbai, heading toward the outskirts of the giant city. Neil, the expat CIA agent, was behind the wheel of an ancient Morris Minor, with Holliday and Lazarus seated behind him. The street, shops, clubs and markets were as bright and alive now as they were during broad daylight.

It felt to Holliday as though they were driving through a never-ending display of screeching fireworks. Cars honked their horns, painted buses drove by in clouds of diesel exhaust and there was always the roar and chatter of the people on the streets. If the roads of Mumbai had been the arteries of the human body, they would have clogged and led to a massive heart attack long ago.

Eventually Neil guided the little humpbacked vehicle through the outskirts and into the countryside. They made their way down an unlit dirt road, then turned and went down another, narrower road that eventually led to a farmer's field. Out of the shadows a shape Holliday had only ever seen in photographs appeared at the end of the field. It was a dull green DC-3, a transport aircraft that had first flown before World War II. The twin-engine plane rested at a high angle on a tricycle landing gear, one wheel under each wing and one under the tail. This was a military version, known as a Dakota. Its wide cargo doors were already open and a ladder had been let down from the interior. Two Pakistani men in overalls were turning the aircraft by the tail, swinging it into the wind.

"This is your irregular flight?" Lazarus asked.

"With five hundred extra gallons of fuel, it'll get us where we want to go," said Neil.

They exited the old vehicle, at which point the two men who had turned the aircraft into the wind climbed into it. They drove the car to the far end of the field, then turned to face the airplane from perhaps three hundred yards away. Holliday could see that the airfield was nothing more than packed earth and grass. It was going to be a bumpy ride.

Neil went up the ladder first and disappeared, heading toward the cockpit. Holliday and Lazarus followed. There was a huge explosive coughing sound followed by a grumbling whine. Then a second cough and then the dull low pitch sound of the propellers beginning to turn and gather speed. Neil came back out of the cockpit. He swung a flashlight into the rear compartment of the plane's interior. There were a dozen fifty-gallon drums, all connected to a single pipe and a hand-cranked pump.

"That's our reserve," said Neil. "You guys will have to do the pumping when the wing tanks are empty."

"Where do we sit?" Holliday asked.

"There are two jump seats on this side of the bulkhead. Strap yourself in for takeoff, and if we actually get this old bus into the air, you can either come up to the cockpit or get some sleep on those two mattresses on the floor." He swung the flashlight toward the jump seats and two wads of bedding and a pair of rolled-up sleeping bags. "Okay. Get in the seats and strap yourselves in."

Holliday and Lazarus did as they were told. Neil vanished into the cockpit. The sound of the engines rattled up to a high grumbling thunder and they began to move, gathering speed with every second, using the headlights of the Morris Minor as a marker for the end of the runway. Two hundred feet from the car, the Dakota lifted into the air and made a broad swinging turn, no more than a hundred feet above the ground.

Out of nowhere there was a sudden slash of heavy machine-gun fire. An instant later there were heavy thumping sounds as the large bullets pierced the side of the airplane just above their heads. Holliday unstrapped himself and crawled on hands and knees into the cockpit. He squeezed into the copilot's chair and sat down.

"What the hell was that all about?" Holliday asked as the sound of the machine-gun fire faded behind them.

"Pakistani army, I'd guess," said Neil. "You're not allowed to fly out of an unlicensed field, for one thing."

Neil guided the lumbering old airplane to the northeast, never exceeding five hundred feet in altitude.

"Where are we going?" Holliday asked.

"The Seychelles. Scuba diving is pretty good this time of year, or so I'm told."

For the first five hours they flew on without incident, always at an altitude low enough to see the waves beneath their wings. At the sixth hour, at Neil's command, they began pumping and transferring the gas in the fifty-gallon drums into the wing tanks. After an hour and a half, the wing tanks were full and Holliday and Lazarus were able to climb into their sleeping bags and get some much needed rest.

Holliday fell asleep almost instantly and had no idea of how much time had passed before he awoke, startled. There was an unpleasant ratcheting sound coming from the left engine, and then it stopped. Holliday climbed out of his sleeping bag and went forward to the cockpit.

"What's the problem?"

"Left wing tank is empty. I had to flutter the engine, or we'd have had a fire."

"How much time do we have?" Holliday asked.

"Hard to tell," said Neil. "We should be pretty close now, but I'm going to climb to get us some altitude. This old bird can glide for miles, especially if I've got a bit of altitude."

"Is there anything I can do?" Holliday asked.

"You'll notice a big barrel-shaped thing clamped to the bulkhead across from the jump seats. It's a rubber life raft. Take the container down and pull out the raft. When you hear the second engine go out, inflate the raft and take it down to the cargo doors. We either reach land or we go down on the water. I think it's probably going to be the water."

Forty-five minutes later the engine fluttered out and there was an eerie silence as the ancient aircraft began a slow, curving dive. The silence went on for another ten or twelve minutes, the air whistling over the wings like an Arctic wind. Suddenly the plane's nose pulled up and a call came from the cockpit.

"We're going in now. I can see the lights of Victoria." Neil's voice rose with excitement. "We may just get this old girl down after all."

They didn't.

The DC-3 hit the water at slightly more than a hundred miles an hour. It slid across the calm seas for a few seconds and then the nose and one wing hit an invisible reef just under the surface. The aircraft swung around on the ruined wing, digging the nose even deeper into the water. It was clearly Ridley Neil's last flight.

The plane came to an absolute halt at a twenty-five-degree angle, water rushing into the cockpit and then pouring into the fuselage. Holliday and Lazarus struggled to open the cargo doors as the water came up to their waists. They managed to open the doors and toss the lifeboat out. Grabbing the edges of the door, they pulled themselves up until they were hanging above the water. Holliday closed his eyes and prayed they wouldn't drop over the reef. They let go of the airplane and dropped, tumbling into the water on the far side of the reef. They resurfaced, coughing and gagging, and swam a few yards to the bobbing lifeboat.

Suddenly out of the darkness there was the sound of an engine roaring to life. A searchlight swung over them and an accented voice called out:

"Stay where you are."

Holliday and Lazarus did as they were told. They weren't going anywhere. A much larger inflatable appeared, carrying four armed and uniformed policemen in the stern with a single man in the bow operating the beam of the searchlight.

"Colonel Holliday, Mr. Lazarus, my name is René Dubois. You are now formally under arrest."

31

Dubois, Holliday and Lazarus sat under an umbrella on the outdoor patio of the Anchor Café, enjoying their Cinzano and lime drinks and their view of the sea. Lunch had already been eaten and their empty plates removed.

"Neil had been working in this part of the world ever since the CIA caught him with his hand in the cookie jar," said Dubois.

"What cookie jar was that?" Holliday asked.

"More than half of the covert operations carried out by the CIA in Afghanistan were paid for by smuggled opium shipments. He started cutting himself into the business on the side. The DC-3 he managed to get you here in used to make regular flights out of Afghanistan, down through Burma to the Golden Triangle, where it was shipped abroad, and made its way to Marseille, back in the old French Connection days. I've known about him for years."

"And the rest of it?" Holliday asked.

Dubois replied, "We'd been investigating my boss, François Picard, on an ordinary corruption charge, which involved tapping his telephone and that of his mistress. Through the tap on his mistress's telephone, we discovered his connection with Neil's people and also with his mysterious assortment of people involved in the smuggling of arts and artifacts. That, in turn, led us to Picard's connection with Cardinal Hébert."

"So you knew about the stolen art at the Vatican?" Holliday asked.

"Not immediately," answered Dubois. "It actually took me years to put all the pieces together. Your arrival on the scene just complicated things even more. I knew Picard's talk of recovering French property dating back to the Bourbon kings was all a smoke screen for something, but I didn't know quite what it was. When your friend Philpot called me three days ago and asked me to give you all the cooperation I could, I accepted, if for no other reason than to find out where you actually fit into this whole thing."

"I guess you could call me the Man Who Knew Too Much," said Holliday, quoting the title from the old Hitchcock movie.

"So are we under arrest or not?" Lazarus asked.

"Of course not," said Dubois. "To get the co-operation of the police here, it was either I arrest you or they do. I thought it would be better if I was the man taking you in. The Seychelles police will be having a field day with the wreck of the DC-3 anyway."

"So where is all this taking us?" Lazarus asked.

"If Potsy and Peter here have done their jobs, it should take us to Geneva within the next forty-eight hours."

Sir Henry Maxim's Mercedes limousine pulled up in front of the Banque Orientale de Genève and stopped. The MI6 official entered the bank and asked to see the manager, Herr Hafner.

Hafner took him personally down to Maxim's large locked room in the basement of the bank and left him there. Twenty minutes later, Maxim reappeared with a small object wrapped in brown paper under his overcoat. He crossed the floor of the bank and stepped outside. The chauffeur was standing beside one of the passenger doors leading to the rear of the car, but there was something wrong. In Geneva he always had the same driver, a man named Henry Poole, who was actually an MI6 operative in the Geneva office. But, as if by magic, Henry had vanished during Maxim's short sojourn at the bank and had been replaced by another driver. This driver was carrying a small automatic pistol in his gloved hand, which was pointed in the general direction of Maxim's midsection.

"What the bloody hell is going on?" Maxim exclaimed.

Suddenly the quiet backstreet was full of people, all of them rushing in Maxim's direction, all of them carrying pistols. The package was taken out of his hands and Maxim was pushed into the limousine, accompanied by three other men.

David Moorhead, the chief of Interpol in Switzerland, walked across the street, with the package Maxim had brought up from the locked room under his arm. He greeted Dubois, Lazarus and Holliday, who were standing in the doorway of yet another bank. Behind Moorhead, the limousine sped off and the street cleared.

"Well done, Peter. We'd almost written you off when you disappeared the way you did."

"What's in the package?" asked Lazarus.

Moorhead carefully stripped off the paper wrapping. The subject matter of the little painting was immediately obvious. It was a study for Vermeer's famous *Girl with a Pearl Earring*."

"Unbelievable," said Moorhead. "He would have made millions."

"Who owned it?" asked Holliday.

"I have no idea," said Moorhead. "This must be one of the lost Vermeers. Maxim could have put this on the market using a proxy and he would have gotten away with it, since there is no possible way he could have a provenance."

"What I can't understand is what a man like Maxim could possibly need, especially with all the money he's made over the years. He's an old man. What more could he want out of his life now? As a high-ranking civil servant in the public eye, he couldn't buy yachts or emerald necklaces or country houses or anything of immense value."

"I suppose for some people enough is never enough," said Lazarus.

Holliday and Lazarus walked back to their hotel and went up their suite. Philpot was already there. Somehow he'd managed to get a couple of Big Macs and supersized fries into the room and he was eating heartily as they came in the door. He put down his half-eaten burger, wiped his lips with a napkin and grinned.

"I heard it all went well," said Potsy.

"Couldn't have gone better," said Holliday, dropping down into a chair across from his old friend.

Potsy chewed his way through a few fries and

shook his head. "Boy, you sure know how to kick up a shitstorm. You've got every intelligence agency from one end of the world to the other falling all over themselves to get to you. I suppose it's your magnetic personality."

"The shitstorm isn't quite over," said Holliday. "One last piece to fit into the puzzle."

"You mean this goddamn scroll everybody's fighting over?"

"That's the one," said Holliday.

Philpot went back to his burger and finished it off. He wiped his mouth and leaned back on the couch.

"One thing really confuses me. When you called me from that hotel in Mumbai, you still had the scroll with you. You even told me you still had it and that you'd carried it all the way through Pakistan without anybody finding it. It sure as hell wasn't in your luggage on the Air France flight from the Seychelles. I know that because I checked. So answer me the Sixty-Thousand-Dollar Question. Where is the scroll?"

"I'd like to know the answer to that one too," said Lazarus.

Holliday smiled. "You remember when we were being picked up by Neil in front of the hotel?"

"Sure," said Lazarus. "You sent me outside to

make sure we didn't miss him while you paid the bill."

"That's right," said Holliday. "I paid the bill and then I mailed a package with the scroll in it to myself. I mean, if you can't trust the post, who can you trust?"

"Where did you mail it to?" Potsy asked.

"Where it all began," said Holliday.

Holliday and Lazarus sat in the kitchen of Holliday's small apartment in Old Jerusalem drinking a coffee. Holliday's apartment wasn't far from where Peggy and Rafi had set up housekeeping so long ago.

"We've come a long way, you and I," said Holliday. "I wouldn't hold it against you for a minute if you wanted to bail out now."

"Not a chance," said Lazarus. "I want to see how this whole thing turns out."

The two men drove through Old Jerusalem and up toward the Mount Herzl Cemetery high above the city. Before they got out of the car Holliday handed Lazarus the package containing the scroll.

"If anything goes wrong, you take this straight to the director of the Israel Museum. His name is James Snyder."

"You sure you don't want me to go up there with you?"

"It would screw things up. You wait here. I have to do this part on my own."

Holliday got out of the car and climbed up the hillside. In some ways the cemetery reminded him of the one in Arlington. A lot of his friends had been buried there, friends he still missed. He finally reached the spot he was looking for, two stones side by side, the names and dates inscribed in both English and Hebrew. This was Peggy and Rafi's home now, a warm hillside in Jerusalem with the smell of orange trees sweetening the hot dry air.

How many people had died because of the scrawled notation that a Templar Knight had left in a cave over two thousand years ago?

Staring at Rafi and Peggy's graves, Holliday could feel history unrolling in front of his eyes. There was no way to tell what that simple scratching in the stone had launched. A bullet spinning its way through a hundred wars and ten thousand battles. For a moment Holliday felt a lurching feeling in his chest. Then, bending down, he picked up two small pebbles and placed one on the top of each gravestone in front of him in the Jewish tradition.

"I came back to see you," Holliday whispered. "I came back to tell you how sorry I was."

Eight hundred yards away Geronimo Caserio stared through the high-powered sight of the .50 caliber sniper rifle, waiting for a perfect shot. The bullets he was using were mercury filled and capable of blowing a man's head off from twice the range there was between him and his target. Caserio looked away from the scope for a second, checking on the leaves on the trees around him. He put his eye back to the sight and slowly adjusted the knob on its top surface.

"You've got maybe three seconds," said Philpot's voice in Holliday's ear. "He's eight hundred yards northwest of you. When I say duck, fall to the left. Remember that—fall to the *left*."

Above him Geronimo's finger squeezed on the trigger.

"Now!" said Philpot in Holliday's ear.

Holliday did exactly what he was told. He dropped suddenly to the left, keeping the bulk of his body behind the two headstones. The crack of the bullet from Caserio's shot rebounded through the hills.

The man Philpot had imported from the Ranger

School at Fort Benning, Georgia, watched from two thousand yards away as Caserio opened and then closed the bolt of his rifle, injecting a new round into the chamber.

The Ranger watched as Caserio put his eye to the sight again. He'd heard apocryphal stories about one sniper killing another by shooting him through the reticle of his telescopic sight, but they'd never made any sense to him. Once your bullet had entered the sight, the variables of its movements were impossible to predict. A round could veer in half a dozen directions. And anyway, the Ranger from Fort Benning was the old-fashioned kind. He fired a shot right between Caserio's eyes. It took a little more than two seconds for the high-powered round to cross the valley, and it hit exactly where the Ranger sniper had wanted it to. The P2 assassin's head jerked back and he fell away from the rifle.

Philpot spoke into Holliday's ear one last time. "It's over. You can get up now."

Holliday climbed to his feet. The circle had now been completed. The man who had killed Peggy and Rafi had been brought to justice. Holliday stared affectionately down at the gray stones, then turned and walked back down the hill.

EPILOGUE

John Holliday stepped out of his newly purchased town house on Berkeley Square and walked up to Piccadilly, where he flagged down a London black cab.

Holliday climbed into the backseat and settled in. It had been more than a month since he stood at the graves of Peggy and Rafi on Mount Herzl—and a great deal had happened since then. The shitstorm predicted by Moorhead, the Interpol chief, had turned into more of a hurricane.

At the Vatican, Pope Francis had declared that full restitution would be made for all the works of art that had been hidden there for so many years, but it did little good. Discovering who owned what and what compensation would be paid would take years. The Vatican Bank was bankrupt and there were fears that the Church

would be damaged to a point that it would decades to regain its credibility. It was an unholy
disaster.

In the art world, the damage was almost just
as bad. Dozens of galleries and auction houses
were implicated in the whole Operation Leonardo conspiracy and their reputations were as
ruined as the Church's.

On the other hand, things had gone rather well
for Holliday. The uncovering of the art forgery
conspiracy and its connection to the CIA Ghost
Squad had earned Holliday not only a Presidential Medal of Freedom, but it had also earned him
a presidential pardon for any crimes he might
have committed in the past or present. In England, the Queen had given him and Lazarus a
formal audience and he was told that he was free
to stay in England as long as he wished.

The cab pulled up at the Bond Street address
Holliday had given the driver. He paid the cab-
bie off and climbed out of the vehicle. He looked
up at the sign, which read "Lazarus Recovery
and Restoration."

In one of the two bay windows a painting that
looked very much like a Rembrandt was displayed
on a large easel. In the other window the painting
was a medium-sized Turner landscape. He smiled
and went inside the small shop. The interior looked

more like a small warehouse rather than a Bond Street gallery. In the rear of the store, there were banks of lights, easels, large worktables. Large, brightly lit magnifiers were neatly arranged as half a dozen men and women in lab coats worked on restoring paintings. In the front of the store, a small greeting area had been arranged with a round table and several comfortable chairs. A coffee service was already laid out and waiting. Lazarus greeted Holliday as he came in the door and gestured to one of the chairs around the table. Lazarus poured coffee and they both sat back in their chairs.

"A lot can happen in a very short space of time," said Lazarus. "They wanted me to stay on at Interpol, but they only offered me a desk job. I made a deal with them to be a consultant anytime they needed me. The signing bonus helped me to buy this place and a variety of banks did the rest, although I'm now shackled to them for the rest of my life."

"The banks didn't buy you those paintings in the window," said Holliday. "Are they fake or real?"

"Quite real," said Lazarus. "One's from a duke trying to keep his country estate afloat and the other is from a Saudi prince who's quietly selling off his father's collection right from under his nose. The bulletproof glass is real too. Throw a brick at that stuff and it'll just bounce back and break your nose."

"That's not why you called me last night."

"No, it wasn't. A young archaeologist sent me something by courier. He wanted me to give him some idea of what it was. I did as much research as I could and then called him back to tell him what I'd found, which was nothing. But when I called him back, a policeman answered. My young friend had been tortured, murdered and nailed to two boards made into the shape of a cross in his garage. Whoever killed him was looking for information. Then, this morning, an object arrived."

Lazarus got up and disappeared into the rear area of the shop for a minute. He returned with an object about two feet high wrapped in velvet. Lazarus set the object down on the table and pulled off the velvet drapery. Holliday leaned forward. The object was in the shape of a rough stone obelisk. At the base of each side of the stone was clearly a Templar Cross. What was carved above it was something entirely different. They were undoubtedly ancient occult symbols of one kind or another. Goat-headed men, horned devil figures, pentagrams, upside-down crucifixes and every other sort of black magic symbol you could imagine.

"Do you know anything about this?" Lazarus asked.

"I'm afraid I do," Holliday replied. "They were a sect within the movement called the Black Templars. Nobody's heard from them for a thousand years."

The Sword of the Templars

Army Ranger Lieutenant Colonel John Holliday has resigned himself to ending his career teaching at West Point. When his uncle passes away, Holliday discovers a medieval sword—wrapped in Adolf Hitler's personal battle standard. But when someone burns down his uncle's house in an attempt to retrieve the sword, Holliday realizes that he's being drawn into a war that has been fought for centuries—a war in which he may be the next casualty.

Read on for a preview of the first installment in Paul Christopher's Templar series. Now available in mass market and e-book from Signet.

1

"In *The Da Vinci Code*, Dan Brown depicted the Knights Templar as being the sacred keepers of the secret of Christ's bloodline. In *Indiana Jones and the Last Crusade* they were portrayed as immortal guardians of the Holy Grail. In the movie *National Treasure*, Nicolas Cage described them as being the caretakers of a vast fortune buried under Trinity Church in downtown Manhattan. According to various religious scholars they were gatekeepers of the Temple of Solomon in Jerusalem after the successful conclusion of the First Crusade as well as protectors of pilgrims on their way to the Holy Land.

"Bull. The truth is the Knights Templar, this self-described Army of God, was nothing more than a gang of extortionists and thugs. As a group they were certainly the world's first example of organized crime, complete with secret rituals and a code not unlike that of the Sicilian Cosa Nostra—the Mafia."

Lieutenant Colonel John "Doc" Holliday, a dark-haired, middle-aged man in an Army Ranger uniform wearing a black patch over his left eye, looked out over the classroom, checking for some sort of response from his students, or failing that at least an indication of interest. What he saw were eighteen "firsties," fourth-year students, all male, all wearing the same "as-to-class" short-sleeved blue uniform blouses with a neat triangle of snow-white T-shirt showing at the neck, all wearing the same gray trousers with a single stripe, all with the same high-and-tight haircut, all with the same sleepy, glassy-eyed expression of young men attending the last class of an academic day that had started almost ten hours before. Incredibly, this was the cream of the West Point graduating class, most of them single-minded ring thumpers who'd already branched Artillery, Infantry, or Armor, and none of whom had the slightest interest in medieval history in general or the Knights Templar in particular. Future Warriors of America. *Huah!*

Holliday continued.

"The big problem with the First Crusade of 1095 was the fact that the crusaders won it. By 1099 they'd captured Jerusalem and they were an army without an enemy. No more godless Saracens to slaughter. Knights of the time were professional soldiers, swords for hire bought and paid for by wealthy noblemen, most of them French, Italian, or German. They were *chevaliers*, literally men who could afford to ride a horse; chivalry and fair damsels in distress didn't factor in the equation. They were killers, plain and simple."

"Warriors, sir." The observation came from Whitey Tarvanin, a tough-looking Finn from Nebraska whose pale skin and even paler hair had given him his nickname. He was obviously Infantry, the crossed idiot sticks on his uniform blouse proud proof of that. When he'd posted a few weeks ago he'd actually chosen Fort Polk, Alabama, the least attractive choice on the roster, just to prove how down and dirty he was.

"No, not warriors, Cadet, mercenaries. These guys were in it for the money, nothing more. No Honor, Duty, Country. Maybe a little raping and pillaging on the side; after all, according to the rules of engagement in the eleventh century non-Christians were going to Hell anyway, so they didn't count. The nobles had promised them all sorts of plunder in the Holy Land, but as it turned out there wasn't enough to go around and thousands of these *chevaliers* came back penniless and a lot of the nobles were close to bankruptcy, as well. Many of them returned home to find that their lands, castles, and everything else had been stolen by scheming relatives or simply forfeited by one king or another for taxes."

Holliday paused.

"So what does an unemployed soldier whose only real skills involve hacking, butchering, and otherwise committing acts of extreme violence on the godless enemy do with himself once that enemy has been vanquished?"

Holliday shrugged.

"He does what men in that situation have done since the days of Alexander the Great. He turns to crime."

"Like Robin Hood?" This was from "Zits" Mitchell, skinny, pimples, wire-rimmed glasses, and a hairline already edging backward into baldness. After watching Mitchell go through four years at the Point, Holliday was still amazed by his stamina. He'd expected the beanpole cadet to wash out after Beast Barracks, if not before. But he'd stuck it out. Holliday smiled. Mitchell's pimples would go away eventually.

"Robin Hood was a romantic fantasy invented by songwriters who came along a few hundred years after the fact. The people I'm talking about, the *routiers*, as these vagabond highwaymen were called, were more like Tony Montana in *Scarface*—products of their environment; an unskilled ex-con Marielito washed up on the shores of Key West doesn't have much choice if he wants to get ahead in his new home: he deals cocaine. A *routier* in medieval France joins a gang of like-minded ex-soldiers and starts plundering the countryside or offering villages and towns 'protection' for a price.

"One of these men was Hugues de Payens, a French knight in the service of the Duke of Champagne. The duke ran short of money and Sir Hugues switched allegiance, fighting with the army of Godfrey of Bouillon until Jerusalem was overthrown.

"Godfrey was installed as king of Jerusalem, and using his prior connection Sir Hugues along with half a dozen other *routiers* petitioned King Godfrey for the job of guarding the new pilgrim routes through the recently captured Holy Land, along with the right to establish their headquarters in the ruins of the old Temple of Solomon.

"Pilgrims were big business back then, and tolls from the pilgrims formed the basis for economy of the newly 'liberated' Holy Land. Godfrey agreed, and Sir Hugues took things one step further, ratifying his position by having Pope Urban II grant him the status of a holy order, thus freeing the newly formed Knights Templar from the obligations of any sort of taxation, not to mention making them answerable only to the Pope."

"He made them an offer they couldn't refuse." Zits Mitchell grinned. "Godfather style."

"Something like that." Holliday nodded. "Sir Hugues and his fellow *routiers* controlled a lot of military might. Godfrey had upset a bunch of his colleagues by accepting the title of king. At the very least Godfrey was buying protection for himself in the fragile little kingdom."

"So what happened?" Whitey Tarvanin asked, suddenly getting interested.

"There had always been rumors about some sort of treasure hidden in the Temple of Solomon, maybe even the Ark of the Covenant, the box that supposedly held the second set of the Ten Commandments brought down from Mount Sinai by Moses."

"Second set?" Tarvanin asked.

"Moses broke the first tablets," said Granger, a football jock with the nickname Bullet, which probably had something to do with the shape of his head. He was also the class's biggest über-Christian. The hefty point guard had been scowling at Holliday since he'd mentioned Dan Brown and *The Da Vinci Code*. A sensitive topic for a lot of people, although Holliday wasn't quite sure why; after all, it was a novel, a work of fiction, not a campaign platform or a sermon. Granger cleared his throat as though he was embarrassed about displaying too much knowledge in front of a teacher. "God wrote them down a second time and Moses put them in the Ark. It's in the Bible."

"It's also in the Koran," said Holliday mildly. "It has a deep significance for Muslims as well as Christians."

Granger's scowl darkened and his big head turtle-tucked down into his beef-slab shoulders.

"Did these guys find it?" Tarvanin asked.

"Nobody's quite sure. They found something, we know that much. Some say it was gold from King Solomon's Mines; others say it was the Ark of the Covenant; others say it was the secret wisdom of Atlantis. Whatever they found, within a year the Knights Templar were loaded. They financed their pilgrim escort service, built castles up and down the pilgrim routes to Jerusalem and sold their muscle to anyone who could pay.

"Because of the distances involved between Europe and the Holy Land, they borrowed an idea from their Saracen enemies and introduced an encrypted note of transfer—a deposit of money in one place could be transferred on paper for thousands of miles. Wire transfers before they had wires.

"The Templars also began making loans at interest, although this was specifically forbidden in the Bible. As time went on the Templars even began financing entire wars. Land and other assets were regularly used as collateral and often wound up being forfeited, expanding the Templars' power and wealth even more.

"Within a hundred years the Templars were into everything: loan-sharking, real estate, the protection rackets, shipping, smuggling, bribery, you name it. By the end of the next century they were the next best thing to a multinational conglomerate, and there's no doubt that much of it came from illicit sources.

"In most major cities of the time, from Rome to Jerusalem, Paris and London to Frankfurt and Prague, you didn't make a major move without consulting the local Templar authority. They controlled politics and banks, and owned entire fleets of ships. They were their own army, and by the beginning of the fourteenth century they had an unsurpassed intelligence network that spanned the known world. By then, of course, Jerusalem was back in the hands of the infidel, and the Holy Land was a battleground once again, but by then it didn't matter anymore."

"So what happened then, sir?" Zits Mitchell asked.

"They got a little too big for their britches," explained Holliday. "King Philip of France had just fought a long war with England. He was broke and he owed the Templar banks a lot of money. They were on the verge of taking over the entire country. The Pope was getting a little nervous, too; the Templars had far too much power within the church and were easily capable of putting their own man on the papal throne if they chose to.

"Something had to be done. Pope Clement and King Philip concocted a plan, laid charges against the Order for various crimes, some real and some false, and on Friday the thirteenth, 1307, most of the Templar leaders in France were arrested. They were tried for heresy, convicted, tortured, and burned at the stake. Eventually the Pope ordered every Catholic king in Europe to seize Templar assets under threat of excommunication, and by 1312 the Knights Templar had ceased to exist. Some say that the Templar fleet took the Order's treasure to Scotland for safekeeping, and other people think that they managed to flee to America, although there's no proof of that."

"I don't see the point," said Whitey Tarvanin. "It's like most of this historic stuff. What's it got to do with right now? With us?"

"Quite a bit actually," replied Holliday. It was an argument he'd heard a thousand times, usually from the mouths of gung ho kids exactly like Whitey Tarvanin. "Have you ever heard the expression 'Those who forget history are condemned to repeat it'?" There were a lot of blank looks. Holliday nodded. He wasn't surprised.

"The quote is generally attributed to a man named George Santayana, a Spanish-born American philosopher of the early twentieth century. In the way that Adolf Hitler forgot the lessons of history and tried to invade Russia in the winter. If he'd remembered Napoleon's disastrous attempt he might have consolidated the Western Front instead and won the war in Europe. If we'd paid attention to history and remembered the decades-long failure of the French in Vietnam, maybe we wouldn't have tried to prosecute that war in the same way they did and maybe we wouldn't have lost it."

"So what does that have to do with these Templar guys?" Zits Mitchell asked.

"They got too powerful and they forgot who their friends were," said Holliday. "Just like we did. The United States came out of the Second World War with a per capita casualty rate that was lower than Canada's, and we suffered none of the catastrophic damage done to Europe and Great Britain. We also had made enormous industrial wartime loans that put us into the world's economic forefront. We dominated the world, just like the Templars. People got jealous. People got pissed off."

"9/11," said Tarvanin.

"Among other things," said Holliday. "And to make things worse we started mixing religion with politics. An old argument just like the Crusades. Our God is better than your god. *'God Is with Us'* on the Nazi belt buckles. Holy Wars against women and children, Catholics killing Protestants in Belfast. We went into Iraq for the wrong reasons and we left our friends behind. More people have been killed in the name of God and so-called 'faith-based values' than for any other reason.

"You can bully people into being your allies, but when things get bad don't expect them to stand beside you, especially when you put God into the mix. The separation of Church and State. That's what the Constitution is for, although we seem to have forgotten that, as well. And as for the relevance of history you can probably trace the troubles in the Middle East directly back to Moses."

"Don't you believe in God?" Bullet Granger asked.

"My personal beliefs have nothing to do with it," said Holliday quietly. He'd been here before, as well—shaky ground, the kind of thing that could get you into trouble.

"You're always knocking Christians and the Bible. Moses, and like that," Granger argued.

"Moses was a Jew," said Holliday, sighing. "So was Christ as a matter of fact."

"Yeah, well," grumbled the big football player, brooding. The bell rang.

Saved.

2

Lieutenant Colonel John Holliday stepped out of Bartlett Hall and paused for a moment, enjoying the early-evening sunlight that bathed the gray stones of the United States Military Academy at West Point. Directly in front of him was the broad expanse of the Plain, the celebrated parade ground that had felt the heels of ranks of marching cadets for more than two hundred years. All the greats had been here, ghosts in cadence from George Armstrong Custer to Dwight D. Eisenhower. To Holliday's left were a score of other stone buildings rising like the protective bastions of some crusader's castle. To the right, beyond the baseball diamond on Doubleday Field, were the bluffs that stood above the wide silver brushstroke of the Hudson River as it flowed the last fifty miles down to New York City and the sea.

There were monuments scattered everywhere on the grounds, commemorating battles, brave deeds, brave men, and most of all the dead, graduates of this place who'd given their best, their all and their lives for one cause or another, the causes now long forgotten, found only between the dusty pages of the history books that Holliday loved so well. That was the problem of course; all wars became meaningless in time. The Battle of Antietam was the bloodiest single conflict in American history with 23,000 dead in a single September day, and now it was a plaque on the side of an old building and a picnic ground for tourists toting cameras.

Holliday had fought his own war, of course, more than one in fact, from Vietnam to Iraq and Afghanistan, with half a dozen others in between. Had his fighting made any difference, or the lives of the men who died beside him in those terrible, lonely places? He knew that the simple answer was no. They kept on growing poppies in Afghanistan, oil still flowed in Iraq, rice still grew in the paddies around Da Nang, babies still starved to death in Mogadishu.

That wasn't the point, of course. Soldiers didn't think that way—they were trained not to. That's what places like West Point were for: to ensure that the next generation of officers in the

United States Army would follow the orders of their superiors without question, because if you stopped or even hesitated long enough to ask that question the other guy would probably put a bullet in your head.

Holliday smiled to himself and went down the steps. All those wars, all those battles and the only injury he'd ever sustained was a blind eye caused by a sharp stone thrown up from the wheel of his Humvee on a back road outside Kabul. The eye had cost him his combat posting and had eventually led him here. The fortunes of war.

He crossed Thayer Road and started down the footpath that cut across the Plain at an angle. A pair of cadets rushed by, pausing just long enough to throw Holliday a rigid salute as they passed. Cows, by the look of the stripes on their tunics—third-year cadets. Firstie year to get through and then they'd be off to their own far-flung outposts of democracy. A long time ago in a galaxy far, far away. Holliday shook his head. Did George Lucas ever wonder just how many West Point Luke Skywalkers he had inspired? A cool gust of wind spun across the parade ground like a shiver. It wasn't even summer yet, but the breeze felt like fall. The leaves rattled in the trees that stood along the path for a few seconds, and then the strange feeling was gone. Goose just walked across his grave. One of his mother's favorite spooky sayings from long, long ago.

Holliday reached the far side of the Plain and the Thayer Statue, then crossed Jefferson Road and walked past Quarters 100, the superintendent's white-brick house, with its twin cannon guarding the front walk. He continued on to Professors Row with its neat cluster of late-Victorian houses and finally reached his own quarters at the end of the block, a little two-bedroom Craftsman bungalow built in the 1920s and the smallest accommodations on the Row.

Stepping into the cozy house was like going back in time. Warm oak, stained glass, and built-in cabinets were everywhere. There was even an original slatted Morris chair and matching ottoman in the living room beside the tiled fireplace, as well as plain painted cabinets and a huge porcelain sink in the simple kitchen at the back. He'd turned the larger of the two bedrooms into a study, the walls lined with his books. The smaller bedroom held nothing but a bed, a chest of drawers, and a bedside table. There was a single photograph on the table: Amy on their wedding day, with flowers in her hair, standing on a beach in Hawaii. Amy when she was young, eyes bright and flashing, before the cancer that swept through her like the cold wind that had rushed across the Plain a few minutes ago. It took her in the springtime, killing her before summer's end. It had been ten years ago now, but he still remembered her as she was in the fading picture on the bedside table, and mourned her and her vanished smile. Mourned their decision to put off having children for a little while longer, because a little while never came and there was nothing left of her in the world.

Holliday went into the bedroom, stripped off his uniform and changed into jeans and an old USMA sweatshirt. He went to the built-in bar in the living room, poured himself a good belt of Grant's Ale Cask, and headed into his study, bringing the drink along with him. He put a Ben Harper and the Blind Boys of Alabama CD into the stereo and sat down at his old, scarred partners desk. He booted up his PC, did a quick check of his e-mail, then opened up the file for his work in progress, a half-serious, relatively scholarly work he had tentatively titled *The Well Dressed Knight*, a history of arms and armor from the time of the Greeks and Romans to the present day.

The book had originally been the subject of his doctoral thesis at Georgetown University back when he'd been at the Pentagon more than a decade ago, but with the passage of time it had turned into the massive, doorstopper epic that he used as both a hobby and a way to occupy his mind when it started to turn into the dark corners of memory that sometimes haunted him. At nine hundred pages he'd just finished with John Ericsson and the construction of the Union Navy vessel *Monitor*, the first American ironclad, and he still had a long way to go.

He'd been interested in the subject of armor since he was a kid playing with his uncle Henry's antique lead soldiers in the big Victorian house up in Fredonia where the old man still lived. Henry had been a teacher at the State University of New York in Fredonia for years and before that something vaguely sinister and hush-hush during the Cold War. It had been Uncle Henry who'd interested him in history in the first place, and it was Uncle Henry who'd managed to wangle him the congressional recommendation that got him into West Point and out of the intellectual desert of Oswego, New York. Not to mention freeing him from a life of stormy alcoholic desperation with his widower father, a railroad engineer on the old Erie Lackawanna Line until he was laid off in the early seventies.

By then Holliday was already off to West Point, and a few years later, gone to war in Indochina. When his father died of liver failure in the spring of 1975, a twenty-four-year-old Holliday, now a field-promoted captain in the 75th Ranger Regiment, was helping the last evacuees board helicopters during the fall of Saigon.

Holliday sat at his desk working until taps sounded at ten o'clock. He got up, made himself a cup of tea, and then went back to his computer and spent another hour checking over what he'd just written. Satisfied, he switched off the computer and leaned back in his battered leather office chair. He intended to spend a few minutes reading the latest Bernard Cornwell book and then head to bed. His telephone rang. He stared at it, listening to it ring a second time. He felt a little lurch in the pit of his stomach and a clench in his throat. Nobody called with good news at eleven o'clock at night. It rang a third time. No use putting off the inevitable. He picked up the receiver.

"Yes?"

"Doc? It's Peggy. Grandpa Henry's at Brooks Memorial in Dunkirk. I'm there now. You'd better get here quick; they don't think he's going to make it."

"I'll be there as fast as I can." It was three hundred and fifty miles to Fredonia, seven hours if he drove straight through. He'd be there by dawn. Peggy was weeping now; he could hear the tears in her voice. "Hurry, Doc. I need you."